TODOS SANTOS

Black Lawrence Press
www.blacklawrence.com

Executive Editor: Diane Goettel
Book Design: Steven Seighman

Black Lawrence Press
115 Center Avenue
Pittsburgh, PA 15215
U.S.A.

Cover art by Faustino Pablo Bautista
Author photograph by Marion Ettlinger

Grateful acknowledgement for permission to quote from *The Dharma Bums* by Jack Kerouac is made to The Viking Press.

Permission to quote from the song "Me Gustas Tu," written by Manu Chao, is courtesy of Blue Mountain Music Ltd o/b/o Radio Bemba Sarl

Published 2010 by Black Lawrence Press, an imprint of Dzanc Books

First edition 2010
ISBN-13: 978-09825204-0-6
Printed in the United States

TODOS SANTOS

A NOVEL BY
DEBORAH CLEARMAN

Black Lawrence Press
New York

To the people of Todos Santos, who gave me a home.

1.

The engines cut, and two hundred tons of metal and plastic and human flesh began the long glide back to earth. Most passengers that afternoon, busy balancing their dinner trash on overcrowded trays, fidgeting with headsets or snapping their lolling heads away from strangers as they drowsed, never noticed the start of the descent. Catherine Barnes, sandwiched in a middle seat, did. She hated to leave the sky. Up here, untethered, free from the gravity of husbands and sons, she stared out the window and saw pure patterns of light, shifting and changing.

"Have you been to Guatemala before?" The clean-cut young man in the window seat broke into Catherine's thoughts. She'd been imagining how she would mix the colors packed in her paint box in the overhead bin—cerulean blue, flake white, ivory black, a touch of sienna—colors for the clouds and sky. Annoyed that he had, after all these hours, intruded through the comfortable privacy that divided them, she answered that she had been to Guatemala several times, but always before on vacation. And then, because she couldn't help herself, because the compulsion to be polite drove her to it, she asked the fresh-faced youth where he was headed.

"We have a mission on the coast. I'm taking the bus there tomorrow."

A missionary. She might have guessed from his white shirt and tie. "Oh, the coast," she said. "It's nasty in the lowlands. Hot. Unbelievably humid."

"So I've been told. A difficult place, full of disease and poverty. I figure we can really make a difference there, amongst indigenous people struggling for their daily bread."

Make that *tortilla,* Catherine wanted to snap. The missionary leaned toward her to speak.

"They have so little. They *need* God's love."

She managed a thin smile. "I'll keep that in mind when I get to Todos Santos." The name of the town meant *All Saints,* but she doubted that its citizens prayed to Mary, Peter, John, and Paul, the pale-faced holy ones of their Spanish conquerors. Surely they would favor older, darker gods. Just the missionary's presence irked her, his simple certitudes, the arrogance of those professing to know right from wrong. Better by far to listen to the silence emanating from her son, Isaac, fourteen, recently flunked out of eighth grade, asleep in the aisle seat.

Isaac shifted. Catherine glanced at her son's loose blond curls straying over his collar, the pale eyelashes against flushed cheeks, so vulnerable in sleep, so precious. Too bad the messy ponytail made him look like the kind of kid gringos are famous for, spoiled and poorly groomed.

Outside the plane window the light show continued. Billowing thunderheads framed the setting sun. The missionary talked on with unstoppable enthusiasm. "I can't wait to see Guatemala City in the sunset."

"You won't," Catherine said, with secret satisfaction.

"In Guatemala it's dark by six thirty, year round. Welcome to the tropics."

A half hour later, when the landing gear finally bumped the tarmac, she was happy to leave the righteous young man behind. She roused Isaac and stretched from the multi-legged flight, ready to be back on earth.

Guatemala City no longer greeted arrivals with mariachi bands and machine guns, the way it had on Catherine's first visit years ago, but it still had the capacity to unnerve. They entered the terminal, shuffled through *Migración*, two foreigners surrounded by natives returning to their homeland. Past Customs, she looked up at the visitors' gallery, searching for her sister-in-law. A teeming mass of short, black-haired people—decked out in everything from designer jeans and platform shoes to colorful indigenous costumes—peered down, waving, whistling, signaling to arriving passengers. Whole families, entire villages, about to be reunited it seemed, and overjoyed at the prospect. Catherine felt a pang of envy. Where was Zelda? She checked over her shoulder for Isaac, as though he might have disappeared in the turmoil at the baggage carousel. His silence made him difficult to track. "Are you okay with those bags?" she asked.

He carried a large duffle in each hand, so that she could handle her cumbersome French easel, the wooden paint box with legs that folded up for portability. Isaac grunted assent. They passed gleaming counters proclaiming hotel and tourist services, currency exchange and tours, all oddly unmanned in the empty room, as though Guatemala had planned on a thriving portal welcoming thousands at a time and the guests had never showed. Instead, the planes dribbled in, one flight at a time. Glass doors disgorged the arriving passengers into the mob, kept outside. People shoved through the human wall, porters shouted, horns honked. Finally she spotted Zelda, tall among the Guatemaltecos, her red hair, wild and kinky, streaming to her waist, a welcome sight. Catherine waved, and then used her French easel to carve a way through the crowd. Isaac followed with the duffles. Zelda, her large body swathed in native cloth, hugged Catherine and got banged in the knee by the paint box.

"Shit, Catherine! What have you got in there?" Without waiting for an answer, she put her arm around Isaac's shoulder and pulled him toward her in a forced embrace. "How are you, kid?"

When he remained silent, Zelda coached. "Say hi, Isaac."

"Hi, Aunt Zelda."

Zelda led the way around puddles in the street, turned iridescent by streetlights in the early night. The air was fresh from the recent rain, sharp from the altitude of five thousand feet, smoky from cooking fires and exhaust from cars and trucks and buses that had never seen emission controls, and tingling with mythology, with a past more exotic than covered wagons and Plymouth Rock. Catherine breathed it in, freed from the atmosphere she'd left behind in Iowa.

She was glad it wasn't raining when they reached Zelda's pickup truck.

"You have to ride in the back with the luggage, Isaac," Zelda said. Without a word, Isaac sprang into the back of the pickup. He arranged the duffle bags and settled himself among them, as if they made a cozy banquette.

"See?" Zelda said, "Kids love riding in the back."

Catherine climbed in front and searched, sticking a hand into the crack between the seat and the back.

"Don't bother looking," Zelda said. "There aren't any seat belts."

Catherine could see Isaac through the back window of the cab. "What if it rains?"

"He'll get wet." This was the woman to whom she planned to entrust her fourteen-year-old nihilist son, counting on her to set limits, read him the riot act, and guard him from danger while she went on her research trip. "He'll be fine," Zelda said.

Zelda negotiated the pickup through the freshly washed but still dirty streets of the capital, neon lights screaming from businesses along the strip: Car Wash La Cabaña, Campero Pollo to Go, Pizza Hut—Llámanos! The mangling of cultures exhilarated Catherine. That she could speak another language felt miraculous to her, like walking through a wall, taking her behind the looking glass. They swerved and screeched through lanes of traffic. Stopped at a light, Zelda shouted "Jesus fucking Christ!," threw open her door, and leapt from the cab.

Through the back window Catherine saw Isaac pulling on one handle of a duffle. Grasping the other with two hands was a wiry man in rags. Horrified, Catherine stared at the strange man, his face contorted in struggle, his mouth gaping in a snarl, like a wild snaggletoothed dog, threatening her son. She heard Zelda's voice shrieking "*Policía! Socorro! Vaya-cabrón-chíngate-hijo-de-puta!*," saw Zelda appear over the back of the pickup, and realized finally that the tug-of-war was a robbery attempt.

Catherine yanked open her door. Her feet hit the pavement. She saw the ragged man dive from the truckbed, dart through the line of stopped cars, and disappear into an alley. Shaking, she climbed into the back, pulled Isaac into her arms, and started to sob, her panic changing to relief. He hugged her back with unusual warmth. "Relax, Mom. He wasn't even armed. He never stood a chance against Aunt Z's charging rhino act."

Catherine felt the beginning of a laugh even as she cried.

Their journey resumed. Isaac insisted on riding in the back, over his mother's objections. Catherine tried to believe Zelda's reassurances that the most dangerous part of the trip was over. The road rose out of the bowl of Guatemala City, snaking upward into the dark forested mountains. At least the Pan-American Highway here, though battered, was four lanes wide and well traveled at this hour.

"How's life in Iowa? What's my dear brother up to?" Zelda asked.

"He's in the studio until all hours every night, painting a metaphoric cycle on the life of Poe," Catherine answered.

"Don't you mean, on the sex lives of under-graduates?"

"Zelda, do you have to be so . . . blunt?" Catherine had been one of those undergraduates once, a painting major in love with the dashing young art professor.

When a friend had told her this spring what the whole campus had apparently been talking about for several years, she'd been stunned. She'd never doubted Elliot's devotion. She'd called her sister-in-law, distraught.

"What should I do?" she'd asked. Zelda always had an answer.

"Do you want to leave him?"

Life without Elliot was inconceivable. In that case, Zelda suggested, why not get away for a little while, get some distance. Guatemala would be the perfect setting for her next picture book. And here she was.

They left the Pan-American on a grandiose cloverleaf, passed stands of pine trees, and started down toward Antigua. Now theirs was the only vehicle on the lonely road. It began to rain. Catherine peered through the window at Isaac in the back of the pickup, rain pelting him. She shivered. "He'll be soaked," she said.

"We'll be there soon."

Zelda slowed to a crawl. The road was steep, the curves were sharp, the mountainside plunged into a deep ravine. Forests of roadside crosses made Catherine think of those who'd gone over the edge and not come back. Rain beat on the roof of the truck as they got to the bottom of the hill and reached the outlying buildings of Antigua. Rain splashed on the cobblestones. They bounced through the streets into the former capital. Narrow sidewalks were bounded by old adobe walls painted in earth red, gold, soft white. At the tops of walls shards of pointed glass sparkled in the scattered glare of streetlights. Wrought-iron bars decorated windows. Hand-painted tiles were set over doorways. Occasional doors stood open, giving glimpses of courtyards into which people dashed from the street.

They stopped in front of Zelda's house, her treasured piece of colonial Guatemala. Catherine got out, anxious to see how Isaac was doing. He stood up and shook his hair, now tamed by the wet, and picked up the duffles.

"Here, Aunt Z. All the inventory accounted for. No more shoplifters!"

He'd just sat in the back of that damned truck for an hour of bone-crunching road, and here he was cracking jokes—Catherine loved that about her son. Put him in a more comfortable setting, a bright and cheery classroom, say, ask him to participate in group discussions, and he'd turn sullen and hostile. Or he'd hide in the closet like a five-year-old and play class goofball. That's why he'd flunked out. At least, that was one reason. He climbed out of the truck with one of the duffles while Zelda unlocked the wooden gate.

Later that night, after dinner, after Isaac had retired to read and sleep, the two women sat in the living room of

Zelda's house, drinking rum. Through the open door and window they could hear rain splashing in the courtyard and dripping off roses and bougainvillea. A cloud of blue smoke hung between them from Zelda's cigarette.

"I don't know if I did the right thing," Catherine said. "Isaac hates school. I didn't think another two months of it in summer was going to turn him into an achiever."

"Of course not," Zelda snorted. "He could flunk out of summer school just like he flunked out of eighth grade. Why second-guess yourself? He's much better off here with me. I'll put him to work." That was Zelda, always sure of herself. In a way, she was very much like her brother.

The phone rang.

"I'll bet that's our lonesome cowboy now," Zelda said, getting up to answer.

It was. Catherine listened to her shoot the breeze with Elliot. Her tough talk didn't fool Catherine, who knew the loyalty that lay beneath it, both to her brother and to her sister-in-law. The miracle was that Zelda wouldn't take sides; she would only listen and point out folly.

"Don't worry. I'm taking care of them. Just keep painting and stay out of trouble. Here's Catherine." Zelda held out the phone to her.

"Hey, babe. I'm reading news stories of murders and abductions in Guatemala. Be careful down there, won't you?" Elliot's voice in her ear sounded tender and wistful. "I miss you already. Ain't no sunshine when you're gone." He quoted the familiar song. It tugged at Catherine. She felt his body against her, dancing, his hips moving, her hand in his, the way it used to be.

"Did you find the pasta sauce I left in the fridge?" she asked. "I forgot to tell you, a notice came from the dealer yesterday. It's time to take the car in for a tune-up. And I left the ticket for the dry cleaning on the kitchen counter."

"You know I can't deal with all that crap. Hurry back, sweetheart."

* * *

The first thing Isaac thought about when he woke up the next morning was his computer. How was he going to survive a month in this unconnected place? He'd tried to convince his mother he could learn responsibility and earn money by designing websites, but she'd said it was Guatemala or summer school. In the past, he'd never minded Guatemala. So he'd agreed to work in his aunt's high-end handicrafts store, where cool stuff from all over the country went for good prices to discerning collectors, while his mother was off having adventures. Even though he knew the idea was some sort of tough-love boot camp. He would start on Monday. Today was Saturday, and his aunt Zelda left them right after breakfast to go to work, saying, "Pick up some bananas and oranges at the market."

That gave his mother a mission. Not that she needed one. She would never be satisfied lying around the house all day doing nothing while Isaac read *Wired, Maximum PC*, and the Games Workshop catalogue from the library he'd brought with him to fend off boredom. They always had to do something. At home that meant weekend picnics and excursions to fossil beds and historical sites, as if there were anything of historical interest in Iowa. Here it meant going to the market.

Isaac had never liked the Latin American market scene. He wasn't crazy about people in small numbers, much less by the hundreds. Much less people who didn't say "Excuse me" and step around you the way they did back home. But his mother bribed him with a promise of ice cream and a visit to a cybercafé later on. They walked across town. Isaac remembered the way to the sprawling building with the low, corrugated tin roof. He led them through crowded aisles, past scores of stalls, deep into the dark maze, trying to avoid stepping on people crouched over their wares. Smells of rotting vegetables, fresh-killed meat, and human body odor filled the air. Isaac pushed through as quickly as he could, wanting to get this over with. They looked at piles of fruit and vegetables so varied and strange he had never learned their names or how to eat them.

"*Cuánto por las naranjas?*" his mother asked a gnarled woman kneeling by a basket of oranges, the big yellow kind that Zelda liked. For some reason citrus fruit in this country was always the wrong color. His mother and the woman started in on the ridiculous bargaining ritual, while Isaac stood there watching them haggle over pennies. He moved away, his eye caught by a display of machetes in a booth at the other side of the produce area. He made his way toward it, and ducked into the booth out of the crowds. The machetes, in different sizes, hung from nails amid tooled leather belts and sheathes. Sombrero-style straw hats were stacked on shelves below.

"*Cuánto por el machete?*" Isaac asked the guy in the booth, just so the guy would lift it down and place it in Isaac's hands, so that he could run his thumb along its honed edge.

"*Bien afilado,*" the guy said. Very sharp. "*Veinte-cinco.*"

"*Tan caro!*" Isaac exclaimed, in imitation horror. So expensive! Isaac knew the bargaining game. Across the aisles, he saw his mother straighten up with her yellow oranges and look around for him.

The guy lowered his price two quetzales. Isaac countered with an impossibly low offer. His mother didn't see him and headed off down another aisle. He calculated her route down that aisle and up the next as he and the guy batted prices back and forth like tennis balls. Finally they met in the middle, as both had known they would. The price seemed cheap to Isaac. "*Está bien*," he said, and handed the guy some frayed five-quetzal notes.

Bearing his purchase, he threaded his way back through the throngs of short people and intersected his mother, coming from the direction he'd predicted.

"Isaac! Where *were* you? I looked all over!" There was panic in her voice, as though he'd been lost for hours behind enemy lines.

"Sorry, Mom. But look what I got." He held up his prize and ran his thumb over its sharp edge once again.

She shuddered. "What are you going to do with that?"

"Ward off bad guys!" He gave her what he hoped was a sweet smile. He was now her height and, when he wanted to, could look her straight in the eye. She sighed. They resumed their course toward an exit and emerged into sunshine. He blinked and oriented himself.

"This way," he said.

Antigua's streets should have been easy to navigate, laid out in a perfect grid, numbered from the central plaza. But there were few street signs, and the ones that Isaac could spot bore names that were no longer used, like Avenida de la Concepción or de la Virgen. So you had to count blocks, because they all looked alike. Isaac was better than his mother at finding the way. In airports and forests and foreign cities she let him lead. He liked that.

* * *

At six forty-five Sunday morning the doorbell rang. Fifteen minutes early.

"I've got it!" Catherine heard Zelda yell from the

living room. "Relax. Take your time." Catherine was still dripping from what she hoped would not be her last hot shower. She'd barely slept all night, panicked about her venture into the wild, and now the tourist guide was here to drive her wherever she wanted to go for the next week, sticking to her day and night.

"Latin men can be assholes," had been another of Zelda's helpful tips last night. "They think all gringas are whores."

"So what you're saying is my guide is going to be a sleaze looking for action on the side?" Catherine had replied. "Great."

Peering into the dark mirror, she struggled to get her earrings in, always difficult when she was nervous, and ran her fingers through her hair, brown sprinkled with gray, cut short so it curled over her ears. She wore no makeup in Guatemala, as if on a camping trip, and her unadorned features struck her as sharp. She gathered her last-minute stuff—bottled water, rolls of toilet paper—with the feeling she was leaving civilization. She nudged Isaac, asleep in the other bed. "I'm going, sweetie."

"Bye, Mom," he mumbled as she hugged him, limp and compliant in his half-conscious state, and went to the kitchen. Zelda had made coffee.

"I should go," Catherine said, thinking of the guide. She gulped the coffee and forced down a banana, all her stomach could handle.

"I've heard there's a phone now in Todos Santos," Zelda said.

"I'll call," Catherine said. She clutched the French easel and her duffle, and Zelda went with her to the gate. The guide was standing by his van. He reached out to Catherine to take her baggage.

"I hope you will have enough room," he said in

Spanish, shoving the easel and the huge duffle onto the back seats of the fourteen-passenger van. Catherine stared at him perplexed. Enough room?

He grinned. A gold tooth sparkled in his wide smile. His black hair stood up like a stiff scrub brush over his forehead. His almond eyes, broad cheeks, and long nose spoke of Mayan blood. He was younger than she was, but she couldn't tell how much.

"Sit anywhere. Please." Still smiling.

Oh. A joke. He'd made a joke, Catherine realized, looking into his laughing eyes. Maybe not a Latin lover on the make after all.

"I'm called Oswaldo. At your service."

With the suddenness of a cat pounce, she felt delight.

"Call me Catherine," she said. "Do you mind if I sit up front?"

* * *

Oswaldo kept both hands on the wheel while he drove. Catherine liked that. "Do you know, the first time I met a gringa was in 1984," he said.

"What did you think?" she asked. She liked the word *gringa*. It set her apart, gave her special status. Zelda had told her that the word was not an insult here, that Americans were welcome.

"She was strange. Very different from what I was used to. I was still a kid. She was a lady journalist, visiting my school." His parents had sent him to school in Nicaragua, he said, to escape the *Violencia*, the civil war in Guatemala.

"They sent you to *Nicaragua* for safety?" Catherine repeated him, astonished.

Oh yes, he confirmed. As if he considered that his responsibilities as guide included entertaining her on the long drive, he launched into a story. He began with the time before the war, which seemed like a dream to him. His father worked regular hours as a shopkeeper. His mother fixed her elaborate hair every morning before facing her world of female friends and domestic tranquility.

The *Violencia* changed all that, although Oswaldo was too young to know much about the kidnappings and the killings. All he knew was that his parents feared for him, packed him up at the age of twelve, and sent him off to Nicaragua. He was the only Guatemalteco in the school. He felt very alone. He had an aunt and uncle in the local town, but they had their own problems and let the school take care of Oswaldo. The story fascinated Catherine. She stopped him and made him repeat the parts she didn't understand. Her Spanish was getting a workout, along with her worldview.

There was never enough food. The students were always hungry. The cook was a belligerent woman with a nasty temper, and that, combined with perennial problems of supply, created an atmosphere of hostility in the cafeteria. But Oswaldo, needing a friend, found a chink in the cook's armor: she liked to chat. When the lonely boy crept into the kitchen by himself to sit on a stool and look up at her with black melting eyes, he made his first friend. Then he discovered other things she liked. Cigarettes. Chocolate. In his weekly letters to his mother, he begged gifts for Cook. His mother sent them.

"Your mother sent you cigarettes when you were twelve?" Catherine asked.

"It was the least she could do," Oswaldo said. He turned to glance at her. She tensed, then saw his twitch of a smile. She leaned her head back and let the pent up air escape through parted lips. The hours passed. They drove west through the highlands.

Armed with contraband, Oswaldo told her, he had gained an ally in the cook. His rations increased subtly. And he had free access to forbidden kitchen snacks. When the gringa journalist visited the school a few years later, she was surprised to find a Guatemalan refugee. And Oswaldo was surprised to meet a woman who didn't hide behind femininity, whose manner was plainspoken and aggressive. In her wraparound skirt, bare toes in sandals, the journalist was attractive, in a straightforward way. She asked him piercing questions. What did he think about the regime? *Which regime*, he asked. Her accent was heavy, but her words were clear and bold.

"I decided then that I liked gringas."

This time when he looked at Catherine it was to smile in a way that might be flirtatious or only friendly, she wasn't sure. She steered the conversation around the smile, like a rough spot in the pavement. "How did you become a guide?"

He returned to Guatemala when the *Violencia* petered out, he told her. His skill at making friends and his attraction to foreigners led him to the travel business, first in a travel agency in the capital, and then to Antigua. He led tours around the plaza, to the ruins of Las Capuchinas, up the Hill of the Cross. Soon he was driving a tourist van to the Lake and further afield. He liked his job. He enjoyed meeting people. To his parents' despair, he had not yet married. He told them to wait, there was no hurry. He asked Catherine about her family.

She had a son, she told him. That was all; no mention of Elliot, although he'd no doubt seen the ring on her left hand. She preferred to talk about her project in Todos Santos, to paint pictures of children for a book.

He had never been to Todos Santos, he said. "But I can help you, nonetheless. I put myself at the service of your art. It's an honor." He was impressed by her, Catherine noticed. Unlike Elliot, who didn't consider book illustrations to be art. There was enthusiasm in his voice. "We'll find children to pose for you. No problem. It will be my pleasure. I like exploring," he said with cheer.

* * *

"Here we are in Huehuetenango," Oswaldo said, five hours into the drive. "Pronounced in Spanish *Way-way*, but tourists like to call it *Huey-huey*. Population, thirty thousand people and one gringa."

"Does that mean I'm not a person?" Catherine directed a sharp look at him.

"A joke," he said with a goofy smile.

"You know, your jokes are a little stupid."

"I know," Oswaldo agreed. "But the tourists like them."

Catherine chuckled. She had to like them, too. He was so ingenuous. With every mile they put between her and Iowa, she felt a little freer.

They passed through the harsh commercial strip of Huehue, where buildings painted toothpaste green and florid pink screamed for attention. Out of town they left the main road and began to creep on endless switchbacks up the great green face of the Cuchumatanes, the highest mountain range in Central America, he told her. They doubled back to look down on the roofs of roadside houses. People stood and watched them pass, as if they were parting seas. Cornfields hung onto the mountainsides. Men with hoes and machetes hacked their way along rows of corn, weeding and cultivating. Clouds lowered onto the altiplano, the high plain far above them.

"We're going to touch the sky, I think," said Catherine.

"How handsome is the Sky," said Oswaldo. "He must be from Guatemala."

* * *

For an hour they traveled the high plateau of the Cuchumatanes, where stone fences sprouting spikes of maguey cactus and brilliant red flowers crossed the wide green moors. Giant rocks loomed in the mist of the altiplano like the bones of ancient monsters. Rocks scorched by smoldering fires reminded Catherine she was in a place where people didn't look to psychoanalysts to explain the inexplicable. In Todos Santos, Oswaldo told her, the affairs of mortals were controlled by the Lords of the Hills. There were four of them, each named for his mountain peak in the guttural Mayan language of Mam. When they emerged from their caves at the tops of the peaks, these four Lords rode on white horses. If a Lord called a man's spirit into his cave, the man died. When the road had been built to Todos Santos in the sixties, the Catholics had sent a priest to banish the Lords from the village and convert the people to Christianity. Later the Evangelicals had come, to broadcast salvation over tinny loudspeakers in cloying chants that echoed from the mountainsides like gnats whining in the face of God. The Lords of the Hills were older than the Christian God, older even than the first ancestor, and more durable than the black rocks of the Cuchumatanes. Still, today, in Todos Santos there were shamans who propitiated the Lords with ceremonies, burning candles and incense, spilling alcohol and blood. Many of these shamans performed good ceremonies, and worked for the benefit of the village, taking only just recompense in return. But some were evil, worked for gain, sold illness and death if the price was high enough. They were the practitioners of black magic, and people knew who they were.

"How do you know so much about a place you've never been?" Catherine asked.

"That's my job. I'm good at it!"

"And modest, too." They both laughed. The guide was worth the price, she reflected. Trust Zelda's pick.

They left the main road to follow a dirt track down an upland valley, going slowly to save the springs and muffler of the van as they bounced over ruts. Green mountains rose up on either side, clouds drifting up like smoke from the ravines. Finally they dropped to a settlement of houses, and a sign told them they'd reached Todos Santos, altitude 2,470 meters. Over 8,000 feet, Catherine thought, high enough to shorten your breath. The sign said they were 51 kilometers from Huehuetenango. She looked at her watch. Two hours to travel those thirty miles. Zelda hadn't been kidding when she'd called this place remote. Far away felt good.

The sun broke through the clouds when they reached the main street of town, as if in welcome. Dun-colored paving stones were bordered by raised concrete sidewalks just wide enough to accommodate a person leaning against a stucco wall, watching the village go by. The buildings were two-storied, and the street-level doorways and windows opened into shops—a hardware, a pharmacy, a foreign mail and package service—unprepossessing shops full of third-world sundries, papers and plastics of a type Catherine never saw in Iowa, thinner, brighter in color, poorer in quality. Oswaldo inched the van along the street against a tide of people walking, all the women in dark indigo skirts and the hand-woven blouses called *huipiles*. In their vibrant magentas, reds, and blues, their long hair black and glossy, the women were almost indistinguishable in their beauty. The men were bright against the dusty street in red-and-white-striped pants, the signature of Todos Santos, and pale shirts with broad embroidered collars. The women balanced bundles and baskets on their heads; the men wore straw hats and short black chaps that swung about their thighs with an alluring swagger. Bands of children scampered among them, the street their playground. The van felt out of place here. Catherine wanted to be walking, among the people, in rhythm with them.

They made a sharp turn up a steep stone street. A few doors up they stopped under a sign for the Hotel Todosantero. A young woman in the doorway struggled with a crying child. The woman's thick black eyebrows wrinkled in a frown. The child, a girl about three, Catherine guessed, with tousled hair and a dirty face, stamped her foot, broke away, and ran inside. The woman's dark eyes reached out and met Catherine's, conveying a wordless message, a communion of mothers. She shrugged and spread her hands.

In that instant Catherine figured out what had scared her so much the night before. Not where she was going, but what she was running away from. Her life. And now, just when she needed it, escape appeared in front of her, beckoning. The woman invited them inside, saying she had available rooms. She took them through a dining room onto a terrace. From here Catherine could see below her the town plaza, its austere white church, red-tiled rooftops left and right, and across the valley, the mountains rising in a green wall, keeping out the world. The woman's name was Nicolasa. Make yourselves at home, she said. Catherine already felt she belonged here, in this high valley, on this terrace. Maybe she would never go back.

2.

Nicolasa had been seven the night her town died. What struck Catherine, the next morning on the terrace, was how she told the story as she wove. The Indian woman was sitting on a low stool, the warp of her portable loom tied to a balcony post and kept tight by a strap fastened around her waist. The air was filled with wood smoke and the tinkle of marimba music from a radio somewhere. Catherine's easel was set up nearby in the bright morning sun, next to a table where her coffee sat, but she wasn't ready to paint yet. She needed to find her subject. So she drew Nicolasa. Drawing kept her hands occupied and gave her an excuse to stare at Nicolasa, watching her brown fingers work and the intricate designs in red and violet, turquoise, black, and pink appear on the strip of cloth. Nicolasa said that the patterns were handed down from the ancestors. But to Catherine it seemed that as the shuttle passed back and forth, Nicolasa's story of that event almost twenty years before was woven into the threads.

All day, Nicolasa remembered, things had been strange. Her mother and aunts were breaking pots. That upset her. Always before, whenever she picked up the big clay jar to go for water, her mother Faustina had said, "Be careful! Don't drop it!" Nicolasa's little brother, Desiderio, was only three and was not allowed to touch a pot at all.

Now her mother was breaking pots on purpose, all the big ones, and burying the shards in the *milpa*, the cornfield just outside their compound. "The soldiers are coming," Faustina said. "If they see big pots, they'll say we're feeding the guerrillas."

The soldiers came in jeeps and trucks, down the dirt road from the altiplano. Nicolasa had never seen so many trucks. She'd never seen soldiers. They wore strange clothes with green and brown spots. They carried big guns that scared her. She saw fear on the faces of her papá and uncles and grandfather.

The soldiers took down the flag of Ché Guevara that the Todosanteros had raised in the town square. They rounded up everyone in town, shouting, waving their guns, shoving people out of their houses, demanding "Where are the guerrillas?" They made everyone go into the church. There the soldiers yelled at them until all the people, even old grandfathers, were crying and shaking with fear. Even the brave young men who never showed fear were whimpering. The soldiers took some young men away, telling the people to stay inside the church, closing the doors behind them. The people inside tried to pray. But their gods weren't in the church. Their gods, Lords K'oy, Xolik, Cilbilchax, and Bach, lived on the tops of the four mountains outside of town. There was no one in the church to help them if the soldiers came back to kill them all.

All night the people listened for the return of the soldiers, for the sound of heavy boots outside the door.

But there was no sound, only silence more terrible than shouting. When Nicolasa and Desiderio whispered to their mother that they were hungry, she just told them to be quiet. Finally morning came, and someone opened the doors. They all went outside.

The soldiers were gone. The town was empty except for the crowing roosters, the roving pack of starving dogs, the pig tethered in someone's yard, and the young men left hanging from trees, dead.

One of those young men was Nicolasa's uncle Porfirio. Her parents burst into sobs. Nicolasa closed her eyes. She didn't want to see those dead bodies slowly turning in the stillness. She didn't want to hear her parents' wails. She wanted to run away. But she went home with her mother and father, her little brother, her aunts and other uncles and cousins to their compound where there were no more large pots.

"The soldiers will be back," everyone said. They packed up their belongings and trudged off into the hills with heavy bundles on their backs.

"Where are you going?" Faustina asked the neighbors.

"To Huehue," some said. "To Guate," said others. And still others, "To hide in the hills."

The rich Ladinos, people of mixed Spanish and Indian heritage, who owned all of the shops and most of the land, also left, sure that the town would be destroyed when the army returned.

"We'll stay," Faustina said.

"They can't drive us away," Nicolasa's father, Benito, said.

Nicolasa's family and some of the other Indian families who were, like them, too stubborn to leave, or too rooted to their town, or too accustomed to suffering, stayed in their compounds. They ground corn on stone mortars to make tortillas until there was not enough corn for tortillas so they mixed the ground corn *masa* with water for gruel and every day the gruel got thinner and so did they.

Nicolasa could never understand why her family had stayed. Even though the Ladinos never came back and the Indians who stayed were able to buy for a song the land and businesses left behind, Nicolasa wished they had left.

Even now, eighteen years later, when they owned the best hotel in town, she thought they should have gone when they had the chance. Because now the problems had gotten more complicated in Todos Santos. In the days when every Todosantero had to do hard physical labor just to eat, you knew your neighbors were honest. When you went down to the coast in November to pick cotton on the plantations where you'd be sprayed with pesticides while you bent in the fields and your babies would die from the poison and the heat and the starvation rations, you knew good from evil.

Now Todosanteros didn't go to the coast any more, and that was good. Instead, they went to the North, crossing two borders illegally to work in the land of gold. They sent back the dollars to build the new houses you saw going up all over town, and that was good.

But the fathers were gone, having journeyed thousands of miles, having risked their lives in the desert crossing. Often they stayed in the North and started new families and new lives there. They sent the dollars, but the children of Todos Santos were growing up without fathers, wild and undisciplined. Now, although people didn't want to admit it, there were gangs in Todos Santos, two of them, made up of these fatherless boys and their friends. Mostly the gangs only harmed each other in youthful brawls. But every time there was a theft, an accusation, some small disturbance in the public order, suspicion fell at once upon the gangs.

Nicolasa didn't think her brothers had stolen anything. After all, their father was right here to beat them up if they stepped too far out of line. Even so, Otto, the youngest, hung out and drank beer on street corners with a gang. Chancho, the middle one, was running with a wild crowd in Huehue, where he was in high school. And as for Desiderio, he was the worst problem of all. Already, at twenty-one, he'd served time for smoking marijuana. Although he was married, with a small son and responsible work as the owner of a bar, he had a reputation as a fighter and a womanizer.

* * *

Nicolasa's daughter Marvella came out of the kitchen onto the terrace. Nicolasa stopped her tale. Catherine put down her pencil. Perhaps her subject had arrived. She had an outline of a plot jotted on two pages of yellow pad. Later, after many sketches, she would write the words and make the finished illustrations for the story. This was her process, images and words complimenting each other, guiding her, holding hands as they worked their way through the hard places, like a married couple.

"I have an idea, Marvella," Catherine said. "You draw a picture. I paint you. *Está bien*?" She tore a page out of her sketchbook and put it on the table in front of the little girl. Marvella looked up at her with the expectant air of a child accustomed to the attention of *turistas*.

"What shall I draw?"

"How about me?" Catherine suggested. Maybe this would keep her still for a few minutes. She gave Marvella her pencil and squeezed a curl of ochre paint onto her waiting palette.

Marvella set to work with an intensity Catherine tried to channel onto her own canvas paper. She dipped her brush into the paint and sketched swiftly in spare lines. The child was three, as she had guessed yesterday, in constant motion, flickering from sunshine to petulance, like the sky over Todos Santos.

Catherine moved her easel into the shadow of the balcony to avoid the glare. She kept her chair in the sun. Its heat was welcome after the cold night she had spent shivering under thin blankets. She glanced back and forth as she blocked in areas of color, deep mauve for shadows, bright gold for highlights on Marvella's face. She studied Marvella against the clouds creeping up and down the mountain wall across the valley, jockeying against the brilliance of blue sky. By afternoon the clouds would dominate.

"How do you like it?!" Marvella held up her page for Catherine's approval. It was a circular scribble with lines wandering toward an unseen goal.

"Good," said Catherine. "Is that my hair?"

Marvella crowed with laughter. "That's not you. It's my mamá, weaving!"

Next to them, on her low stool, Nicolasa shifted and leaned back slightly, adjusting the tension on the weaving stretched in front of her. Her long black hair was tied into a ponytail with a red bandanna. She wore her traditional *huipil*, similar to her weaving, the blouse's elaborate patterns symbolizing corn and beans and birds and water, its white stripes radiating from the neck opening like rays of sunshine. Here, thought Catherine, the women wear their art.

"I see," she said, looking from Nicolasa to the drawing.

"See, Mamá!" Marvella whipped her drawing into her mother's face, blocking Nicolasa's view of her weaving.

"Very good, Marvella," the mother said, raising her thick eyebrows, gently pushing the drawing aside. "Now make another so that I can finish this collar for your father."

Catherine tore out another sheet from her pad. If Marvella was to be the character for her book, she was going to need a lot of pads.

Oswaldo had gone off after breakfast to do some business in the town. Catherine had asked him as he left what business could possibly get done in such an out-of-the-way spot. He'd informed her that there was a bank on the town square and three telephones for public use in stores along the main street.

She painted in the pinks of Marvella's *huipil*. The servant, Cecilia, lifted a plastic tub out of a large stone sink and carried it to the clothesline strung from a peach tree in the center of the terrace. She spread wet sheets on the line. They flapped over Catherine's head.

"Do you have children?" Nicolasa asked Catherine.

"A son," Catherine answered. "He's staying with his aunt in Antigua."

"And are you married or divorced?" A question that seemed presumptuous, but understandable, Catherine supposed, since she was traveling alone. She would hear it again many times.

"Married," she answered, "I guess. My husband seems to have lost interest in me."

"Does he have a girlfriend?"

"He's had more than one, I'm afraid." Although she didn't want to talk about Elliot with Zelda, somehow to unleash her worries to a stranger seemed easier. "I don't know what to do about it."

"Do you still love him?" Nicolasa drove straight in.

"We've been married a long time. It's hard to know what you feel after a while. Angry, hurt. Or just tired and disgusted. How do you love someone who cheats on you and all the world knows it?"

"The men of Todos Santos are never satisfied with their wives," Nicolasa said. "They're always looking for women on the side. A lot have two wives: one in town, one out of town; one up the hill, one down the hill. You go to look for a man, you have to ask his neighbors, 'Which wife is he with today?' I'm lucky my husband's not a Todosantero. He's German, came as a tourist and never left. At least he's faithful."

The terrace was filling up. Nicolasa's ancient grandmother shuffled out and knelt on a straw mat under the peach tree. She shelled nuts from a basket. A plump young woman with a placid face came out of the hotel and tied her weaving to the balcony post next to Nicolasa. Her toddler clasped her knees. Quick as a lizard, Marvella danced over to the little boy and said something Catherine couldn't understand. They were speaking Mam, their Mayan language. Suddenly the boy was crying and Marvella ran off.

Nicolasa sighed with exasperation.

"Marvella is always causing trouble. She gets it from her father. Maya children are usually quiet and happy. Not Marvella! She teases her cousin Celestino all the time. And she has tantrums. Rolfe had them too, when he was little, his mother told me."

"Has she been here? Your husband's mother?" Catherine asked.

"Oh, yes. And we have been to Frankfurt to visit Rolfe's parents. Marvella speaks three languages," Nicolasa boasted, "Mam, Spanish, and German. She makes fun of my German."

Kneeling in her ancestral sun, weaving on an ancient loom, was a woman who had traveled to Europe.

Did she wear her *huipil* and indigo *corte* skirt in Frankfurt? Catherine studied her, contrasting Nicolasa's lighter skin, golden instead of brown, and angular face with the dusky moon face of Celestino's mother, who had quieted Celestino and gone back to her weaving. Marvella was gone from the scene. Trying to paint her was like trying to tie a ribbon on a bolt of lightning. Catherine filled in the background of her oil sketch.

"Rolfe's parents want him to move back to Germany to work in the family business. A car dealership. It would be good for Marvella. The schools are better there, and women have independence. But Rolfe likes it here, the clean mountain air, country life. He likes planting his corn and working with wood. He says Europeans have forgotten how to live. He's building us a house outside of town."

"Life here seems pretty good," Catherine remarked. From what she had seen so far, the people appeared well fed, close to nature, proud of their traditions, wise about the world.

"I want something better. I don't want to raise sons here, if we have them. Look at my brothers!" Catherine had not yet met Otto, Chancho, or Desiderio. Nicolasa lowered her voice and nodded in the direction of Celestino's mother. "If you only knew what Esperanza puts up with from Desiderio!"

The moon-faced woman noticed, shrugged, and continued weaving.

"I want to go. I argue with Rolfe about it all the time," Nicolasa said. "So you see, marriage is always travail, one problem after the next."

* * *

The main street of Todos Santos continues past the square with its small concrete fountain, its tidy plantings, its scruffy shoeshine boys always on the ready to give you a polish for a quetzal. It rounds a bend and descends through the other end of town to the school, Escuela Nacional Urbana Mixta, which stands behind a wrought-iron gate and a lone pine tree. Beyond the school the street turns into a dirt road that winds down the valley seventeen kilometers to Chanchimil. Late in the afternoon of the same day that Catherine painted Marvella on the terrace of the Hotel Todosantero, Don Roberto, the principal of the school, dusted off a chair beside his desk.

"Please, have a seat. It's good to see you, *compañero*. What can I do for you?"

Domingo Pablo Pablo, mayor of Todos Santos, sat down and sighed. "Have you heard the latest news?" he asked the older man.

"I've heard rumors," Don Roberto said. Domingo had been his student once, as had all the educated people in town. The mayor still addressed the school principal with the respect that had been drummed into him as a child. "*Profe*, people are talking about the devil-worshippers again."

He paused, awaiting a response, perhaps an insight. Don Roberto nodded and rationed out his words. "So I've heard. This has happened before."

"This time the evil ones are coming from the United States to steal babies. The devil-worshippers will arrive at the full moon, remove organs from the babies, and it's said they will perform their blasphemous rituals right here in Todos Santos. On the anniversary of the cult gathering in Huehuetenango, when a schoolgirl was sacrificed."

That murder, Don Roberto knew, had never been solved. The police were not having much success cracking down on gang violence in the department capital.

"The governor has brought in extra police for Huehue," Domingo Pablo Pablo said, with some agitation, "but for Todos Santos there's nothing."

Don Roberto sat tall in his chair and clasped and unclasped his hands on the desk in front of his large Underwood typewriter. He pondered the information and studied his fingers, longer, more finely wrought, than those of the indigenous mayor. "How are the people taking these things?"

"They're frightened," said Domingo Pablo Pablo. "I'm very worried. We must protect our children. We can't afford to have something happen to destroy the tranquility of our town. We can't afford to scare away the tourists. We have five hotels and three Spanish schools for foreigners. They must be full."

"We need the tourists," Don Roberto agreed, although he knew they would never have enough gringos to fill three schools, even if the tourists came as usual. He also knew the local rivalries that had created three competing schools. He had been in Todos Santos for thirty years, although he was not a native, but a Ladino from the department capital. He'd lived with these people day and night, going up into the mountains with them to hide when the soldiers came. He celebrated and suffered with them, and shared their fears. He was as much of the place as a person could be who did not claim direct descent from the four gods dwelling in the hills outside of town. "More important is the safety of our children. Just today I had a visitor, a gringa who is interested in meeting children. I invited her to come tomorrow and see some classes. Is it possible that I'm inviting a kidnapper into school?"

"What's this woman's interest in the children?"

"She says she's an artist, painting children for a storybook. She doesn't look threatening. But what do I know? There's evil everywhere when people are stirred up."

"We must reassure them," the mayor said. "Talk to the children. Warn them of the danger. Tell them to stay indoors, not to talk to strangers. Tell them the municipal government will not permit Satan-worshippers to steal Guatemalan babies. Keep your eye on this woman tomorrow. We must be vigilant."

This was the message the mayor wanted Don Roberto to give his students, all eight hundred of them, to caution the children, and to pass on to their parents. They must be on their guard. They must trust their mayor.

"Guatemalans have always been afraid of baby-snatchers," the principal said. He thought that Todosanteros were unlikely to be reassured by the vigilance of their mayor, although he did not say this to Domingo Pablo Pablo. They had no confidence in police or politicians, who all too often, although not in the case of this mayor so far as Don Roberto knew, were thieves and murderers themselves.

"Warn them," Domingo pleaded. "They'll listen to you."

Don Roberto promised to try, and the mayor left. The principal got up to ring the bell hanging in the school courtyard to signal the end of classes. The bell was not activated by electricity but by the cord hanging from its clapper, and as a result was somewhat haphazard in its regularity.

* * *

On her second day in Todos Santos, Catherine woke up in the dark, startled out of sleep by a cacophony of horns. She felt an instant of alarm, disorientation, not knowing where she was. Then she remembered and checked her watch: four thirty. The same thing had happened yesterday, and she'd asked Nicolasa at breakfast what caused the predawn bedlam. No one had heard it, so she'd asked when the first bus left from the town square. Four thirty. She wondered how long it would take before she, too, was deaf to bus horns.

This morning she gave up the comfort of blue jeans, ideally suited to this cold climate, for a cotton skirt and sandals. She didn't hope to blend in with the women of the town, but rather to express the formality of her first visit to the school. After breakfast she and Oswaldo crossed the square, bordered on two sides by the colonnaded arcade of post office, bank, and municipal offices. Its other two sides, because of the steep angle of the hillside, were high above the level of the street. Here, people sat on concrete benches and kept an eye on everyone who walked up or down the street, as well as those on arriving and departing buses.

"Look at those two guys over there. What do you think they're saying?" Oswaldo asked Catherine.

"I have no idea." She looked at Oswaldo.

"There goes Paco, on his way to Cristobalina's house. Her husband just left on the Huehue bus, so Paco slips in the back door while her mother watches the kids."

"You think the mother would go along with this?"

"She doesn't know anything. She thinks Paco's chopping firewood."

"Come on," she laughed. "You have too much imagination."

They had an appointment at the school, made the day before when Oswaldo had brazened them into the principal's office and introduced Catherine as an artist from the United States in a way that made her feel important. Now, as they walked back to the wrought-iron gate, he seemed just as eager as she was to explore the world inside.

Don Roberto welcomed them with old world formality and led them through the central courtyard of the school. He pointed to a line of homemade brooms lying on the dusty concrete. "When the students arrive in the morning, first they sweep the schoolyard. Then they wash their hands and faces and brush their teeth. Personal hygiene is their first class of the day."

Don Roberto was proud of his school. Its student body was 96 percent indigenous, its faculty 50 percent, and they believed in bilingual education. The children were taught in Spanish and Mam. Even Ladinos learned the Mayan language. It had not always been this way, Don Roberto explained; there had been a shift in philosophy from the old days, when the only language acceptable in school was Spanish. He brought them to the first door, a kindergarten class. They went in, and all the children rose with respect at the sight of their principal. He introduced Catherine. Some of the children looked down at the floor and avoided the eyes of the stranger. But most were excited by the break in the routine and answered Don Roberto's questions eagerly, with innocent enthusiasm.

"Do you love your mamá?" he asked.

Forty-five voices chorused back, "*Sí!*"

"Do you love your papá?"

"*Sí!*"

"Do you love your teacher?"

"*Sí!*"

The classroom was spartan and crowded with roughly built wooden tables and benches, though colorful posters on the cinderblock walls reminded Catherine of an Iowa preschool. The children were ragged, and she could see the importance of the morning hygiene class. Cups with toothbrushes lined the windowsills.

"Will you sing a song for our guests? What is your favorite song?"

"*De Colores*," a number of voices shouted.

The teacher counted to three, and with no conductor the children began to sing in a medley of keys and rhythms. By the end of the first line they were together, singing in unison. Catherine could tell they did this often.

Oswaldo was delighted with the performance and led the applause. The ritual was repeated as they went from class to class, up through sixth grade, with variations in the questions the principal asked and the songs the children sang. Oswaldo requested a song in Mam, and the students complied. Sometimes the visitors watched a lesson in progress.

Then, Don Roberto would ask, "Do you love mathematics?" or Spanish, or history.

"*Sí!*" the students answered together, delivering the expected response without irony.

What Catherine saw in these classrooms bursting with students, fifty or more in a class, thrilled her. In the principal, the teachers, the children, she sensed a community working together against great odds with exuberance and humility to attain the miracle of a sixth-grade education. She wondered how her paintbrush could possibly capture this feeling.

Crossing the courtyard again, they passed an open door. A teacher at a blackboard glanced out at them. His face darkened and he scowled. Catherine thought she heard the hiss of "gringo" among the babble of student voices. Don Roberto shut the door of the classroom. "You have seen enough," he said, and led them back to his office to say goodbye.

"We are a poor country," said Don Roberto in closing, "But we are rich in spirit. And besides, not one of the students is barefoot now.

On their way back up the hill toward the Hotel Todosantero, Cathcrine remarked to Oswaldo on the contrast between these children and the cynicism and rebelliousness of Isaac and his schoolmates.

"It wouldn't be like this in Antigua, either," he said with a hint of laughter.

"Do you think I'm an idiotic foreigner, in love with the exotic natives?"

"Oh no," he said grinning. She noticed the gleam of his gold tooth, the sparkle in his eyes. "I liked the school, too. Those red pants the boys and men wear. I want to get some for myself."

* * *

Don Roberto took out a handkerchief and dabbed his face. He was relieved when the gringa had gone. She had not noticed the looks that followed her across the courtyard, or the anxiety on the faces of the children when she entered the classrooms. He had managed to convey to her the essence of the school without its dark undercurrent. What he had kept from her was also true. These days, one could not be too careful. He had not taken his eyes off her. Fortunately, she had approached none of the children. She appeared to be what she said. He had done his job. Now he would go deliver the mayor's message.

* * *

By Wednesday, Catherine had already stayed longer in Todos Santos than the average backpacker tourist, who has to keep to a tight schedule to cover all seven countries of Central America before moving on to other continents. After lunch she and Oswaldo walked up the street that went past the hotel and climbed up toward the altiplano. Oswaldo insisted on carrying Catherine's French easel. She wanted to paint a panorama of the valley. On the way out of town they stopped to look at the Mayan ruins, grassy mounds that covered buried pyramids. A small fire burned at the base of two wooden crosses set side by side.

"Looks like the Christians have staked their claim," Catherine said.

"It's a shared claim," said Oswaldo. "Only one cross is Catholic. The Maya have a cross, too, the world-tree, *Wak Chan*. The tall one is theirs. The story goes that fifty years ago, when the Ladinos came to Todos Santos and tried to replace the Indians' cross with their own, a terrible wind came. The weather turned colder than it had ever been, and all the sheep died. Then drought set in and the corn dried up. So the Maya sent their shamans to the mountaintop to find out what was wrong. Our old friends, the Lords of the Hills, told them they were being punished for casting down the cross of their forefathers that had come into being when the world was born. The shamans convinced the Ladinos to let them put the old cross back up beside the new one. Ever since then, Todos Santos has had two crosses."

"Really, Oswaldo, you continue to amaze me."

"Look at this." He led her up the grass hummock behind the two crosses. "We're standing on a buried temple," he said. "This has been sacred ground to the Todosanteros since the beginning of time. That's why the two crosses are here. People in town are upset that the crosses aren't better maintained. There used to be a roof over them. Now they have to put a plastic sheet over the ceremonial fire to keep the rain off. You'll hear from the Lords if that fire goes out."

"You think the Lords talk to gringas?"

"Probably not." He let loose a suppressed smile.

They left the ruins and continued up the road. They crossed a bridge over a mountain stream, and the paving stones ended. The dirt track zigzagged between cornfields and adobe houses up the precipitous valley wall. The road was so steep and the bends so sharp that Catherine was breathless and stopped often to rest. The sky was brilliant blue, with no hint of afternoon clouds.

At one of their pauses Oswaldo said, "Always in the rainy season there is a spell of dry weather, the *canícula* it's called. It can last a day or two, or a week. Up here in the Cuchumatanes, it frequently comes in July."

"So," said Catherine, "you've also become an expert on the climate of the Cuchumatanes."

"What did you think I was doing this morning, while you were painting?"

"Sitting in the library, maybe?" An improbable guess, she thought.

"No. I did that before we left Antigua."

Conversation was impossible while climbing at this altitude. They walked side by side in silence, mounting higher and higher. They conquered false summits to see further rises ahead. Behind them the town disappeared into the cleft of the valley. Catherine abandoned herself to the smell of pine trees and wood smoke in the thin cold air. She felt the heat of Oswaldo's body next to her. How easily he matched his pace to hers as they climbed. She let the past fall away, her long marriage, her current doubts, and felt a glow of pleasure. This place was so far removed, so complete by itself. They reached the top of the ridge; the rim of the valley disappeared in the blue toward Mexico. Mountains stretched before them. They saw the cones of distant volcanoes.

Catherine set up her easel. She could not hope to convey the vastness and emptiness of the place on a single sheet of canvas paper. But she laid in the curve of the road twisting down toward Todos Santos, passing a lone house, the shoulders of hills plunging into the valley. Oswaldo wandered off to talk to a shepherd while she worked. She glanced back and forth from her scene to her canvas to Oswaldo. She listened to their quiet voices and the *baas* of the sheep.

A while later Oswaldo was beside her again. "*Qué bonito!*" he said, looking at her oil sketch.

"You say *all* my work is beautiful," she observed.

"Do you mind?" he asked.

No, she didn't. It had been so long since she'd heard a compliment from Elliot.

That evening they sat on the terrace of the hotel to watch the sunset and drink a beer. Nicolasa joined them and asked where they had walked.

"Be careful," Nicolasa told them when she heard about the afternoon. "Normally it's very safe here. But people in the *campo* are superstitious. Don't take pictures of them without asking first. They're easily frightened. Some of them think the camera steals their souls."

"Oh my!" Catherine said. "Am I stealing Marvella's soul when I paint her?"

Nicolasa waved a finger, cautioning her to be serious. "There are rumors going around now that make the people fearful."

"What kind of rumors?" Oswaldo asked.

"About satanic cults and foreign baby-snatchers."

* * *

When the stars and moon came out and washed the mountain ridges in silver light, Catherine began to feel chilled. Coldness had always been a problem for her. She wore a sweater when other people were in T-shirts. Elliot, who was her mentor in the bedroom as in the classroom, had long complained of her cold feet. Recently he'd complained of other coolings. Her responses to his ardor were inadequate. Her orgasms were not loud enough. Here in Todos Santos at least, she didn't have to worry about his criticism. Only about the cold.

She said good night on the terrace and went up to her room, where the wind blew through the plywood walls and shook the loose frames of the windows. She had forgotten the cold nights in Guatemala when she packed her light summer nightgown. She shivered and thought about Oswaldo's warmth beside her on the ridge.

* * *

Next morning, the dry spell held. The sky was clear and blue. Marvella flitted in the sunshine from table to table, as if each tourist were a flower and she were gathering sweetness. She was in her charming mode, irresistible and impossible to pin down. Here it was Thursday, and Catherine had many starts but no finished pictures of Marvella. She had to hope the quick sketches of various angles and poses would give enough information for careful paintings later.

"Marvella, aren't you going to sit still for the artist? She's promised to give you a portrait to hang on the wall." Rolfe spoke to his daughter in his accented Spanish. She orbited within range and alighted at the table next to Catherine.

"Thanks," Catherine said, and started working fast, while she had the chance. Rolfe watched her. The other men of the family were rarely around. Nicolasa's portly and affable father, Benito, greeted her when he saw her, but seemed to spend his days in meetings with no time to

45

spare for the hotel's guests, who were tended to by the women. Rolfe, on the other hand, had stopped to speak to her every morning as he left to work on the house he was building. He wore the red pants and embroidered shirt of the Todosanteros, gaudy compared to his thin European face, scraggly brown hair, and Teva sandals. But Catherine thought he'd earned the right to wear *traje*, as they called the native costume. He'd adopted the culture as his own.

Discordant music reached the terrace, a hymn that sounded familiar to Catherine, sung out of key and broadcast from a nearby temple. The temple's speakers were aimed at the church, as though Evangelicals and Catholics were doing battle in song for the souls of Todos Santos. Hallelujahs ricocheted off the façade of the sixteenth-century church, its windows and doors closed in stately forbearance. Nicolasa came out onto the terrace and tied her weaving to the post. Her grandmother took up her spot on the mat under the peach tree. Another woman knelt beside the old woman and grasped her arm in both hands, at the wrist and elbow.

"What's she doing?" Catherine asked Rolfe.

"Reading her pulse. To tell her future. Everyone here, no matter how well educated, believes in the powers of the *pulsera*. Even my wife." He winked at Nicolasa. "After you've been here long enough, you'll believe, too."

Nicolasa shook her ponytail and sniffed. "Liar!"

"Doña Margarita is asking Doña Juana if she should journey to Quetzaltenango to visit her other grandchildren. At that age you don't undertake a trip lightly. At my age, either. For example, a trip to Germany could have all kinds of hidden dangers." Nicolasa sniffed again.

"Perhaps, my love, you should ask Doña Juana to read your pulse," Rolfe said. "You might not be so happy a European wife as you think. Sometimes it's surprising what the *pulsera* can tell you about yourself." He exited before his wife could retort.

"He thinks he's so clever!" she said when he was gone. "He's learning about medicinal plants from Doña Juana and thinks the world of her. She's a *comadrona*, a midwife, also. She delivered Marvella."

The child looked up from her drawing at the sound of her name. She'd been sitting remarkably still for a remarkably long time. The period of grace was over. She dashed out after her father, shouting, "A hug! Papá, a hug!"

Catherine felt good about the rapid likeness she'd snagged while listening to the conversation. The nice thing about painting was that it used the part of her brain that didn't think in words. She could listen to a talk show on the radio, carry on an imaginary argument with Elliot about Isaac, or learn about the rivalry between the Catholics and Evangelicals while her visual mind was free to soar.

Oswaldo came out onto the terrace, his hair wet from a shower, brushed up straight and stiff.

"I'll see you at lunchtime," he said.

"Where are you going?" Catherine asked.

"Wouldn't you like to know?" he teased. "To visit my friends in town."

"Are you getting bored here?" When she had hired him for the week, it had been with the idea that she might want to travel around and see more of the Cuchumatanes. Since she had not left Todos Santos, there was no real need for him to stay. But somehow, she hadn't wanted him to leave before Sunday, the day they had agreed upon. So the subject hadn't come up. This was the closest she'd come to broaching it.

"Not at all," he said with his gold-toothed smile. "I enjoy seeing your new painting every day and walking with you in the afternoon."

"You're easily amused."

* * *

"A Gallo," Oswaldo said. It was Friday evening.

The bartender passed him a bottle of beer without comment. In the Bar Sin Nombre on the main street of town, a bottle of the native brew was the most common order. Occasionally someone would splurge on a rum and Coke, but not often.

There were no women in the bar, only a few young men in those red pants sitting at wooden tables. Oswaldo liked the red pants so much that he had ordered a pair from a local tailor the other morning while Catherine painted Marvella. Loud strains of merengue filled the room, which was decorated with bamboo and corncobs and crudely painted abstract patterns in black and white.

Oswaldo had tried both of the bars in town. He and Catherine had eaten in the one across the street, upstairs, with a carved wood balcony. It served gringo food, pasta dishes and salads washed in bottled water. But he liked this one, the No Name.

A man in red pants waved Oswaldo over to his table and clasped his shoulders in an overfriendly greeting. "*Compadre!*" he exclaimed. Oswaldo could smell the alcohol on his breath. "Where is the North American woman? Or don't you want to share her with us?"

"She likes to spend the evening reading and working," Oswaldo said. He knew already that he was with the local group of studs who flaunted their adventures with foreign women.

"Don't be so selfish. Look at us. We have no women here."

"Take it easy, Juan," another at the table said. This one was drinking *aguardiente*, Guatemala's powerful sugarcane liquor, called *rum* but cheaper and more to the point, mixed with Sprite. "You're just back from Lívingston. Give your little friend a rest."

"I'll tell you about Lívingston." Juan kept his arm around Oswaldo's shoulders.

"I know Lívingston," Oswaldo said. It was the town with the English name on the gulf coast that attracted tourists with its blend of Caribbean culture, Indian villages, and seedy nightclubs.

"I went down there with a girl from Canada. Man, she was fat. But she was lonely."

"They come here with their pockets full of money and their hearts full of emptiness," the *aguardiente* drinker said.

"*Hombre*! So we empty their pockets and fill their hearts," another at the table chimed in.

"So what did she give you, Juan?"

"Two hundred dollars. That doesn't last long in Lívingston. Good thing I had five hundred quetzales in my back pocket she didn't know about. I was only going to sleep with her once. She was too fat for me."

Oswaldo sipped his beer slowly and listened without comment. He noticed the bartender watching them gravely, drinking a Coke. Oswaldo recognized the bartender with his long black ponytail, his necklace of lion's claws, his discreet nose piercing. Oswaldo had seen the man at the hotel. He was Desiderio, the owner's oldest son, and Oswaldo had wondered if he were a drug dealer.

"So then what?" the talk about Lívingston continued with a lot of drunken laughter.

"We fucked," said Juan as a matter of not-too-interesting fact.

"Just once?"

"Yes. I tell you, she was fat. Then we had a fight over money. So I went to a bar, and the bartender, she was very pretty."

"Did you fuck her, too?"

"But why not?"

The door of the Sin Nombre opened and two young women walked in. Immediately the atmosphere in the bar changed. Even the music shifted, by magic, from salsa to rock. The girls were tall and blonde, booted and layered in khaki for their third-world expedition, the way rugged European youth always came to Todos Santos. Oswaldo had met them earlier at the hotel, two Danes.

Juan detached himself from Oswaldo as the girls drifted toward them with cries of friendship—*Hola! qué tal, Juanito, Basilio, Florindo, Felícito, cómo estás?*—and kisses on cheeks. They sat down and Oswaldo watched the predators cluster around them, lovely loose girls from Europe. The bartender brought them beers and plates of food which they readily offered to the men at the table. It was as if they couldn't be generous enough. Their good will poured out of them like liquid gold and splashed over the men, who laughed and drank it in. The two girls put their arms around the men and pressed their bodies against them and pulled them up to dance between the tables in the room hung with corncobs in the ancient Mayan custom. The girls danced from man to man as everyone grew drunker except Oswaldo and the solemn bartender.

Oswaldo was about to leave when the door flew open again and two men marched in. The first was on a mission. The second was trying to hold him back.

"Baudilio! Hey! What are you doing here? Join the party." Greetings were tossed toward them from the dancing revelers. But the angry man ignored them, threw off his friend's flimsy hold, and went straight toward the bar.

"The curse of the Lord is on the house of the wicked!"

Baudilio stormed behind the bar. He clutched the bartender's shirt in two fists and leaned toward him. Desiderio tried to push him away, and said something Oswaldo couldn't hear.

"Desiderio, you bastard, *cabrón*, I'm going to break your bones!" Baudilio shouted. "It's not enough you destroy men's bodies with alcohol and get rich off the ruin of their souls. Your family's hotel brings the godless foreigners into Todos Santos to spread their sin and their diseases. This hellhole of yours is a blemish in the sight of God! And that's not enough! You fornicator, now you're messing around with my daughter!"

Baudilio shook Desiderio by the handfuls of shirt he held. The bartender pushed him back hard, breaking his grasp. Baudilio fell against the bar.

"Baudilio, you asshole, get out of here. Desiderio doesn't need to fool with your daughter. He has a wife of his own," someone said. The men from the dance floor tottered toward the bar, leaving the Danish girls to watch the altercation.

"That never stopped Desiderio," someone else said with snicker. Baudilio straightened up.

"Lay off, preacher-man. I wouldn't be surprised if you've gotten into a few daughters, yourself!" another onlooker volunteered, and they all guffawed.

Baudilio slugged Desiderio once in the mouth before hands grabbed him and shoved him toward the door, where his friend pulled him out onto the street. The men tried to pick up where they'd left off, but now it was becoming difficult for many of them to dance.

Oswaldo carried his empty bottle to the bar where Desiderio was wiping his mouth with a damp cloth.

"That Baudilio is an angry man," Oswaldo said.

"Baudilio is scum. He has blood on his hands, just like his hero, Ríos Montt. He preaches his venom to his Evangelical congregation."

"It doesn't look like he has many friends here." But Oswaldo noticed that no one had come up to Desiderio after the brawl to inquire about his bleeding lip.

"Even here they listen to him. People like anyone who speaks evil of his neighbors. They pretend to ignore him, but they're drawn to him, hypnotized, as to the hissing of a snake. He'll have them believing whatever he wants about me. Before long he'll have them forming vigilante groups to patrol the town, to guard it from troublemakers, he'll say. But he's the one brewing trouble, with his warnings and accusations. Something's going to happen in this town." Desiderio turned away and disappeared into the back room.

Strange man, thought Oswaldo. He wore red pants like the rest of them, but he was no peasant. He looked like a drug dealer, drank Coke, ran his business, played with his toddler son on the terrace of the hotel, but ignored his quiet and demure wife.

Oswaldo left the bar and walked up the dark and empty street. He carried a rock in one hand; wild packs of dogs roamed the town at night. He thought about the rage and fear smoldering in the town. He would have to warn Catherine. It was his job to protect her.

The men at the Bar Sin Nombre had circled those Danish girls like coyotes at a chicken shed, just waiting to pluck them, the way Juan had done the fat Canadian. Oswaldo, too, had occasionally had a fling with a passing tourist. But these men disgusted him. He was not like them. Particularly not when it came to Catherine. He liked being with her, talking to her, carrying her paint box up the mountain and feeling her close to him. He liked watching her work, seeing her smile, sensing her sadness. Someday he wanted to give his whole heart to a woman who would care for it, and make tortillas for him and give him children scampering around his knees. So far that woman had not come along, and he was in no hurry. That woman certainly wouldn't be Catherine.

* * *

On Saturday morning Catherine and Oswaldo worked their way through the packed market. The street to the hotel was lined with vendors, their wares spread on the pavement, enamel bowls, pitchers made from industrial-sized tomato juice cans, plastic containers of every description, barrettes, hair ribbons, bandannas and handkerchiefs, baskets of rice and peppers and fruit and live turkey chicks, sacks of potatoes, the shells of dead armadillos.

"What do you use those for?" Catherine asked the little boy minding the armadillo shells.

He regarded her as if to say, If you have to ask, don't bother. "I'm looking after them for my uncle. He'll be back soon," was his explanation.

Oswaldo laughed in her ear as they pressed through the dense crowd trying to make its way down to the corner. "They bang on them, like drums, at dances and celebrations," he said.

She loved that he knew that.

Finally they escaped to an area where they could actually shop, the crowd was thin enough. The town was extraordinary today, with people decked out in costumes from their native villages, lacy *huipiles*, pleated *cortes*, white pants from San Juan Atitán. Oswaldo sported his new red pants of Todos Santos, strutting a bit. Up a side street Catherine saw what she was looking for.

"*Sobrepantalones!*" She pointed them out to Oswaldo. The black wool chaps she had noticed her first day in the town, that the men of Todos Santos wore over their red pants, cupping their buttocks and opening with silver buttons at the tops of their thighs. "You have to have them," said Catherine, "They look so. . ." She couldn't say it: sexy. "Cute," she finished.

"You think so?" Oswaldo cocked an eyebrow.

"Oh, yes!" Catherine giggled and picked up the *sobrepantalones*, holding them up to Oswaldo, asking the vendor how much. She counted out the quetzales from her money belt and gave Oswaldo her purchase. "A gift from me."

"Thanks," he said. "When I wear them I'll remember you." They were close together. He touched her lips with his in a brief, Spanish kiss, the kind that said hello, goodbye, and thank you, but not I love you.

Catherine wished the kiss could have lasted just a little longer. Perhaps it might have, in another setting, where a hundred eyes weren't watching them. She thought about the kiss later, in the afternoon, when Oswaldo took her hand to help her climb over rocks beside the river. They were alone now. The water rushing by them made a symphony of gurgles and splashes. Grass spread out on the bank in an invitation. Which they declined, walking on down the trail. She thought about it again that evening on the terrace after supper, when the stars came out and she shivered with cold and wondered if she could wrap Oswaldo's arms around her instead of putting on another fleece jacket. He was standing so close to her it would not have been difficult. But he turned away and said goodnight.

This time, if he'd kissed her again with that Spanish kiss that can also say goodnight, she would have pulled him to her and not let those lips escape so fast. But he didn't, although surely the kiss must have been on his mind too.

"A long day tomorrow, Catarina," he said instead. "I'm going to turn in early, if you don't mind."

And even if she did mind, what, really, could she say?

3.

L ate in the afternoon in the Cybercafé Acción on Antigua's Calle de la Sin Ventura, also known as Fifth, Bernie Schwartz had been watching the kid next to him long enough to have a pretty good idea of where he headed on the Net. First he'd grabbed his mail off the POP3 server. While he was waiting for the download, he checked k10k for the latest updates, and logged onto the Ars Technica message board, no doubt to see what the gossip was in the DC forum.

The kid appeared to be about Bernie's age. He kept pushing stray blond hairs out of his face while his fingers flew over the keyboard. The fact that some of the letters were in weird places on account of the keyboard being Spanish, and that some of the keys had their letters worn off them so you just had to know or guess what they were, didn't seem to bother him. That long ponytail was a mess. He obviously wasn't into personal appearance, not like Bernie, who was fastidious in his grooming. The kid's light blue eyes glowed with fervor at the screen. Back at Yahoo! it seemed he had gotten nothing but spam, so he closed that.

Bernie got up, went over, tapped him on the shoulder. "Hey! Wanna come over to my place and play Quake?"

The kid looked up, took him in, realized Bernie was speaking to him in English. "Where's your place? Here? In Antigua?"

"Yeah, of course. What do you think, we're gonna fly back to New Jersey to play Quake? It's just a few blocks away." He picked up his backpack and slung it over his shoulders.

The two boys, two gringo boys, the one in typical jeans and T-shirt, Bernie preferring khakis and a polo, left the Internet café and headed out across the plaza. Afternoon clouds were looming over the peak of the volcano Agua south of town, over the gracious arcade that faced the square, over the avenues of manicured trees and luxuriant flowerbeds and climbing bougainvillea. The throngs of international tourists, *ricos* from the capital, and local businesspeople, who would in sunshine be ambling by the fountain and lingering on benches, scurried to get where they were going before the rain. The boys, however, sealed in their adolescent bubble, were oblivious to both the scene's colonial charms and any impending downpour. Bernie continued his social overtures.

"So I'm Bernie Schwartz and you already know I'm from Jersey." He waited for the kid's reply. It was long in coming, and Bernie was impatient. "Who're you? What are you doing in this shithole?"

"Isaac Barnes. I'm from Iowa. My mom dropped me off here while she goes on a trip to find herself. My aunt's supposed to be straightening me out."

"Yeah." Bernie laughed. "Don't you love the way they think we're the ones need to be fixed?"

The rain began, with big drops pelting the boys and splashing on the cobblestones.

"Rats!" Bernie swore and quickened his pace. "Hurry! Let's get out of this." He led them at a clip beyond the plaza, along a straight street lined with expensive shops selling jade jewelry and handicrafts adapted to the tourist trade. Restaurants boasting international cuisine opened on the sidewalk. They rounded a corner and Bernie came to a halt in front of a massive wooden door and took his key from his pocket.

"Home sweet home," he said, and ushered Isaac inside. They darted through a narrow strip of garden where impatiens and hibiscus bloomed in a profusion of pinks under a lime or lemon tree—Bernie could never remember which was which down here—and reached the shelter of the roof overhanging the front door of his house. He threw his backpack onto a wooden bench by the door, removed his wire-rimmed glasses, and tried to dry them on the tail of his polo shirt. "I'm soaked!" he announced with disgust. "Frigging rainy season. It does this every day."

Isaac squeezed his wet ponytail and grinned. "Me too."

Bernie tried the doorknob. Locked.

Good. That meant the maid had gone. They had the place to themselves.

He unlocked it and took Isaac in through the living room, grabbed towels from the bathroom that, like all the rooms in the house, opened onto the inner courtyard, and chucked one to Isaac. Bernie's room was in the back. He peeled off his shirt and tossed it into a basket on the terra cotta tiled floor.

"You want dry clothes?" he asked, eyeing the T-shirt sticking to Isaac's skinny frame. Isaac's jeans hung loose on him. Bernie wasn't fat, just stocky and rounded.

"That's okay," Isaac said. "I'll air dry."

Bernie shrugged. "As you weesh, *señor*." He took out a fresh polo, also light blue, from the antique wooden wardrobe, put it on, and checked his reflection in the wardrobe's mirror while combing his short, dark hair so that it curled correctly around his forehead. Then he pulled a second of those clunky wood chairs this place was littered with up to his computer, on the antique table by his bed. His computer was the only thing in the room that didn't look like it belonged in a museum. The two sat down and booted up. "What are you supposed to be straightening up from?" Bernie asked while they waited for Quake to open.

"Flunking out of eighth grade. Are you here on vacation?"

"I wish," Bernie said. "I've been here since January, going to school in Guat City. Ninth grade. I just got back from school when I saw you in the cybercafé. Can you imagine, school in July? This place sucks. And I'm stuck here for two years."

* * *

Isaac could have played Quake for hours, but after a while Bernie suggested they take a break and smoke some pot. Isaac hadn't ever smoked pot, but of course he didn't want Bernie to know that and think he was some hick from the Iowa cornfields. So he said sure. As off-handedly as possible he added, "You're not expecting anyone home soon, are you?"

"Nah. My mom doesn't get back from teaching English until after six. Dad commutes from the City. Hotshot bankers work late. My parents have no idea how early Floridalma takes off. Not that they'd care. Maids are dirt cheap down here. And if they're paying her to keep an eye on me, that's a joke. Suppose I wanted to burn the place down, she'd help me find the matches. She doesn't hate my parents or anything. That's just the way it is here. I'm her young *caballero*. Gentleman."

"I know Spanish." Isaac was watching Bernie roll the marijuana into the paper and lick it shut like a pro. He let Bernie take the first drag so he could imitate the slow inhalation, try to keep it in as long as Bernie did, try to stifle the urge to cough. It was a while before there were any more opportunities for conversation. By that time Isaac thought he could feel a bit of buzz, but he wasn't sure. The sensation was not as radical as he'd expected. He was a little disappointed.

"My aunt's going to wonder where I am soon," he said.

"We'll just finish this up," Bernie said.

The joint was so small now you couldn't hold onto it. Bernie picked it up in a tarnished silver clip like a short tweezer, only fancy. Isaac wondered where he got the thing. Isaac was a loner at school, avoiding the druggies as well the jocks. They were all morons in his opinion: slaves to their teachers, or their coaches, or the latest teen fad. Bernie seemed like maybe he didn't follow the pack either. Instead of the usual collection of sports trophies and rock paraphernalia, the shelves on the wall by the computer table displayed an eccentric mix of Chinese robots and Warhammer figures. Isaac picked up one of the figures. It was a little over two inches high and heavy, made of metal, not plastic.

"Did you paint this Bloodthirster?" he asked. The paint job was really good. Bloodthirster's great bat-like wings were red shaded with black. His horns had gold tips. Silver chains wrapped around arms meticulously veined in purple. His battle ax gleamed silver. He looked every inch a Chaos Demon.

"Yeah." Bernie gestured toward the jars of paint on a smaller table in the corner of the room. Slender brushes with only a few hairs lay scattered among the jars. "Most of my stuff is back in New Jersey."

"I have a Dark Eldar Army." What amazing luck that the one kid Isaac met in Guatemala was into Warhammer too.

"No shit," Bernie said. "Do you play Fantasy?"

"Mostly Forty K. Too bad I don't have my army here so we could play."

"Come over again tomorrow. We'll play Quake," Bernie said.

* * *

Zelda was heating the pot of black beans left over from lunch when her nephew came in. She noticed his bloodshot eyes but didn't comment on them. Instead she asked, "How was the cybercafé?"

"Fine."

"You were gone quite a while. What did you think of your first day on the job?"

"Good," said Isaac. He was a master at the one word answer, she had already discovered.

"Hungry?" she asked.

He was ravenous, even though they'd eaten a big meal in the middle of the day, closing up the shop for an hour to do so. Zelda watched him shovel in the black beans. "Worked up a big appetite, didn't you?"

He met her eyes and seemed to reflect, as if calculating how much she could see below the surface. "Well, I'm a growing kid, you know?"

"That you are."

She'd been impressed by what a willing worker he was, following her directions with unexpected docility, unfolding, refolding, and stacking cloth after cloth for her as she went through her inventory of hand weavings, brightly colored fabrics from Sololá and San Pedro Necta, from Chichi and Ixta, Patzun and Patzicía, every little village in Guatemala, each with its own distinctive pattern. Isaac learned the designs rapidly, and even appeared to appreciate their beauty.

But one thing she knew that he wasn't going to do was open up and engage in conversation.

* * *

Isaac didn't mind the job, as he explained to Bernie the next afternoon. Hard work was okay, and for some reason taking orders from Aunt Zelda didn't piss him off. Strange, since there was no one else on the planet he could say that about, which was why he had flunked out of eighth grade. Teachers were always telling you what to do. The dumbest things, too, like "Homework is 30 percent of your grade." Never mind that you did all the classwork and aced all the tests and quizzes, demonstrating to any idiot that you could learn the shit without putting in the after-school drudge time when you had better things to do, like install a new operating system. No, with homework at 30 percent they'd hit you with a C or D or worse. Just to teach you a lesson. What lesson, he wondered. How small-minded they were?

Aunt Zelda wasn't stupid. And she didn't make you do stuff without a reason.

"We had a sit-out in school," he told Bernie. "They thought I started it. That's what it was really about, not my grades." It was their dishonesty that angered Isaac, the dishonesty of the adult world.

"And did you?" Bernie was rolling a joint again. Like yesterday, his mother wasn't home. Floridalma was out behind the kitchen washing clothes, but Bernie said that didn't matter, she wouldn't notice if a bomb dropped.

"No. Well, kinda. My friend Andrew really thought it up." Andrew was his one friend, the only kid at school who was up to his intellectual standard. They were designing a Web page together, trying to start a business online. "Teachers all talk about gender equality, then they let the girls get out of taking wrestling. Doing dance while we're on the mat grabbing onto each other's sweaty bodies. Yuck. Even the girls signed our protest petition. The administration said they would give it to a study group. Right! In ten years they'd fix the problem. But the faculty grew up in the sixties, or wished they had, so they thought it would be cool to help us organize a civil protest. A sit-out of gym." Talk about mixed messages! The boys passed the joint between them. Isaac felt it more today than he had yesterday. Bernie's room began to pulse and sparkle a little. Nice.

"They did? What a joke!" Bernie whooped with laughter.

"Yeah, really. They said it would be okay to sit out of gym and accept an F for the day as long as we didn't interfere with the learning of others. But the gym teacher didn't think it was okay. He must've enlisted for Vietnam while the rest of them were at Woodstock. I thought he was gonna have a stroke, he was so mad. So it ended with me in the principal's office, getting suspended." The suspension put to rest any hope that he would jump through the year's remaining academic hoops. Isaac won the battle of wills. Eighth grade crashed and burned.

"Did your parents flip?"

"No. My dad's an artist and wannabe rebel. He thinks the principal's an asshole. Anyway, he's too busy chasing girls at the college where he teaches to worry about me. I'm not supposed to know, but I overheard my mom talking on the phone." Isaac affected a breezy tone, to show that even in Iowa kids could be worldly on the topic of parental infidelity.

"No shit. That's too good." Bernie collapsed in another fit of giggles. Isaac figured it must be the effects of the pot. Come to think of it, maybe it was the pot that was making him run off at the mouth so much.

"My mom doesn't think so. She's run away," he said.

"Even better. You've got a great setup. No parents!"

Isaac watched Floridalma out the back window, pinning the wash on the clothesline while the clouds piled up overhead. Looked like the laundry would get a second rinse. Nobody had dryers here, although it would have made their lives so much easier if they had. Floridalma appeared to be used to drudgery, accepting it like an assignment. It seemed unfair, in his clear-cut judgment of the world. Isaac wasn't used to servants. "Yeah, but my aunt, Sergeant Z, checks my room every morning to make sure my bed is made."

"That's a drag. Floridalma makes mine. She won't let me lift a finger."

"Zelda's not so bad, really. She chain-smokes and says *fuck* in front of me. And she's paying me to work in her shop."

"Oh yeah? How much? I'm broke now. My allowance doesn't cover nearly all my expenses."

"A hundred bucks a week."

"Wow!" Bernie rubbed his hands together. "A hundred bucks can take you far in this country. We'll have to figure out what to do with it. You have Saturday off?"

* * *

"Listen to this." Bernie opened the paperback to the dog-eared page. "'I believed that I was wandering the world in order to turn the wheel of the True Meaning and gain merit for myself as a future Buddha (Awakener) and as a future Hero in Paradise.' Jack Kerouac." Bernie jumped up from his bed, where they'd been munching from a box of Cheerios. They were sick of Quake and out of marijuana.

"Let's go," he said. "Do you have money on you? We need to start getting outfitted for the weekend."

The week was wearing on and they didn't have a plan yet. Bernie said he was still thinking. But Isaac had some dollars. They walked out into a sunny afternoon, no showers today, so the atmosphere around the fountain in the center of the plaza was bright and celebratory, as was usual in this land of eternal springtime. Light-hearted tourists poked among handicrafts spread out on the paving, dickered with Indian vendors, snapped pictures. The boys dawdled by the fountain, listening to some revivalist nearby trying to harvest souls. They couldn't follow his Spanish too well at the rate he was haranguing, but there was no mistaking the message. "Karl Marx was right," Isaac said. "Religion's the opiate of the people. Look at that guy. Brain dead."

"They love religion here," Bernie said. "Jesus, voodoo, the Pope, it's all the same."

"No it's not," Isaac argued. "At least the Catholics leave people alone, let them practice their old customs as long as they call their gods Mary and Jesus. The Protestants want to take them over and brainwash them. Reminds me of the US government."

"What are you, an anarchist?" Bernie was looking around, searching for someone.

"Libertarian," Isaac said.

"What's that?"

But before Isaac could explain that it was government that corrupted people and turned them into slaves and criminals, that without government people tended to get along, Bernie became distracted. Past the preacher and his little knot of earnest listeners he had apparently spotted someone.

"Come on," he said, again leading the way.

Isaac tensed. He felt nervous about the upcoming transaction, especially since it was his money they were using, which he slid into Bernie's hand as they approached a nondescript guy with the greasy Latin look. Bernie knew him, that was obvious. Isaac tried not to glance around for cops toting automatic weapons while Bernie whispered with the guy. Then Bernie passed the sleazoid the folded bills and got in return a small package wrapped in dirty brown paper. They walked away.

"Great. Now we're set for the weekend," Bernie said. "I've got it figured out. We're going to Lívingston."

"Lívingston? Is that in Guatemala?"

"Yeah. It's down on the Caribbean Coast. It's got black people, they call them Garífuna. There's discos, music, action. We'll take a bus."

"Just the two of us? My aunt will never let me go. Guatemalan buses are always getting hijacked and falling into ravines."

"Don't tell her. I'll think of something. Don't worry. I'm used to handling bandidos. Remember, I go to school in the capital. Everyone I know has been robbed there, some more than once. You just watch your back." Bernie cuffed him on the back. "I'll take care of Auntie Z. We have to wander the world and gain merit as future Buddhas."

Kerouac had become their bible, as he had for generations of young men eager to shake the shackles of boyhood. Isaac had borrowed the book from Bernie and read it straight through in one night. He liked that in Bernie he at last had someone he could talk about ideas with, not like the kids in Iowa. Still, when Kerouac had written *Dharma Bums*, he'd at least been old enough to have a driver's license.

* * *

Zelda was glad Isaac had found a friend his age. She hadn't met Bernie Schwartz, but from what she managed to squeeze out of Isaac she figured him to be a smart kid with a bad attitude. Maybe not the best influence on Isaac, but clearly a soul mate, which Isaac needed. There was an aloneness about her nephew Zelda didn't like. She wanted him to break out of his shell, care more about the people around him. From what Catherine had told her, she didn't think he had any real friends in Iowa, just cronies he hung out with, cut classes with. From the bounce in his step as he set out from the shop at the end of the day to meet Bernie, Zelda guessed that the kid from New Jersey had breached Isaac's defenses. So if he came home stoned, she didn't worry. Better to experiment here, under her watch, than back where there were teachers and principals and parents to go ballistic.

Isaac came into the kitchen just as Zelda finished frying the pork chops. That was the other thing. He managed to get home every night in time for supper, no matter what he and Bernie had been up to.

"How's your friend Bernie today?" she asked as they sat down at the kitchen table to eat.

"Good. His parents have invited me to go with them to Livingston this weekend."

Isaac didn't like to waste his imagination. He believed that the best lies were closest to the truth. So even though Bernie had fabricated an elaborate story about his parents' beautiful condominium in Panajachel for Isaac's benefit, the fiction went unused at the critical moment, facing Zelda's X-ray vision.

"Lívingston! That's a long way to go for a weekend," Zelda replied.

"That's why we're going to fly to Puerto Barrios. They said it's just a half hour boat ride from there, so we'll get in before lunch if we leave Antigua at five in the morning."

Two taxis, a plane, and a high-speed launch just to get there, Zelda thought. Then the hotel and repeat the process to get back. "Who's going to pay for all this?" she asked.

"Ed and Cynthia. Mr. and Mrs. Schwartz." Isaac had just met Bernie's parents for the first time that evening, and was glad he remembered their names. "But I'll take along my own money to pay for extra stuff."

"That's pretty nice of them," Zelda mused. She hated the lowlands, too hot, and would never take Isaac there herself. This was a chance for him to see a new place and spend time with his friend. "It still seems like a lot of traveling for one night."

Isaac thought fast. They hadn't planned on an extra day, but why not? "That's what I wanted to ask. Could I have Monday off? Bernie doesn't have school, some saint's day, and the Schwartzes want to stay over." It seemed even when you wanted to keep your lies simple, things could get out of hand. Would Aunt Z bother to check the schedule of the American School in Guatemala for unusual saints' days?

"That sounds like a more sensible schedule. But I won't pay you for Monday if you're not at work."

"Of course not. I'll tell Bernie tomorrow."

Zelda had swallowed the story. Now he had to go.

* * *

The worst thing about the lie was having to leave at five on Saturday morning, supposedly to catch the six a.m. flight out of Guate they'd read about in *Lonely Planet*, when really they were going to catch a bus that ran at all hours of the day. But Isaac had stuffed a few things into his backpack the night before, and was up way before dawn to get last admonitions from Aunt Z.

"Remember," she said, "you get into any situation you don't like, call me. Any hour of the day or night. And don't keep your money in your back pocket."

Looking less like a drill sergeant than she sounded in her sleeveless nightgown, her large arms spilling out of skimpy straps, she gave him a quick hug and let him out to walk by himself through the dark streets of Antigua to the fountain, where he met Bernie. People were up and about already, getting a jump on the day, Isaac figured, in the middle of the night. He wasn't at all pleased when Bernie paused in the cathedral ruins to light up.

"Just a couple hits for the journey," Bernie whispered. Isaac wondered what the Guatemalan police did with gringo boys caught in possession. But he weighed the risks against the fun, and fun won. A few hits later they continued on their way, their thoughts charged and swirling like the bats circling the streetlights of the old capital. Their adventure took on an epic importance. Isaac felt excitement overcoming his fears; he felt the boldness of the two of them venturing into the unknown.

"Odysseus sets out from Troy," he said.

"Oh yes!" Bernie cackled, "you gotta tie me to the mast so I can listen to those Garífuna sirens, mon." Bernie was convinced that the black women of Livingston were voluptuous and available. That he was a shortish, bespectacled boy not yet shaving didn't seem to dismay him.

They waited on the corner for the bus to the capital. It pulled up, an ancient American school bus painted in brilliant designs of red, yellow, and green and spangled with iridescent decals across the windshield: the notorious Guatemalan chicken bus. Isaac had never been on one, although he saw them all the time in Antigua, discharging diesel fumes and black smoke, horns blasting.

"*Hay lugares!*" called the *ayudante* hanging from the open door, but if there were spaces in the bus, Isaac couldn't see them. Seats designed for two American children were packed with three adults, many with kids on their laps, and the aisle was jammed as well. Bernie shoved his way resolutely into the crowd. Isaac followed in his wake down the aisle.

"*Atrás, jóvenes!*" the *ayudante* screamed. Get back! Bernie pressed harder into the mass of flesh. More people piled in behind Isaac, smashing him against Bernie's backpack. The bus lurched up the street, bouncing over the cobblestones, and Isaac grabbed the back of a seat for support.

"It's like this on Saturday because people are taking stuff to the market in Guate," Bernie said in his ear. Isaac's senses were overwhelmed by pungent body odors and the sharp scent of vomit from a nearby baby. Sounds of laughter, children crying, and people chatting battled with the over-amplified bus radio. Outside of town, the bus continued to take on passengers, defying credibility. Huge bundles tied in net bags and plastic crates of animate and inanimate cargo were wrestled onto the roof by the *ayudante* and lashed to a metal rack that had not been there when this bus had plied the streets of suburban Peoria. As they mounted the steep hill out of Antigua, the engine ground and wheezed, as if it was about to die. The bus inched up the mountain while the *ayudante* forced his way down the aisle, collecting fares.

"Three Q's each," Bernie told Isaac. "Not too much to pay for all this festivity, hey?"

Isaac dug for the heavy gold-colored coins in his front pocket, then tried to lean out of the way to let the *ayudante* worm past. There was no place to go. Isaac watched with astonishment as the *ayudante* hoisted himself up onto the backs of the bus seats and clambered past him, collecting fares as he went.

Forty-five minutes later the bus descended into Guatemala City and rumbled to a stop in a grimy downtown park.

"Welcome to beautiful Zone 1," Bernie said, when they had debarked. "Crime pit of the capital." They swaggered down the street like they knew what they were doing and carried switchblades in their pockets. Isaac noted that they were the only foreigners to be seen, possibly for miles. The city stretched out before them, huge and shabby—potholed streets, crumbling sidewalks, cinderblock buildings all screamingly third world. It was impossible for Isaac to tell who among the milling pedestrians might be criminals, who victims. Fortunately Bernie knew where to go, and led them without hesitation.

"How many hours to fucking Puerto Barrios?" Isaac felt done-in already.

"Five!" Bernie's energy was undiminished. "Don't worry. No more chicken bus."

The Pullman to Puerto Barrios was, by contrast, normal. Soft, reclining seats all to themselves were pure luxury. Bernie talked non-stop for the first hour, about the wheel of existence and the creeps at the American School who had nothing weightier on their minds than football and gossip and getting into snob schools in the States. Isaac eventually dozed off in the middle of a sentence, and woke up dripping with sweat.

The bus pulled into a dirt area in front of some buildings. Steam appeared to be rising from mud puddles. The boys staggered off the bus and into the heat. Their pants stuck to their legs. The dozen blocks to the pier proved that Puerto Barrios—the town that United Fruit built in the early twentieth century, when its tentacles held Central America's international commerce in their grip, owning vast jungles, building railroads and fleets, deposing democratically elected presidents—was, as the guidebook promised, a dump. Even the sight of the harbor, with container ships floating in oil-slick water, was oppressive. The two boys stood in the shimmering glare, almost unable to open their eyes. A tall black man wearing almost nothing pointed out a launch. It was an open boat with a fiberglass awning, a large outboard motor, and four wide bench seats already filling up with passengers for Lívingston.

"*Cuánto?*" asked Bernie.

"*Veinte.*" Twenty quetzales.

"Let's go," Bernie said. "The ferry's cheaper, but it doesn't leave till five o'clock and I can't take another five minutes in this place."

Not until the launch had cleared the harbor and revved up to speed, throwing an arching wake, did Isaac feel like he could breathe. Moist Caribbean wind beat his face. He looked out at the shoreline, jungle growing down to the water's edge. An occasional thatch-roofed hut slumbered in a yard of packed dirt. Dugout canoes nestled in the roots of palm trees. They zoomed past Q'eqchi' Maya Indians fishing from dugouts so low in the water Isaac thought the wake of the launch would overturn them. They rushed toward the mouth of Río Dulce, where the sweet river emerges from its lush green gorge and flows slow and flat into the sea. Where the guidebook told them that Caribbean blacks speak their own creole, Garífuna, and bake coconut bread in metal drums over fires in forest clearings. Where Lívingston, accessible only by boat, dreams in lowland torpor. This was not the Guatemala Isaac knew. He had descended from the crispness of the highlands into something murky and mysterious. This was adventure. This was freedom.

* * *

Isaac and Bernie, the Kerouac boys, left the launch at the municipal dock and joined the flow of tourists and locals—Indian, Ladino, and permanent ex-pats—passing ramshackle wooden buildings painted pastel pinks and blues. They turned from the main street that led up the hill away from the harbor and headed down the riverfront street, moving slowly through the noonday swelter. A faint exhalation came off the water. "We've got to find an air conditioner or a swimming beach soon, or I'm gonna pass out," Bernie said.

"Doesn't look like an air-conditioner sort of town," Isaac observed.

It wasn't. They passed a number of hotels they vetoed for reasons of style—cinderblock bunker around a cement patch didn't suit their Caribbean fancy—or apparent price—climbing gardens and waiters by the pool spelled big bucks, although Bernie was sorely tempted by thatched bungalows clustered near a long dock that ended in a gazebo. "Let's ask the price," he suggested.

Isaac only rolled his eyes. "You're delusional," he said.

Finally they came to a funky establishment on stilts, perched beside a stagnant stream. They figured they'd found a bargain. *La Iguana*. Bernie liked the name. They were shown to a room in back. Its walls were wooden slats with spaces between to let the insects in. A single bare bulb hung from the ceiling. Two narrow cots, a wooden chair, and a small electric fan furnished the room. They took it for twenty-five quetzales a night and were given a padlock to put on the door. A sign suggested in Spanish that they leave their valuables in the hotel safe.

Bernie threw down his pack and dug out the joint they had started that morning. He lit it and sprawled out on a bed. "Sweet," he said, passing the joint to Isaac. "The heat's not so bad if you don't move. We have to prepare for the next leg of our journey to enlightenment. This is just the beginning."

Isaac held in the smoke and looked out the window into jungle. There was no screen or glass, only a dirty curtain to pull for privacy. Below, the water in the stream was dark and thick for breeding...what? Mosquitoes, crocodiles, monsters? Salsa music pounded from the room next door, which was just as well, Isaac thought. Otherwise their neighbors would hear every word they spoke. It was hardly a comforting spot, yet Isaac felt, with a tingle of pleasure, promise stealing in. "Some beginning," he said, to get Bernie's goat.

Bernie exploded in a paroxysm of giggles.

After finishing the joint they were hungry. They changed into cutoffs, walked back along the riverfront to town, and turned up the main street in search of food. They sat at a streetside table, ordered spicy mystery fish, and ogled the passersby. European blondes wore bikini tops, long skirts, and athletic shoes. Americans covered up in safari garb. But the Garífuna girls stole the show, with short shorts and silky stretch tops that gleamed over their breasts and butts. Their dark skin poured out of brief confines in a siren song.

"Later, baby," Bernie murmured as the girls walked by, in a voice that only Isaac could hear. "See you tonight."

After lunch they followed the main street away from the river and down to the Caribbean side of the town, where the jungle met the water's edge. They picked their way along the shoreline out of town, stepping over tree roots and mudholes in search of a beach. This was a walk the guidebook had advised against, for reasons of safety. Passing houses in dirt yards strewn with trash, they felt dark eyes watching them. Women, children, powerful young men in dreadlocks turned to stare at the two tender white boys. The young men walked slowly on cat feet in groups of three or four, their muscled arms hanging loosely. "Lots of barracudas around here. Aren't you glad we left our money in the Iguana's safe?" Bernie said.

They still felt the eyes on them when, a half-hour out of town, they reached a narrow strip of sand under a row of coconut palms. Leaving Bernie's backpack hidden under their towels on the beach, they waded out into the shallow sea. The water was clear and warm, refreshing compared to the heavy air. Brown clumps of algae floated in the gentle waves. Isaac checked back over his shoulder to see the pile of towels on the beach. Bernie splashed him, and they dove in and swam, Isaac maintaining a mental vigil over their belongings, until they were exhausted. Then made their way back to shore to lie on the towels and let their cutoffs dry. Bernie took out his glasses from the safekeeping of his pack and lit a new joint.

Isaac studied the snack bar set back from the beach, a shadowed empty building with outdoor plastic tables. The place looked vacant and abandoned, despite a lone couple sitting under a large umbrella. Little kids roughhoused in the water a short way off, while their mother watched.

Nearby, a man prowled, perhaps another barracuda.

"Relax, mon. We're in Lívingston!" Bernie lay back. "This is the life. I'm not going back, how about you? Days in the sun. Nights in the discos. There must be opportunities here for a couple of enterprising guys like us."

"Sure," said Isaac, "Maybe we can wash dishes." He was glad the prowler hadn't come near the backpack while they were swimming.

That evening they returned to the main street parade. Music throbbed from bars along the strip. El Malecón, Tucán Dugú, Bahía Azul. Garífuna drummers pounded out hypnotic rhythms from table to table. Isaac felt the syncopation in his heartbeat. They followed the tide of glistening bodies into a dark and smoky room. Dancers flailed to the drumbeat on the crowded floor. They drank a beer, and then another. The alchemy of drugs and music and smoke and body heat worked upon them; they felt their courage rising and calling them to turn another wheel of meaning. Bare arms and legs beckoned from the dance floor, and they gravitated toward enlightenment.

4.

Sunday morning Catherine handed Nicolasa a sheet she had pulled from her sketchbook. On it she had recorded every meal she and Oswaldo had eaten at the hotel in the last week, every cup of coffee they had made from the hot water urn and powdered instant that stood ready in the dining room, every bottle of water or beer or Coke they had taken from the refrigerator that was used as a cupboard but was not cold. How casual was the service here! Improvisational, like Guatemala. Catherine loved that they trusted the guests to help themselves and pay on the honor system. Nicolasa wrote down prices for each item and tallied them up. "I'll be staying another week," Catherine told her. "Oswaldo's leaving today."

"You're letting him go?" Nicolasa asked.

They were in the shop, the room between the terrace and the street where Nicolasa sold her weavings, as well as those made by her mother, cousins, aunts, and others in their cooperative. Catherine fingered a gorgeously woven bag on the table in front of her. "I can do my work here without him. He'll be back to pick me up."

"He likes you. He's a good man."

Catherine stared at the bag in her hand. "My sister-in-law in Antigua wants me to bring back five bags. It's so hard to choose."

"Men are fickle. In our town, they go to the North, or to the next village; it doesn't matter, they're always on the prowl. Here the man keeps a picture of his girlfriend over his wife's bed. Our women know what to do when their husbands wander. A woman must look for love where she can. Good men are rare. I wouldn't let him go, Catarina."

Catherine jerked impatiently at the bag's zipper, caught on a thread. The Todosanteros never stopped amazing her. Here was Nicolasa, so young, so knowing, and so free with her opinions. No boundaries of propriety to what she would say. "What makes you think he's different from all the rest?" Catherine asked, keeping her eyes fixed on the frustrating zipper.

Nicolasa took the bag from her hands and freed the zipper with nimble fingers. "There are ways of looking into a man's heart," she said. "You don't have to be a *pulsera* to know them. The pattern of coffee grounds in his empty cup. The flutter of leaves when he passes under a peach tree. Just the other day on the terrace, a bird came down and landed right on Oswaldo's head. A sign of good things to come."

"This sounds like witchcraft, Nicolasa!" Catherine exclaimed. "Suppose I'm not superstitious?"

"How about the look in his eyes when he's watching you and thinks no one sees?" Nicolasa glanced past Catherine to the doorway. Catherine turned around. There was Oswaldo with his suitcase in hand.

"I hope I'm not interrupting," he said.

Patting the bag smooth with a flourish, Nicolasa invited him in. "Here at the hotel, you are always welcome— you are *en su casa*. But we hear you're leaving us. Todos Santos is too tranquil for you."

"I like Todos Santos. My client is sending me away." He nodded to Catherine. She felt her cheeks burn. Annoyed that her face might give her away, she picked up another stack of bags from the shelf to spread out on the table and examine.

"Which is your favorite?" she asked Oswaldo.

He picked a green one.

"I don't think so," Catherine said. "Zelda doesn't like green."

"*Pues*. You'll have to decide for yourself. You have a week."

"You'll be so busy back in Antigua," she said. "You won't forget to come for me next Sunday?"

"I won't forget."

* * *

That afternoon the *canícula* ended suddenly. A violent thunderstorm knocked out the power all over town. Catherine knew that natural forces were not influenced by the puny actions of men, that powerful systems of low and high pressure were colliding as air masses rushed up the high walls of the valley and down from the altiplano. Still, she could not help but feel that Oswaldo's departure had somehow robbed the terrace of sunlight. Why ever should she be lonely, just because a somewhat charming Guatemalan guide had gone back to his usual line of work and left her exactly what she was before, a married woman on the cusp of middle age, with a son? To fill the unexpected void, she accepted

Nicolasa's invitation to attend the crowning of the school princess that night.

In the blackness of the storm-struck town she crossed the street with Nicolasa and her parents and brother Desiderio to the *salón*, a cinderblock building that served as gymnasium, meeting place, dance hall, and auditorium. The large room was lit by candles and oil lamps. The mayor and school principal had tried in vain to hook up a generator to the *salón's* lights. As a result, the crowning ceremony was starting an hour late. Catherine and the family from the Hotel Todosantero passed rows of people sitting on folding chairs—women pulling their shawls tight to keep out the night chill, men stiff in their uniform embroidered collars and striped pants, restless children jumping out of their seats to run up and down the aisle—and found places near the front. Alone on the stage, a man gripped the lectern and fixed his eyes on the audience. His long, beaklike nose cast a shadow across his face in the glare of a kerosene lantern.

"Friends, neighbors, citizens of our dear country, our poor, beloved Guatemala, welcome. May this evening find you in good health, showered with the blessings God has promised to all those who obey Him: 'Blessed shall you be in the city, and blessed in the country. Blessed the offspring of your body and the produce of your ground. Blessed your basket and your mortar.' I am honored that the mayor, our esteemed Domingo Pablo Pablo, has asked me to speak to you tonight at this glorious occasion to celebrate the pride of our town and our traditions with the crowning of our princess, Señorita Instituto."

The man onstage paused to breathe, and Catherine whispered into Nicolasa's ear, "Who is he?"

"His name is Baudilio. Schoolteacher, Evangelical preacher, and my father's rival for mayor in the next election. Prepare yourself for a sermon."

Baudilio's voice thundered, even without amplification. "Yes. It is pride that brings us together, pride in our town, and in our marvelous National Cooperative Institute of Middle School Education, that for eighteen years has been educating the flower of our youth." Just the flower, Catherine thought, certainly not the whole crop. She'd found out from the principal on her visit to the school that out of eight hundred primary school students, fewer than two hundred went on to middle school. Of these, only a handful left Todos Santos for high school in distant Huehue or Xela. Education was still a luxury in Guatemala.

When she tuned back into the speaker's torrent of formal Spanish she heard, "But before the beautiful and talented young miss chosen as this year's Señorita Instituto enters, I must bring you some disturbing news of events that threaten our precious children. Today it is my duty to set before you, as Moses did, a blessing and a curse."

Baudilio paused, crossed his hands over his heart, and leaned forward toward the audience. "I don't like to darken your happy mood on this festive night. But our mayor himself requested me as your servant, and a servant of God, to issue this warning from Scripture: 'The one who practices sin is of the Devil.' Someone, dear friends and neighbors, someone in this room right now," and he lowered his voice and looked around, "is practicing sin. We know this, because the Devil has come to Todos Santos." With this electrifying news he paused.

Mystified, Catherine glanced down the row of faces at her side to see how people would react to this curious turn in the speech. Past Nicolasa, her mother Faustina wore her usual somber expression that said she'd already seen more than enough of the world's pain. Nicolasa's father Benito, the hotel's normally jovial proprietor, scowled.

"For it is the Devil himself who works day and night, even now while we celebrate, to lure our young people away from their studies and their honest toil in their homes and *milpa* fields, to lure them with television shows from Mexico and video games from the United States, advertisements and products from wealthy and corrupt societies, so that they disobey their elders. They join gangs, they pierce and disfigure their bodies, they destroy their lives with drugs and alcohol." Baudilio's accusing finger stabbed the air to emphasize each sin. "This is the Devil's work! And who are his agents, practicing sin here in Guatemala?'

He stared out at the hushed audience with burning eyes, challenging them to come up with an answer.

"The Scriptures tell us, 'The children of God and the children of the Devil are OBVIOUS.' The children of the Devil, my friends, are Mexicans! the coyotes who take away our youths. They are Europeans! who bring their development projects and their depraved morals. They are North Americans! who entice us with their riches to travel north into their slums, their factories, their prisons, where we suffer and die. And where our children learn to be delinquents! Where did the gangs of Guate and Huehue come from? The streets of Los Angeles!"

Where was Baudilio heading, Catherine wondered, with this tirade? What did it have to do with Señorita Instituto?

"And now, tonight, Los Angeles sends us a new terror." He paused and looked around the room. "A SATANIC CULT." Catherine felt the intended chill. "This cult is so deadly that the FBI has expelled it from the US. It is making its way through Mexico, we're told, in a black bus. Its destination?" Another pause. "I don't want to frighten you, my dear neighbors. Our town is so small and so remote; its obscurity is usually our protection. But not now.

Now, practitioners of the black arts have determined that Todos Santos lies at the intersection of powerful magnetic and gravitational forces needed to perform hideous satanic rituals. No longer can we hide in our mountains. The Satanists will find us. They are coming. To Todos Santos. Any day now, they'll arrive. Already there are harbingers, owls circling the town in daylight, signs sent by God. And when the devil-worshippers come, they'll steal our children! tear out their organs! and sacrifice them to the Evil One."

Baudilio paused to let the horror sink in. A wave of murmurs ran through the audience. Catherine saw a man grasp the cross hanging on a chain around his neck; a woman shushed a crying baby. *Jesus!* she thought, this was a nice image to present to a room full of children. How many would be having nightmares tonight? Good thing Marvella was home in bed under Rolfe's care. "Are these the rumors you were telling me about?" she whispered.

Nicolasa nodded. "This speech is ugly," she said. "Worse than I expected."

Baudilio raised both arms and stretched out his hands, palms to the people. "God said to Jeremiah, 'Behold, I am bringing a nation against you from afar, a nation whose language you do not know, nor can you understand what they say. Their quiver is like an open grave. They will devour your harvest and your food; they will devour your sons and your daughters. Your people will ask why—why has the Lord our God done all these things to us?' He brought his hands down to grip the lectern.

"The answer, dear friends, is that we have allowed foreign gods into our land. Foreign greed and corruption into our hearts. And now the Devil comes to take our children. TO RIP OUT THEIR ORGANS! We must trust no foreign face, no Peace Corps volunteer, no tourist in our hotels. Anyone could be the Devil's servant, in secret confederacy with this powerful cult. Anyone with a white face, I tell you, even someone in this room right now!"

Catherine suddenly felt eyes on her. A woman near her clutched her child and turned away. This was crazy. And scary. People were twisting in their chairs, looking around. Looking for white faces, she thought. She glanced back at Baudilio, saw him staring at her, caught a flicker of a smile as he savored his power.

Then, all calm and gentleness, he spoke again. "With God's help, the Israelites drove the foreigners out of their land and rid themselves of the influence of sin. We can do the same. The mayor and I talked earlier tonight about perhaps closing our hotels temporarily and cleansing our town of foreigners."

Catherine looked past Nicolasa again to see Benito's reaction to his rival's speech. His mouth opened in shock, as if this tactic were unexpected, even in this small town with its ancient divisions. Beyond him, Nicolasa's brother Desiderio, the toddler Celestino's elusive father, got up and left. Heads turned to watch him go. Catherine wondered if he was trying to make a point, to show people they didn't have to listen. Maybe he wanted others to follow his example. None did, and Baudilio, having let fly his poisoned dart into the heart of his town, now spoke to them almost tenderly, like a kind uncle. "I assure you, our mayor will keep us safe. He is vigilant. And so must we all be. The Apostle Paul tells us, 'Put on the full armor of God, so that you will be able to stand firm against the schemes of the Devil.' Stand firm against the Devil, Todosanteros. Be vigilant, unified, proud, and brave, Todosanteros!"

He stretched his arms out to the crowd, calling on them to show their kind uncle how much they loved him. They erupted into applause, echoing his battle cry, "Todosanteros!"

"And now, with great pride, I introduce the beautiful young ladies of our glorious Institute. Would the musicians please play!"

Three men next to the stage struck the marimba. The tinkle of melody spread through the room, as if to dispel the shock of Baudilio's message, as if its foulness could be covered over in sweet perfume. Up the aisle between the chairs, between rows of candles, on the cement floor strewn with pine needles, six teenage girls in their finest *traje*, reds and blues glowing in the candlelight, their hair braided with satin ribbons, stiff straw hats perched on their modestly bowed heads, danced trippingly the ancient dance of the Maya.

5.

I saac woke up with a powerful headache and looked at his watch. Almost noon. His mouth felt thick and his throat was sore. He was dying for a drink of water. Bernie came through the door and tossed him a bottle. *Agua pura.*

Bernie sat on his messy bed and chugged back his own bottle of water. "Oh man, it's hot in here. We gotta get down to the beach ASAP for another day of fun in the sun. Tonight we're going to find us a better watering spot than the Blue Butthole, someplace where there's more girls and fewer barracudas."

Getting into the club the night before had been easy. Age was no barrier to alcohol consumption in Guatemala. But for every nubile Garífuna girl in the Bahía Azul, there had been a pack of men. The boys had looked on as Latin Romeos and dreadlocked hipsters put their hands on girls and gyrated their hips. Two gringo boys went without notice here, minnows in the shark pool. After many beers and more marijuana, they had ended up in the small hours of the morning back in their room by the slough, their throats raw and their goal unattained.

Bernie's optimism was undaunted by reverses. Isaac had a more realistic assessment of their chances with the girls. But once again he dragged himself after Bernie, through the noonday heat, down the river road, up the steamy main street, out to the sultry Caribbean, to stumble for thirty minutes along the jungled coast to reach the beach, where they had a long, restorative swim in the cool blue Caribbean water, then sat at a plastic table at the outdoor snack bar breakfasting on ham sandwiches and Coke. Isaac felt his appetite for adventure return.

"Hey!" he said, looking at a sign by the snack bar, "They rent kayaks here. You ever been kayaking? It's great."

"How would you know? You go boating in Iowa?" Bernie asked skeptically.

"Camp, in Minnesota. Land of a Thousand Lakes, remember?"

"It's worth considering, I suppose. I've never much been into boats, but this is the time for expanding horizons and drinking deep from the cup of life," Bernie replied. "Only thing, how's the exchequer? We may need to go in search of supplies later. Our stash is getting low."

"Money's no problem. I still have fifty dollars in the hotel safe. Enough for pot and bus tickets home," Isaac assured him.

"Should we decide to forsake these sunny climes."

"You've been in too many Shakespeare plays. Let's go." Isaac got up from the table. *Cayuco*, they discovered when they asked about the sign, turned out to mean not kayak, but one of the native dugout canoes. They paid the thirty Q's for the afternoon in advance and wrote their names in a tattered register, along with Hotel La Iguana.

The canoe looked as if it had been hacked out of a block of wood by a child. The snack bar guy pulled it into the water for them, handed them two paddles, and warned them to stay close to the shore and head up the beach. They would see *mucha naturaleza*, he promised.

The snack bar guy held onto the dugout while they threw in Bernie's backpack, stocked with towels and Cokes, and scrambled in, trying not to tip the boat over. There were no seats. They sat on slats on the floor, Isaac in the back so that he could steer, and pushed off carefully with the paddles. The sides of the awkward craft rose only inches out of the water, and it rocked treacherously from side to side as they tried to paddle together.

"Whoa!" Bernie exclaimed. "This thing's gonna flip right over any minute. And no life jackets. Where I come from, there's laws against going out in a boat without a flotation device."

"Hey, this is Guatemala. Land of liberty and tippy canoes. They don't tell you how to take care of yourself here. So keep your ass in the middle of the boat," Isaac laughed, leaning right to compensate as the dugout rolled violently to the left.

They fell into a rhythm of paddling and leaning left and right, and made their way along the shore in the direction the snack bar guy had advised, away from Lívingston, until they came to the mouth of a small and placid river cutting through the sand beach to enter the Caribbean. The Quehüeche, he had told them. Feeling like Congo explorers they turned, paddled under a swinging footbridge, and headed up the sluggish stream into a universe of still water, mangrove roots, herons and cormorants. The hum of insects rose around them, almost drowning out the cries of birds. The further they went, the more oppressive the heat and hum grew. After twenty minutes of slogging away, Bernie put down his paddle. "Okay. I think I've memorized this place. About face. Let's beat it out of this furnace."

They turned downriver. Soft puffy clouds gathered overhead, giving them some relief from the sun. When they reached the footbridge again, a cool breeze off the Caribbean welcomed them. Invigorated, they shot out past the beach through mounting chop into the sea. The dugout bucked and plunged over the waves.

"Yeehaw!" Isaac shouted. "How do you like this?"

"Oh yes! Much better. Ride those waves, surfer boy!"

Isaac, on his knees in the rear of the canoe, drove his paddle into the water and grinned with excitement. This was fun. Now they were truly heroes in Paradise, on their own, free of the chains of authority—survivors, thrivers. Leaning and twisting with the rock and plunge of the boat, they beat through the freshening wind toward a dark gray line on the horizon. "Looks like it's going to rain," Bernie yelled back over the whistle of wind and splash of surf.

"Sounds good to me," Isaac called in reply. "I don't mind getting wet. Do you?"

A few more minutes of the sport, and Isaac noticed that the black line on the horizon was moving toward them, under a thick pile of clouds.

"Maybe we better turn around," he yelled. "A storm's coming."

Turning around proved tricky. They fought to keep the unstable canoe upright as they turned it broadside to the surf. Water broke over the side, drenching them and pooling in the bottom where they knelt. When they were finally turned, their backs to the waves, they were surprised at how small the strip of sand and palm trees was. They had gotten so far from shore in so short a time.

The wind was at their backs. They paddled hard, glancing behind them often to see the black line of the squall chasing them, the white line of breakers at its foot. Isaac's arms ached, but he wanted to beat that squall. "Faster!" he shouted to Bernie. The older boy wore out quickly, looked back at Isaac, put down his paddle to wipe his glasses with his shirt. "Faster!" Isaac yelled again.

But no matter how hard they paddled, the storm advanced on them. Isaac could hear its howl over the sound of wind and waves. Its shriek got louder, and Isaac kept turning around. The storm was a curtain of blackness, getting closer. Up front, he saw Bernie put his paddle down again. They were only halfway back to shore. This was no time to rest. "Paddle! Paddle!" Isaac screamed.

A blast of wind hit them with a roar. Surf crashed over them, rolling the canoe, throwing them into the sea. Isaac plunged through the turbulent water into the angry depths, losing all sense of up or down. Seaweed and bubbles swirled around him. Energized by fear, he struggled to find his way to the surface, thrashing against the power of the wave. He saw light and kicked toward it, breaking free into air. He gasped to fill his lungs. Around him the sea boiled. Rain beat on the waves. A short way off, he spied the canoe pitching in the surf, upside down. With all his strength he swam toward it, grabbed it, and held on. He panted hard to catch his breath, then looked for Bernie. Around him all he could see were mountainous waves and foam. Water everywhere. He clung to the inverted canoe. It rode the back of a wave, then slid down into a trough.

"Bernie!" he yelled at the walls of water, "Where are you?"

The canoe rose again, and from the top of the swell he finally saw Bernie's head in the foam out to sea. His glasses were gone. Without them he looked naked, scared.

"Bernie!" Isaac bellowed into the wind. "Come this way! Over here!" He waved.

"Isaac!" the reply blew back to him. Bernie raised an arm out of the seawater. "Help!"

He let go of the canoe and started to swim toward Bernie, striking out against the weight of heavy clothes, feet trapped in sneakers. A breaker appeared over his head and he lost sight of Bernie. Water slammed down on him, and he dove. The force of water grabbed him and tried to drag him to the bottom of the sea. He opened his eyes on cascading bubbles and torrents of algae, twisting around his pale arms. He fought the water for what seemed like hours. It fought him back, holding him in its grip, pushing him down. Finally he burst free and reached the surface again. Panicked, he looked around for the canoe. It was still a short way off. He had to rest. He swam back to it, hung on, and sucked air in through his salt-seared throat.

At the top of the next swell, he saw Bernie again, no closer.

"Hurry up, Bernie!" he shrieked. "This way!"

"I can't! Isaac, help me!" came the faint reply.

He had to try again. He scraped at his sneakers, but they refused to loosen. With no time to waste, he rallied his energy, gave a great push, and struck out toward Bernie. It was all he could do to swim through the mountainous waves. He kicked and stroked with all his strength, losing sight of Bernie, then seeing him again. He was getting closer. He wondered if Bernie could see him, and tried to wave. Another big breaker was coming. He dove before it reached him, but couldn't escape its force. Once again he was dragged through the foaming water. He fought toward the light over his head. Each battle under the sea drained more of his strength. He was getting weaker and the waves were getting stronger. His lungs ached from holding his breath. He longed to give in to the wave, let it fill his lungs. At the last possible instant, he made the surface and gulped in air. He gasped with exhaustion and saw Bernie, farther away than ever. He couldn't make it. He had to choose between his friend and survival. In the saddle between two waves, he swam for the canoe. It had drifted away from him. His arms and legs flailed in the water, desperate to make the canoe. His shoes and shorts pulled him down. In a final lunge, he grabbed the canoe. He clung to it, afraid to let go. The canoe was his only hope of staying afloat.

Far off, he saw Bernie, a lone head in the raging water. Behind the head loomed a monster wave, towering over it, blotting out the sky.

"Bernie, look out!" he screamed, almost splitting his lungs in his effort to make his voice carry into the wind. "Look out behind you! Dive!"

The wave advanced relentlessly on the lone head. Its summit gathered, curled, and exploded, crashing down on Bernie in an avalanche of foam. Isaac watched with horror. The broken monster roared toward him. Then the sea of foam began to rise on the back of a newly formed roller. The new wave rose up, gathered momentum, and broke over the canoe. Isaac clung on, barely aware of what was happening. His vision cleared of water again, he looked around for a head in the water. Out to sea he saw only breaking waves and blowing foam.

"Bernie!" he yelled. "Bernie!"

Isaac and the canoe rose up and sank down, and at each rise Isaac searched the sea, snorting salt water out of his nose and spitting it out of his mouth. Then a breaker drove the canoe against the bottom with a jolt. Isaac felt hard sand scrape against his legs. Mud churned around him. The canoe rose, and fell again with more impact. Isaac let go of the boat and let the force of water carry him onto the beach. He dragged himself out of the water and crawled up the beach to collapse at the foot of a palm tree. Rain beat down on him and wind howled. He lay shivering in the roots of the palm until the storm subsided, as quickly as it had struck.

When the wind died Isaac sat up, soaked and chilled, covered in salt and grit. He brushed sand out of bloody scrapes on his legs and arms and side. He struggled to his feet and peered out to sea, straining to see over the waves. The surf was beginning to calm. The dugout lay a little way down the shore among scattered seaweed, garbage, and other flotsam. There was no sign of the backpack. Or of Bernie.

"Bernie!" he called out over the water, his voice screeching and breaking.

He pictured where he had last seen Bernie, out to sea and off to his right. He waded into the foam, in a desperate urge to swim out to the spot. Salt stung his cuts; current tugged at his legs. He backed out, and trotted down the beach toward Lívingston, hoping at any moment he'd see Bernie climbing out of the waves, shaking off the water, cleaning his glasses on his shirttail, lighting up a joint. He called repeatedly, fighting tears of panic. The snack bar came into view at the end of the beach. He stopped calling and made his way toward it. The snack bar guy was setting up the plastic tables and chairs that had been knocked over in the storm.

"Have you seen my friend?" Isaac wanted to believe that Bernie had already checked in at the snack bar and sauntered on back to the hotel for a hot shower, leaving a casual message with the snack bar guy. Even now Isaac pictured Bernie with his feet up on the bed, smoking pot and waiting for Isaac's return so they could rehash their passage through the squall together. "We had an accident," he admitted.

"Your friend hasn't come. Where's the *cayuco*?"

Isaac pointed up the beach toward the place he'd left the canoe. The snack bar guy frowned. "Were you out in the storm? I told you to stay close to shore. Now I must go fetch my *cayuco* while you look for your friend. If I see him I'll tell him to go back to your hotel." He seemed more concerned for his canoe than for Bernie.

Isaac continued past the beach and along the shore toward town, scanning the sea for a struggling swimmer, picking his way among the debris the storm had left. He was afraid of what he might find in that debris. He was also afraid of finding nothing. A few people were out in their yards, cleaning up from the storm. He asked them if they'd seen a gringo boy. No one had. When at last he reached the main street through town, exhausted, he had found no sign of Bernie.

His pace slowed by exhaustion and despair, he made his way past the strip of bars and restaurants, sodden and filthy with mud as he was. No one seemed to notice him. He wondered if he should go to the police, but decided to check the Iguana first. Maybe a boat going to Lívingston had picked Bernie up and dropped him at the town dock. Maybe he was already in the shower. On the long walk back to the hotel Isaac tried to avoid seeing in his imagination the lone head in the gray sea, the wave towering over it.

He stopped at what passed for the front desk, the bare room with mildew-covered walls, a glass-fronted refrigerator of drinks, and two plain wooden tables with chairs. He asked at the bar for his key. The *dueño* handed it to him without comment, oblivious to his bedraggled appearance. The key meant that Bernie wasn't back. Isaac's spirits sank even lower. He went to the room, closed the door behind him, and sat down on Bernie's bed. It was a tangle of sheets and jeans and yesterday's dirty T-shirt and the empty water bottle left from the morning hangover. Isaac poked through Bernie's stuff, as if he could find a clue there to what had happened. He held the dirty T-shirt up to his face. On it he could smell Bernie, the faint musk of a boy just becoming a man. He bent over, shaking with unbearable sobs, covering his face with the shirt. Then he balled the shirt up and threw it across the room.

He moved to his own bed, untied his shoes, still full of wet sand, kicked them off with a vengeance, peeled off his wet clothes, and wrapped himself in the small scratchy towel the hotel had provided. His beach towel was in Bernie's backpack, which was gone. Like Bernie.

He should take a shower, but he didn't have the energy, couldn't face more water again right now. He lay back and thought. He could go get their passports and papers out of the hotel safe. He could call Aunt Zelda and ask her what to do. He could call Mr. and Mrs. Schwartz and tell them their son wasn't in Panajachel after all, as Bernie had told them, he had maybe just drowned in the Caribbean off Lívingston. Or he could get the launch for Puerto Barrios, take the bus to Guate, to Antigua, go tell them in person. He looked at his watch. It had stopped at 3:27. How many hours ago was that? It was too late to leave Lívingston today.

He toweled himself off and put on clean clothes. They grated on his salt-crusted skin. He dumped the sand out of his soggy shoes and put them back on. He left the room, locking the padlock behind him, and dropped the key off with the *dueño*. That way Bernie could get in if he showed up while Isaac was out. A telephone sat on the rough wooden bar. He thought of calling Aunt Zelda. She'd be furious. What would she say? *You and Bernie ran off to Lívingston on your own? You lied to me! You took a kid who could barely swim out in a canoe in a storm? You're a murderer!*

Even if she didn't say it, that's what she would think. She'd be right. He couldn't talk to her. Not yet.

Darkness was falling with tropical abruptness as he walked into town. He considered looking for a policeman. Could the cops help him find Bernie? This was a country where everyone was afraid of the police. Zelda said they were all either incompetent or worse. Isaac was pretty sure they killed people. What would he say to them? That his friend was missing? That their parents had given them permission to travel alone? He wondered if the booze and pot were still in his blood. Would they do a blood test? He passed the Bahía Azul and turned back. He was hungry. The urgency of hunger was comforting. He'd get something to eat and think about what to tell the police. The evening entertainment hadn't started yet. The place was almost empty. He went in and sat at a table far from the dance floor. After a long time a waitress drifted his way. He didn't notice her tight blouse, just ordered the same mystery fish he and Bernie had eaten the night before. As though he could turn the wheel of True Meaning back a day.

"*Y a tomar?*" she asked.

"A beer," he answered.

6.

In the kitchen of the hotel, Catherine and Nicolasa discussed the events of the previous evening while Faustina kneaded cornmeal dough, *masa*, on a stone mortar. Catherine took a bit of *masa* between her fingers and rolled it experimentally. She wanted to learn how to make tortillas.

"When the soldiers came in the spring of eighty-two, they had a list of names," Nicolasa said. "Everyone on the list died. My uncle Porfirio's name was on the list. People knew who had given names to the government, so afterward the Guerrilla Army of the Poor executed most of the informers. But Baudilio slipped through the guerrillas' fingers and made it over the mountains into Mexico."

"Baudilio, an informer? How could he ever show his face again in Todos Santos? Weren't the families of the victims angry?"

Nicolasa shrugged. "You explain, Mamá."

"By the time he came back, five years later, people just wanted to forget about the war," Faustina said. She pressed down hard on the stone rolling pin as she spoke. The muscles in her arms and neck strained with the effort, as though she could grind away the bitterness of her memories. "On orders from the government, all the men in town had to serve on the Civil Patrol, to root out subversives. No one wanted to be thought a guerrilla. They were frightened. The government blamed the *Violencia* on the guerrillas, and people started to believe. People who had supported the guerrillas felt betrayed. Instead of bringing liberty and justice to Guatemala, they brought massacres of whole villages. Even though some, I among them, held Baudilio responsible for the deaths of their fathers and brothers, many others had come to agree with him that the *Violencia* was God's punishment."

Nicolasa and her mother began patting out tortillas and slapping them onto the hot metal surface of the big cinderblock wood stove, under the gaze of the gray cat that sat right on top the stove, among saucepans pushed back next to the metal stovepipe. At a table by the window, Esperanza put Celestino into a homemade high chair and started feeding him runny oatmeal. The smell of toasting corn filled the dark kitchen.

Catherine watched Nicolasa intently, knowing it was harder to make a tortilla than it looked. Nicolasa wet one hand in a plastic bowl of water next to the mortar, shook off the excess water, grabbed a handful of *masa*, and formed it into a small ball. Then with great speed she patted the ball back and forth from hand to hand to flatten it. She used the heels of her hands, the smoothest part, to keep the fragile *masa* from sticking to her palms. Midway through, she rotated the tortilla in her fingertips, gently massaging to thicken the edges. Within seconds she tossed the perfectly smooth and round disc of corn dough onto the wood stove. Catherine imitated her with difficulty. The *masa* stuck to her fingers and her tortillas came out thick, lumpy, and misshapen.

"The time for vengeance has passed," Nicolasa elaborated. "Baudilio was able to return, same as the former guerrillas did. He got a job at the school, Urbana Mixta, teaching fourth grade. His preaching drew a big congregation of followers. People started leaving the Catholic Church and becoming Evangelicals."

"Before the war," Faustina said, "there were no Evangelicals in Todos Santos. We were all one people. We celebrated our holy days and fiestas together. The Evangelicals preach against our traditions, no matter what Baudilio said last night. He called for unity against the devil-worshippers. What a liar he is! The Evangelicals are dividing the town, brother against brother, father against son."

"Devil-worshippers," Catherine said. "How can people take that seriously?" She couldn't disguise a degree of condescension, try as she might.

"You don't understand," Nicolasa explained, patiently, as if to a child. "The devil-worshippers are real. There was a rally of Satanists last year in Huehuetenango. I don't know how they got permission to meet. They love to frighten and offend people. In addition, there's been a series of murders of teenagers in Huehue in the last year, kids grabbed on their way to and from high school. One murderer left behind severed hands of his victims. The murderers haven't been caught. Gang wars may be responsible, but people blame the Satanists."

Chilled, Catherine felt chastened. Still she protested, "But baby-snatching? Stealing organs?"

"Guatemalans have always feared baby-snatchers. Baby brokers roam the countryside like predators, looking for pregnant girls to buy their babies. We have an extraordinarily high rate of foreign adoptions. There is much money to be made. Officials are easy to bribe. In the past, no one even checked to find out who the real parents of babies were, if the babies were stolen, or if the mothers were forced to give them up. Here, where babies are plentiful, poor people wonder why the foreigners pay so much for babies. Perhaps for their organs."

Catherine stared at the stove and mulled over this disastrous history. Poor Guatemala! So many threats. No wonder people were easy to scare. Nicolasa and Faustina turned over the cooking tortillas one by one. They plucked them off the stovetop without burning their fingers and flipped them back down. The finished tortillas they piled into a basket, to make room for more on the griddle.

"What are you going to do with mine?" Catherine asked. "They're so ugly." She was distressed that she had ruined *masa*. You don't waste food in Guatemala.

"Don't worry," Nicolasa answered, piling the deformed tortillas into the basket with the perfect ones. "The tourists won't notice."

Desiderio stalked into the kitchen and went straight to the stove. All eyes followed him; he was so seldom seen in the mornings. He grabbed the cat and sent it flying with a kick. Esperanza, who was wiping oatmeal off of Celestino's face, winced. He didn't even glance at her. What a brute, thought Catherine.

"What tourists?" he said. "If Baudilio has his way, they'll all be barred from town and we'll be out of business."

He picked up one of Catherine's tortillas from the basket. "What's this? Is Marvella learning to *tortillar*?"

Marvella wasn't even in the room. Catherine didn't know why she felt hot with embarrassment. She didn't care what Nicolasa's brother, a self-centered lothario by his sister's account, thought of her tortillas. Nicolasa snatched the tortilla from his hand. "None of your business," she said.

Desiderio looked at Catherine. Her face got hotter. "You'd better stay away from the school." How did he know she'd been there? Was he checking up on her? The idea gave her the creeps. Too many people were watching her. "If Baudilio catches you there, he might get the mayor to throw you in jail. Satanic conspirator. Of course, if the hotels are all closed, maybe jail wouldn't be so bad. A roof over your head, at least. Just you and the drunks."

"Desiderio! Don't talk such garbage," Nicolasa exclaimed.

"Your father's gone to speak with the mayor," Faustina said. "The hotels aren't going to close." She looked grim.

* * *

Nicolasa didn't know which was worse: her brother's rude behavior or her mother's gloom. She was glad that Rolfe was almost finished with the house. Soon she'd get out from under her family's roof. The first step toward a better life. The next would be moving to Europe. Her brothers aggravated her so. Her father should have sent Desiderio back to the North after his arrest and gotten him out of Todos Santos. Instead, he'd bought him the bar and married him off to Esperanza. What a mistake.

While she baked banana bread, she watched Catherine out on the terrace painting a portrait of Marvella. It didn't seem to be going well. Marvella fidgeted and refused to be bribed by sweets. Catherine wiped sketch after sketch off the canvas to start again. Finally she gave up and came inside, saying a kitchen scene would come in handy somewhere in the book. But even that effort failed.

"The paint may as well be mud today," she complained. "I feel like I've never held a brush before." She began cleaning up her paints.

"You miss Oswaldo. That's why you can't work. You need him here to flatter you and take you for walks in the afternoon," Nicolasa observed.

"You seem to forget I'm a married woman."

"You're an American. You don't have to stay married, thanks be to God. If your marriage weighs on you like the yoke of an ox, throw it off." She said this lightly, as if it could be taken as a joke. But she meant it.

"It's not so easy. There's my son to consider, for one thing. Besides, maybe I like life in the harness, keeping those furrows straight." She snapped her paint box shut like an exclamation point. Subject closed.

Nicolasa saw her sink into thought. She changed the subject. "Today is Rolfe's birthday. We're going out to the new house to make lunch, my mother and Esperanza and I. My father may join us if he finishes his meeting in time. Why don't you come?"

Catherine shook off her mood and agreed to join the party. They loaded market baskets with chicken, pineapples, and vegetables. Walking up the street out of town, Catherine took one handle of a heavy basket, while Esperanza took the other. Celestino was tied onto her back with a shawl. Marvella ran ahead of the group. The women stopped frequently to rest. They passed the Mayan ruins and walked uphill another five minutes. The road crossed a bridge, changed from stone to dirt, and passed through cornfields.

The house was tucked back, away from the road, behind tall corn in a sunny yard green with grass and bright with flowers, a little oasis. Marvella and Celestino went immediately to a wire enclosure in front to feed the rabbits and ducks. Rolfe came out.

"Happy birthday," Catherine said.

"How do you like it? The house is nearly finished. I'm just working on putting in a shower in back. A heated shower."

She loved the house, its freshly painted adobe walls, its varnished woodwork gleaming with newness, its high eaves a blending of the simple local style with a Swiss chalet. "It's beautiful!" she told Rolfe.

They unloaded the baskets of food onto a table on the porch. Rolfe went inside to light a fire. The women set to work washing the chicken and vegetables in the *pila*, the large concrete sink that sat in front of the house, facing the view of fields and mountains. A deep well in the middle held clean water. They used plastic bowls to scoop the water into the two shallow sinks at either side. Catherine enjoyed learning sink etiquette here, so different from scraping plates and loading the dishwasher back in Iowa. If the wood stove was the heart of the Guatemalan home, the *pila* was its soul. Here the women spent much of their day, washing food, dishes, clothes, in the sunshine outside of their dark houses.

"I've noticed that the Todosanteros always put their *pilas* in a spot with a view," Catherine said.

"I guess that's true," Nicolasa answered, "Usually a view of the road in front of the house. That way, the women can chat with passing neighbors while they work. We're going to cook the chicken Mexican style, the way we learned vacationing in Cancún." She had shown Catherine the photo of the family, dressed in *traje* in the slick modern kitchen of their rented Mexican condo. The family looked out of place in the photo, as if they belonged in a Guatemalan kitchen, dark and smoky, where whole families sat huddled close to wood stoves or open fires on dirt floors. And yet, Catherine knew they were at home wherever they went, whether it was to faraway Cancún or up the hill to the kitchen Rolfe had built, cozy and warm with its terracotta tile floor and a hooded stove to keep it smoke-free.

Nicolasa and Esperanza began to cut the pineapples, while Catherine peeled and sliced onions. Faustina had gone out to sit on the grass. She took off her shoes and stretched her bare toes out in the sun.

"Nicolasa, this is so idyllic," Catherine said.

"A mountain paradise. How could I give it up for Europe? Cities and factories and crowds and traffic jams. That's what you're thinking, I know. You don't see these mountains holding in the suffering. My mother's bitterness suffocates me. She only thinks of sad things: the war, the deaths of her brothers, the troubles with her sons, the envy of our neighbors. People here believe there's only so much good fortune in the world. They blame my family for taking more than our share. They blame us for their suffering. That's why they're attacking us now."

Americans, on the other hand, think that good luck is limitless, that everyone should be happy, Catherine thought. Fumes from the onions filled her nose and throat. Tears ran down her face. Her eyes burned. Onions always did that to her. She rinsed her hands, blew her nose, and kept on slicing.

"Who do you cry for, Catarina?" teased Nicolasa. "Your husband or Oswaldo?"

"A good question," Catherine shot back. "For all women who have problems with their men."

The strange thing about onion tears was that once they started to flow, they triggered the emotion that came with crying, as if the process were working in reverse. Tears causing sadness. Catherine felt like she *was* weeping for someone. Who? A lonely wife hungry for her husband's love? Esperanza? Herself? In her mind's eye she saw Oswaldo's laughing gold-toothed smile, and under it Elliot's worn image. Catherine felt her life coming apart in stinging layers.

7.

arlos had noticed the boy with the blond ponytail the night before, when he and his friend were trying to make it on the dance floor without success. After five years in an LA street gang and several more as a river guide out of Río Dulce, plus some extracurricular activities that brought in cash for his wardrobe, Carlos was a pretty good judge of people. These two struck him as runaways. The sidekick wasn't with the blonde boy tonight. The ponytail was wet and matted, and the boy had a haunted look. Carlos wondered what had happened between the two of them. When the kid was on his second beer, Carlos moved over from the bar and sat down next to him.

"Hey, dude," he said in his faintly accented English. "How's it hangin' with you?" Carlos spoke with an easy lilt, infusing ordinary conversation with a warmth and charm that immediately disarmed the most guarded tourists.

"Good," Isaac said. But he didn't sound good.

"Where's your friend tonight? Did you guys have a falling out?"

Isaac regarded the intruder apathetically. A light-skinned black in his twenties, Issac judged—you really couldn't use the more politically correct *African-American* here—with flowing kinky locks neatly contained in a bandana, wearing a loose, colorful print shirt and baggy knee-length shorts. It was a nice look, stylish but not fussy. There wasn't enough accent for Isaac to place: Garífuna, Spanish, or generalized Caribbean.

"Not exactly," Isaac said. "He just went off for a while."

"Hey, man! This ain't no place to be on your own. My name's Carlos. Mind if I join you?"

"Okay." Isaac wondered what Carlos wanted from him. "I'm Isaac."

"Isaac! You know you're the first Isaac I ever met! Great name, man, right out of the Bible, right?" Carlos waved over the waitress. "You tried the *coco loco*, Isaac? Rum and coconut milk, just like a milkshake. You're gonna love it!"

Isaac knew he should say no thanks and get the hell out of there. He'd finished eating. It was time he looked for the police and got some search parties out for Bernie. It was dark now. The police would want to know what'd taken him so long. That was hard to explain. He was scared of what they would ask him, or maybe of what they would find. Maybe a drink would give him the courage to face the cops.

By the second round of *coco locos* the Bahía Azul was jumping. Everyone who passed their table greeted Carlos by name. People joined them, first a Dutch girl, then an Australian, then two local guys. Carlos introduced Isaac to everyone, then let him sink into silence as the conversation flowed around him in English and Spanish. The music grew louder and the beat more hypnotic. Finally Carlos broke into the pool of chatter with a general invitation.

"Who wants to go over to my place for some blow?"

Cocaine. Even a kid from Iowa knew that was a big step up from *coco locos*. Now was the time for Isaac to get away and go look for the police. Although he still hadn't figured out what to tell them. They wouldn't hurt a kid, would they? Not an American kid. Trying to make his brain work, trying to get a hold on what to do, he left the restaurant with the others, thinking he would maybe break away from them and go for help. Outside, he found the street rotating slowly. He was shit-faced, in no condition to face a police interrogation. The cops would smell alcohol on his breath. They'd lock him up. It was too dark to look for Bernie. Anyway, Bernie was probably holed up in one of those scenic shacks under the palm trees by the waterfront. Someone had rescued him and was feeding him chicken soup or whatever they had down here. Some nice family was taking care of him. Some granny had tucked him into a big, soft bed, covered him with a blanket, some kids were playing around him, some mama was shushing them, singing him lullabies. Probably Bernie was tired out from all that struggling in the water and nearly drowning and getting rescued and he needed to sleep. Better to wait for morning. First thing.

Isaac followed the gang to Carlos's place, which turned out to be a budget hotel on the waterfront. His boat was tied up at the hotel dock. In the faint light from the hotel Isaac could see its name, *Good-Times Charlie*, stenciled in block letters near the bow. They all climbed aboard and sat on the floor of the boat around an upturned box that served as a table. Carlos tapped out a line of white powder while the Australian girl held a flashlight. One by one Isaac watched them place a finger over one nostril and inhale the line into the other. His turn came.

"You done this before, Isaac?" Carlos said, putting a reassuring arm around his shoulder. "Don't you worry, man. This is a white-collar drug. Very up-scale. Only doctors and lawyers and bond traders do this shit. It's good for you."

Isaac grinned. Good for you. Oh yeah, he thought. A drug so highly addictive monkeys had been known to starve themselves to death, preferring cocaine to food. You had to wonder who did that experiment, he thought. He put his finger over a nostril. What the fuck. He sucked the powder into his nose, felt a metallic sting, felt his lips go numb. Numbness felt good. His mind cleared of turmoil and tuned in to the immediate present. He focused on the faces bending over the upturned box, beyond them the calm night, the sparkle of light on the water from a three-quarter moon low in the sky. There was no trace of the storm.

After they finished the cocaine Carlos handed out beers. The Dutch and Australian girls made merry plans to go to Belize the next day. "Take us along," the local guys badgered. "You don't want to be alone." Everyone, even Isaac, laughed. "You can come, too" they told him. They were all the best of friends. No one worried about what Isaac was doing on his own in a place like this. Carlos would be their guide to the best beaches, the best reefs, the best diving. Isaac drank thirstily, letting the beer soothe his hyperactive synapses, watching the moon set, until finally he had to lean over the side of the boat to vomit. Carlos took off his beautiful bandana and used it to clean Isaac up with water from the harbor.

"Hey, it's late, my friend. You staying nearby?" he said. "Let me take you back to your place so you can get a little shut-eye." On the walk back to the Iguana, Carlos asked what his plans were for the next day, really.

"We not going to Belize with those girls. That was just party talk," Carlos said. "I'm taking a boatload of tourists up the Río Dulce to see the sights. Come with me. You'll love it, man. Jungle beauty. You can be my first mate. No charge."

Isaac studied Carlos with bleary eyes, wondering what his angle was, why he was being so nice.

"I like you, Isaac, is all." Carlos seemed to read his mind. "I was young once and got help from a friend. You strike me as a guy needs a friend. I'll be by in the morning to pick you up."

Carlos left Isaac at the dark and empty bar of his hotel, where the night watchman gave Isaac his key. Still no Bernie.

* * *

Isaac woke to the sound of pounding on his door. Sunlight was pouring in through the gaping hole of the window, sunlight green with the jungle morning, spilling onto the pile of clothes and jumbled sheets on the empty bed beside him. Isaac's head was splitting with his second hangover in two days. He was becoming an expert at morning pain.

"Isaac! Isaac, my man, it's morning. The birdies are singing, time to rise and shine, boat leaves in an hour, buddy." Carlos's voice on the other side of the door brought memories from the night before filtering back. With memories came another kind of pain, worse. He stared at the empty bed, desperate to see Bernie lying there, reassuring him that this was just a normal hangover, that yesterday was just a nightmare. No Bernie. He felt sick.

"Isaac! You in there, my friend?" Carlos again. The last thing he needed right now was a new friend. "He needed Bernie, so they could get their shit together and get back to Antigua and to their afternoons of playing Quake, no one the wiser.

"Yeah, okay Carlos. I just gotta get up. I'll be around in a little while."

"You remember where to find me, Isaac? You were pretty fucked up last night. How are you now?"

"I'll be alright. Your hotel where the boat is, I remember. I'll be there."

He said that to make Carlos go away. Then he dragged himself into the shower. He used the hotel towel. His towel had gone with the backpack to the bottom of the sea. Was that where Bernie was now? After the shower, another bottle of *agua pura*. There were advantages to being a hangover veteran, to knowing how to manage the pain. While he drank the water he thought about his options. They all looked bad, the same as they had the night before. Go to the police. Call Aunt Zelda. They would want a lot of explanations. How could he explain that the search for enlightenment had gone off course? The authorities would think he and Bernie were a couple of really bad kids. They'd think he was a murderer. He had to believe that Bernie was still alive, as he had thought last night after the *coco locos*. He had to look for Bernie. That was his only hope. To find Bernie. Taking it easy in that shack by the water. It was still early, way too early for Bernie to be up and getting back to the Iguana. It was only Monday morning; Zelda wasn't expecting him yet. He had time. He packed his things into his knapsack and left Bernie's stuff on the bed. At the front desk he asked for his money and both passports from the safe. He paid for the two nights they'd spent there, but didn't check out. He left the key with the *dueño*. Bernie might show up for the key. The *dueño* of the Iguana was used to not asking questions.

Isaac walked up the street toward town. He was thinking about going to all the houses that lined the shore to ask if Bernie was inside. But suppose he was lying on the shore somewhere with a broken leg, or unconscious, and no one had found him yet? There was no time to lose. He wanted to get back up the shore again right now. Bernie might have been swept a long way up the coast. He could have ended up anywhere. A boat would be useful for the search, a boat with a motor, to cover distance in a hurry. One boat came to mind. Isaac went in through the hotel to the dock where Carlos was cleaning up the *Good-Times Charlie.*

"Hey, Carlos. A question. How soon are the tourists showing up? Do you have time to help me look for my friend?"

* * *

Carlos didn't have much doubt about what had happened to Bernie, once he heard the story. But he put the tourists off until afternoon, so that he and Isaac could spend the morning motoring slowly up and down the coast, stopping often to talk to people along the way. He wasn't surprised when they found nothing. He suggested that they delay going to the police, not his favorite people, and that Isaac join him on the afternoon run up the river. They could return later to see if there were any signs of Bernie. That's what he told Isaac. An idea was starting to take shape in his mind. He wanted to give it time to come into focus, while he won the boy's confidence.

The hours of searching deepened Isaac's despair. Little by little the vision he'd constructed of Bernie in bed, some nice local woman nursing him back to health, was replaced by the last real image he had: Bernie's head, the wave. He couldn't get that picture out of his mind. His brain was stuck. When Carlos asked him to come along on the trip upriver, he couldn't think of anything to say except "Sure."

Sitting in the back of the launch with Carlos, speeding up through the green gorge of Río Dulce, passing vertical forest walls hanging with vines, he sank into a black hole. He'd lost his one true friend, let Bernie go under that wave, when what he should have done was swim out to him. He'd taken Bernie out there where he never should have been, and then he'd let the wave suck him under. When people found out, everyone would hate him, with good reason. When Aunt Z told his parents, they would fight over him, as they always did. His mom would cry. His dad would say his mom was too soft on him and would send him to military school, or to one of those boot camps for delinquents. It almost didn't matter. Right now, it looked like his life was over for real.

* * *

That afternoon a Guatemalan family from the capital staying at Las Brisas del Mar, the only hotel in Livingston to face the Caribbean rather than the mouth of the river, suffered a shock. Their two small children, three and six years old, discovered, hung up on the roots of a palm tree down by the hotel's small beach, the bloated body of a boy. Their mother, who had been following right behind them to guard them as they played in the wet sand by the water's edge, immediately grabbed their hands and rushed them back to the hotel, where she alerted the manager. The manager and a male employee lifted the body from the roots, carried it far enough from the water that the tide would not wash it away, and left it on the ground, fearing to further disturb any evidence of how this misfortune had come to invade the calm of the guests at Las Brisas del Mar. The manager went for the police while the male employee, whose normal job it was to sweep and mop the floors and water the plants in the garden and carry the guests' suitcases, kept watch over the body.

The drowned body of a gringo boy promised to be a major headache for the Lívingston chief of police. Because no one had reported him missing, the boy would have to be kept in town until he could be identified, instead of being removed immediately to the department capital in Puerto Barrios, where they had much better facilities for these things. Not only must an investigation be launched into the cause of death, which so far appeared to be drowning, the body showing no signs of distress other than hours of immersion in salt water, but endless forms must be filled out, and worst of all, an embassy would have to be notified. Death among locals was no matter of great concern for the chief, whether it came suddenly and with violence or after a long period of decline and suffering. Death, after all, is always close at hand, waiting just over the shoulder of the living to snatch the unwary. But deaths of foreigners, who for some reason consider death to be unnatural and grounds for outrage, always caused trouble. Most especially, he hoped this boy would not prove to be an American, because the US Embassy was already up in arms over a number of unexplained deaths of its nationals in recent years.

Groaning inwardly at his burden, the police chief had the body packed in ice at the station and commenced asking questions. By the end of the day, after interviewing at almost every hotel in town, he had tracked the boy down to La Iguana. There the owner had copied down passport numbers for two boys, both American. The police chief groaned again. On asking to see the passports, he was told that the second boy had left in the morning with the passports and all his money. Cursing the naiveté of the *dueño*, the chief took the key and went back to the room, where he gathered up Bernie's belongings. He escorted the slow-witted *dueño* to the station, where the official identification of the body was completed. He then sent the *dueño* back to La Iguana with harsh instructions that in the unlikely event of the other boy's return, both passports were to be confiscated immediately and he was to be delivered to the chief.

The chief was satisfied with an unusually full day's work and went home to his supper, a few beers, and his favorite *telenovela*. In the morning he would attack the mountain of forms and the ordeal of placing a phone call to the US Embassy.

* * *

After they had dropped the tourists at the municipal dock at the town of Río Dulce, at the head of the river Río Dulce, where the river issues out of the wide inland lake Izabal, Carlos said to Isaac, "You want to head straight back to Lívingston, or take a little spin around the lake first?"

"I guess I should get back. Maybe they've found Bernie by now."

The launch idled out slowly over the water, away from the shore, into the quiet of late afternoon.

"You got to prepare yourself, Isaac, my man. They're not going to find him alive." Carlos draped his arm over the boy's shoulders, to soften the impact. Isaac winced anyway, as if the truth he'd been trying to avoid, coming now from the river guide's mouth, were a physical object, like a chisel, maybe, getting hammered into his brain. Soft and easy, Carlos said, "We got to think what's best for you."

"It's my fault." Isaac's voice quivered. He fought against tears.

"No, it isn't. These storms come up out of nowhere like that, nothing you can do. Your aunt, she's not going to blame you for running off and getting your friend killed, is she? Even if the cops try to frame you, won't she back you up?"

"What do you mean, if the cops frame me?"

"That's what they do here, these Guatemalan cops, they're rotten. They'll say you guys had a fight and you took Bernie out in the canoe and dumped him on purpose, or some kind of shit. That way, one gringo boy kills another, it's not their responsibility, fewer problems for them."

His dread ratcheting up another notch, Isaac said, "Do they put kids in jail here?"

"Hold on." Carlos took his arm from Isaac's shoulder and tapped his forehead with his index finger. "I'm getting a brainwave, a fucking inspiration, man. A way out for you." Carlos spoke slowly, with pauses, as if he were thinking out loud. "All you got to do is convince them you been detained against your will, which is why you didn't go to the authorities right away like you should have. You were in the power of a third party, perhaps this third party was even responsible for Bernie's demise, I don't know, we got to think on that one. However it turns out, you are now being held some kind of prisoner. Once your aunt hears you're the victim and not the perpetrator, she'll be on your side. She'll protect you from the police." Carlos looked at Isaac, excited. "It's brilliant. This plan can't lose. What do you think?"

"I don't get it. What are you talking about? How do we make me the victim, not the perpetrator?"

"Easy, man! We call up your aunt tonight, tell her you been kidnapped. You talk to her, tell her you're okay but you don't know where you are and she shouldn't say nothing to the cops. Then I demand a ransom, just to make it realistic. That's all."

Isaac stared at the river guide. Was he serious? Could he pull off this crazy scheme?

"Of course, if you don't like it, Isaac, we can head back to Lívingston right now. You can turn yourself in to the police and take your chances they don't poke something up your ass in jail tonight."

Maybe it could work. Maybe this was his best option. Maybe Carlos had just given him an out.

* * *

That evening on the dusty main street of Río Dulce, they found a phone in the back of a store. At the request of Carlos, the storekeeper retired to allow them privacy to make their call. Following instructions, Isaac kept his remarks to Zelda brief, only telling her that he was blindfolded but otherwise fine.

"Okay, Isaac. Don't do anything to make them mad. Don't be scared. We'll get you out of there." She didn't sound like Sergeant Z, even though her words were calm enough. The tremor of fear in her voice made him feel weird, grateful that she wasn't angry at him, but creepy that he was deceiving her.

Carlos took the phone from him. "You have four days to get five thousand dollars in cash. No tricks. Wait for further instructions. Call the police, and you'll never see your nephew again."

He sounded remarkably convincing.

8.

Tuesday morning Desiderio appeared on the terrace, sullen and taciturn, while Catherine was painting Marvella. The little girl's sunny temper had returned. She prattled on while her uncle peered over Catherine's shoulder at the canvas like some hostile art critic. Catherine ignored the chatter and Desiderio's somber presence, feeling the power surging through her brush. At last the painting was going well. She liked to paint standing up, so her energy could flow through her body unimpeded by angles. At times like these she worked effortlessly, knowing exactly what colors to use and where to put them. The knowledge seemed to come from outside her, from some force that seized her, telling her what to do, filling her up with joy.

"It's good," Desiderio said, and walked away.

Well! The stone speaks, she thought.

By afternoon, the painting was finished and Catherine was exhausted. She strolled down the main street, intending to take a walk and unwind. She was lost in her own thoughts, her mind still on painting, not keeping an eye out for unfriendly glances or suspicious stares. A hand grabbed her shoulder from behind and spun her around.

"'Those who indulge the flesh in its corrupt desires are springs without water and mists driven by a storm, for whom the black darkness has been reserved. A DOG RETURNS TO ITS OWN VOMIT!'" Baudilio hissed the words in her face, squeezing her shoulder until it hurt.

"What do you think you're doing?" Shocked at the preacher's audacity, Catherine froze and looked around for help. People on the sidewalk and in doorways looked on but didn't react.

"Why are you here? I saw you at school last week, looking at the children. Now I hear you're painting children. What else? Are you in touch with your friends from Los Angeles? God sees you worshipping the Evil One. God is stronger than Satan. 'The Lord knows how to rescue the godly from temptation and keep the unrighteous under punishment for the Day of Judgment.' Have you no fear?"

"Let go of me!" There was menace in his grip. She tried to shake his hand off her shoulder, but he held on tight.

"I speak for Todos Santos." He squeezed so hard she yelped with pain.

"No, you don't! Not for everyone. I have friends here." This was outrageous. The man had no right to grab her in the street, to threaten her in public view. Why didn't someone stop him? "I heard you Sunday night in the *salón*. Why are you stirring everybody up? I'm not here to hurt anyone, or steal anyone's children. You're the one doing evil around here, not me!"

"Let me teach you to fear God's wrath." With his free hand he slapped her hard across the face.

There was a crash of breaking glass.

"Leave her alone!" Desiderio appeared at her side with a broken-off bottle held high and threatening. Baudilio released Catherine and swung at Desiderio. He struck back with the broken bottle, slashing Baudilio across the cheek. Blood spattered onto the street. Catherine shrieked. Someone pulled her back, onto the narrow sidewalk. Baudilio punched Desiderio in the gut and went for the hand holding the bottle. Desiderio swung it again, missing this time. He danced back out of Baudilio's reach. They glared at each other. Baudilio lunged forward. Desiderio held the bottle high and slammed his opponent's jaw with his free hand closed into a fist.

"Stop them!" Catherine screamed. "Someone stop them!" Red blood splashed from Baudilio's wound onto the dun-colored dust. Why didn't someone run for the police? The sidewalks were now lined with onlookers. The two men circled each other, making jabs that missed the mark as the other dodged. Finally Baudilio grabbed the arm with the bottle with both hands. They struggled. Desiderio dropped the bottle and kicked Baudilio in the groin. Baudilio fell back and was caught by two men. They held onto him, dragging him away from the fight.

Desiderio put his hand on Catherine's arm and guided her through a doorway, into the empty bar. He seated her on a bench, drew purple curtains across the windows, and disappeared into the back. Catherine put her head down on the table. Her cheek, where Baudilio had hit her, was throbbing. Her heart was still pounding; she didn't know whether from fear or anger. Desiderio came back with a basin of water and sat next to her. She raised her head.

"Are you all right?" he asked. He held her face in one hand and pressed a hot, wet towel against her bruised cheek. Several times he soaked the towel and wrung it out, to wipe her face again. As the pain in her cheek subsided, she began to shake. She couldn't stop the tears. He put his arm around her. Startled but oddly comforted, she rested her head on his shoulder, sobbing. When she was done, she pulled back, and he wiped her face again. The water was cooling off. Finally she could speak.

"I feel better now." She said, chagrined that her revulsion for him had softened. His metamorphosis from churl to Galahad unnerved her. She felt ashamed. She didn't know why. "And you? Did he hurt you?"

"I'm fine."

Catherine didn't believe him. She'd seen Baudilio's fists hit him. "No one was going to help me until you came. Does everyone agree with him? Do they think I'm a devil-worshipper?"

"People here don't interfere. They're used to fights. They're used to men beating up their women."

"I'm not Baudilio's woman. What makes him think he can get away with attacking a foreigner that way?" An American! she thought. She had assumed that her membership in that privileged club made her untouchable, safe, at least in broad daylight in the center of town. Baudilio had ignored her immunity, the fact that she was protected by the world's most powerful nation.

Desiderio didn't answer. Instead, he walked behind the bar, found a CD and put it on. Bob Marley played softly over the sound system. In the dim purple light sifting through the curtains, Desiderio poured out two glasses and came back to Catherine.

"What is it?" she asked when he gave her a glass of clear liquid.

"*Un trago*. Drink."

She took a sip. Rum and Sprite. Jesus! They were having cocktails, the last thing she expected. He sat across from her. "The broken bottle," she said, keeping a grip on the facts. "Why did you do that? You could have really hurt him."

"When I fight, I fight to win."

"You humiliated him in public. He'll want revenge. It's an endless cycle. You have a wife and child to think about," she reminded him, wondering if he ever did think of them, and if he did, what those thoughts were.

His eyes narrowed, removing kindness. "My father bought my wife."

"He what?"

"Bought her. It's the old custom. No one does it anymore. But my father thought marriage would make me responsible, settle me down. So one night he took me and my mother and sister and brothers to Esperanza's house. He knew I'd fooled around with Esperanza. But he never asked if I wanted to marry her. Instead he took two thousand quetzales and plenty of alcohol and cigarettes and pounded on the door and demanded that we be invited in. That's the traditional way to buy a bride. They kept the door bolted for hours and yelled at us to go away. Then sometime after midnight Esperanza's father opened the door and we went in and everyone drank the alcohol and partied. Esperanza's father took the money. After that I was a married man."

Catherine was appalled. Nicolasa had chosen her own husband, she knew. She couldn't imagine such barbaric behavior from the same family. "Why didn't you object?"

Desiderio shrugged. "It's not easy to go against my father. He's a big man in this town. I had just gotten back to Todos Santos from Los Angeles. I was deported. I wasn't ready to leave my town again so fast. Too many are leaving. They all go to the North to get rich. I tried that. All I found was trouble. Gangs, fighting, drugs. I want to live here, where I belong, in the land of my ancestors, to prove it can be done. But it's hard to earn enough to hold up your head around here, and *cabrones* like Baudilio make it harder."

Catherine's head spun. This was not what she had expected from him. He was full of contradictions. And so bitter. She sipped her drink.

Bob Marley crooned over the speakers, asking if he was feeling love. Catherine felt a memory appear, a cold winter day long ago, when Isaac was a baby. She and Elliot had put him into the baby seat in the back of the car and driven to the Mississippi. They'd parked on the bluff, drinking beers, listening to Bob Marley on the car stereo, holding hands and making out, while Isaac slept. The sun had reflected off the water of the wide river and off the blinding whiteness of snow everywhere. So much sunlight and the music gave them the illusion they were far away, at some tropical beach. In the midst of all that cold, they had felt warm, with each other. Ever after, they would refer to that drive as their one-day Caribbean vacation. The song in the dark bar ended. The vision evaporated.

Desiderio went behind the bar to change the CD and came back with fresh drinks. Just what she needed, Catherine thought, to get drunk in the afternoon. But she couldn't leave. She was compelled to understand this man. She sipped to the Latin rhythms.

"Do you like to dance?" Desiderio asked.

"Yes," Catherine answered. What a time for honesty.

"Merengue?"

"I don't know how."

"I can teach you."

A dancing lesson. How absurd. Oh well, thought Catherine, why not? There was no one there to see her. And besides, he was so young, she could almost laugh. Next to him, her forty years felt wise and ancient.

Desiderio held out his arms and led her into the moves of the dance. He was a skilled dancer, and easy to follow. She felt their synchronicity with the pleasure of a connoisseur. He guided her in slow, sinuous spins, under his arm, back to back. She flowed with him and the music.

"You're good," he said, and held her closer.

His dancing became more sexual. But that's the nature of dance, after all; that's the fun. Catherine still felt wise. She let him press her into his body. Suddenly his lips were on hers, sucking hungrily. She was astonished. A surge of warmth like liquid pulsed through her body. To be kissed, to be desired, how long had it been? Like something elemental and necessary, water in the desert, fire at the poles, the kiss of a young man.

They danced slowly, with lips locked. He slid his hand under her turtleneck, inside her bra, and fondled her breasts. Her heart beat under his fingertips. His hand went down into her pants. All the hardness in her melted at his touch. He fumbled with the button on her jeans. She pulled away.

"I have to go," she said.

"As you wish." He shrugged. He watched her with impenetrable eyes, his face like the masks that decorated the walls of the bar. She tucked in her shirt and ran her fingers through her hair. Another moment, she thought, and they would have been fucking. It was madness. What had come over her? What was he thinking?

"*Nos vemos*," she said, goodbye, and hurried outside. The light of afternoon struck her full in the face. The blood on the street, the purple dimness in the bar, burned up in the light of a sun so much stronger, so much closer here than in Iowa. Its brilliance could vaporize mist, eradicate darkness, consume memory. By the time she reached the plaza and turned up the street to the hotel, Catherine was no longer sure which of the events of the afternoon had really happened and which were figments of her wishes and fears. And if real, if blood had flowed in the street, and other almost forgotten juices in the bar, should she be afraid, or ashamed? She wasn't. She was glad to be alive.

9.

It was dark. Isaac couldn't see, couldn't breathe. Somebody was yelling. Something wrapped around his neck. Seaweed? Water all around him, bubbles swirling, glowing in the dark like luminous eyes, water churning and crushing him, waves pounding him. Someone yelling. Why couldn't he breathe? His heart pounded. He rose to the surface, he broke. Still it was dark. Hands on his shoulders, shaking him. He was breaking free, but still no light. Somebody yelling for Bernie.

"Isaac, my man, wake up."

His eyes opened on streetlight coming through an open window. A dark face in shadow. Carlos. Shaking him awake.

"Who was yelling?" Isaac asked.

"That was you, man. Woke me up. You having a nightmare, but not to worry. Carlos is here for you. You okay, Isaac?"

"Oh, yeah. A nightmare. Sure, I'm okay." He gulped in air and waited for his heart to slow down. Sheets were tangled around him on the mattress on the floor of Carlos's room, a second-floor cubbyhole crammed with stuff. A large wardrobe looming in the corner held an extensive collection of outfits he'd seen the day before. Many of them lay scattered around the room now. A full-length mirror reflected the streetlight. A double bed beside him filled the room. Carlos got back into it.

"You sure you're okay?" he said. "Sweet dreams, then. I'm going back to sleep."

They had arrived in the afternoon in Río Dulce, a town that was not much more than a bus stop with a very active prostitution scene and Central America's longest, dreariest bridge. They had walked across that bridge last night after the call to Zelda and passed the evening in Carlos's favorite watering hole, the bar of the Backpacker Hotel.

Isaac had been on automatic pilot all through the evening. A beer sat in front of him, but he didn't drink much. Carlos chatted up a dark-haired blue-eyed beauty from Holland and an English girl with dreadlocks and introduced them to Isaac, but he barely nodded at them. He was trying not to feel much of anything or think about where he was. He was trying hard not to think about what he'd just left behind him, down the river, on the Caribbean shore. If he'd gone to the cops right away, maybe they could have found Bernie before it was too late. He wouldn't be in a shitty bar with a near stranger in some dubious kidnapping scam. He'd be on the beach with Bernie, heroes in Paradise.

When they had ended up in his room over the bus stop, Carlos had said, "Sorry, man, it's not the Ritz. But we got to lie low a bit. Enjoy a little R an' R in beautiful Río Dulce."

Going to bed last night, Isaac had thought for the second time that if he could just go to sleep, maybe the whole thing—the day they had spent on the boat looking for Bernie, and the day before, the storm and the big wave—would just be a dream, and he'd wake up in the Iguana with Bernie still alive. Instead, the nightmare came. Even after his heart calmed down, he couldn't get the sensation of water out of his mind. He lay still, trying not to make noise, to let Carlos sleep. Morning finally came. Fumes rising from buses idling under their window woke Carlos up, and they went downstairs for breakfast: pizza and Coke at the dockside restaurant Pizza del Río. Tourists climbing out of the buses and coming into the restaurant would see them there together, the golden-haired gringo boy and the flamboyant Negro, chowing down on a hot and dusty Tuesday morning in a lowlife Guatemalan river town, but Carlos didn't seem concerned. "World looks a lot brighter in the morning, don't it Isaac?" he said. "Eat up. We got a busy day ahead."

The world didn't look bright to Isaac, but he tagged along after breakfast when Carlos loaded up the *Good-Times Charlie* with tourists, buzzed under the bridge between the river and the lake, and zoomed out over the broad expanse of Lago Izabal. Schmoozing with the tourists one minute, his arm around Isaac's shoulders the next, Carlos taught Isaac to run the outboard. Even with the tourists in the launch, Carlos made a game of driving the boat. He made it fun. As if the power of speeding across the lake, throwing a huge tail of spray behind, swerving the boat to dive across its own wake with just a flick of his wrist, could give Isaac a feeling of being in charge. No teachers assigning stupid projects, no Aunt Z issuing commands, no giant wave sweeping in to steal his only friend.

Carlos hung out in the front of the boat with the tourists, pointing out the sights and flirting with the European girls, while Isaac drove. He took the helm again to steer past the old Spanish fort, through the Bocas del

Polachic delta, and finally to Denny's Beach for a swim in the late afternoon.

Over dinner that evening at the Pizza del Río— pizza and beer—Carlos asked, "How do you like the life of the launch captain, Isaac? Swimming, girls, beer, that's all I do. Not too bad. Maybe you want to be my partner on a permanent basis?"

Isaac looked at him with alarm, wondering what hidden motive this guy had, taking him in, being so friendly, so big-brother. Helping him out with this kidnapping scam he hoped wasn't real, but maybe it was. The thought made him nervous. Carlos laughed.

"Just kidding, man. One more day of this, then I think it's time we head up to Todos Santos."

"Todos Santos! I thought we were going back to Antigua, to my aunt."

"I got a better plan. Your mom is in Todos Santos, right? Mohammed goes to the mountain. I return you to mom, your grateful family hands over the cash, I disappear. They don't know nothing about me, the bad guy, and the whole thing is history. No problems for you. I got a friend in Todos Santos I knew in LA, he can put us up and help me with the little disappearing act so you don't have to worry."

Thoughts reeled through Isaac's head. So Carlos really intended to take the money. Did that make Isaac an accomplice in a crime? Stealing from his own mother. That was pretty crummy. On the other hand, his mother would be happy to see him alive, would maybe even forget what he had done. When he and Bernie had left Antigua, they'd thought they were embarking on an important journey to turn the wheel of True Meaning and find enlightenment. Would his mother understand that?

Suppose he told Carlos he'd changed his mind.

He just wanted to go back to Antigua, forget about the kidnapping scheme. Would Carlos let him go? A creepy feeling prickled his spine. Maybe it was safer not to cross Carlos, to play along with him for now and wait for an opportunity to slip away. He agreed to the itinerary change, and after dinner they made another call to Aunt Zelda. She must have been close to the phone, to pick up so fast. Carlos spoke to her first. "Three days left. We coming to Todos Santos. Have the money there."

He handed the phone to Isaac who repeated his line, "I'm okay."

"Where are you, Isaac?" Aunt Zelda asked. She sounded calm and precise, like she always did. He didn't know what Carlos would do if he answered that question. He didn't want to find out.

"I don't know," he said.

"That was good," Carlos said when they hung up. "She trusts you. She trusts me. We doing fine. She sounds like a good lady, not going to give us any problems."

They took the launch to the Backpacker Hotel for another night at a table full of friendly travelers sharing drinks and jokes, and later, on the launch, lines of coke and marijuana cigarettes. This time Isaac didn't throw up, and the world didn't spin so badly. The pain subsided some, and Isaac started to think that maybe Carlos didn't have an angle, he was just full of *joi de vivre*, with a kind heart for a kid in trouble. But he still felt a deep uneasiness.

10.

atherine held up the painting she had just finished, the gift she'd promised Marvella as a reward for long days of sitting still, for more patience than seemed possible. "Here's your portrait, done at last! This is you."

The three-year-old studied her painted image seriously. She frowned. "Is it beautiful enough to be me?" she asked.

Catherine laughed.

"*Egoísta!*" Nicolasa chided her daughter. "She's impossible, this one! Thank you for the beautiful painting, Catarina. We'll treasure it."

With a proud air of ownership Marvella watched the two women tack the wet painting to the dining room wall, then ran off, free. Catherine felt satisfied. Finally she had enough paintings of the girl. It was still early in the day, time for more work.

"Now I need school scenes," she told Nicolasa. "Photographs won't give me enough information." And anyway, she hadn't taken her camera into the school. She didn't want any kids to think she was stealing their souls. They already had too much to fear. "I need to lug my easel in and actually paint in the school. Baudilio will be there. Do you think he can keep me out?"

Catherine's face still ached where the preacher had struck her yesterday. When she had gotten back from the bar, she had told Nicolasa about the assault in the street. Nicolasa had dressed her cheek with a poultice of aloe and heard how Desiderio, to Catherine's astonishment, had fought in her defense. She had left untold what happened afterward: the drinks, the dance, the kiss that now, in the clear morning light on the terrace, seemed so wanton, so unlike the Catherine Barnes she knew herself to be. And so unlike Oswaldo's Spanish kiss.

Nicolasa had railed against Baudilio. "That animal!" she had fumed. Now that she'd calmed down she said, "Speak to Don Roberto. Didn't he invite you to come to the school? Don't let Baudilio scare you."

Catherine didn't intend to. She marched through town with her paint box, her bruised face held high, rage simmering at the preacher's gall. Too many people in this town were under his influence, she thought. It was time someone launched a campaign against ignorance and superstition. Maybe it took someone from the outside, who could see things for what they were. Seeing was her profession. Open your eyes, she would tell the Todosanteros. Instead of color and shape, they would discover a demagogue. She would love to rid them of Baudilio. Tensed for action, as if she might meet her enemy at a barricade, she swept through the gate to the school. It was unguarded. The door to the office was open. The school principal waved her inside, courteous and friendly, as before.

"Please believe me, I'm only here to paint," she said to Don Roberto. "Do the parents really think I'm going to kidnap their children? Someone is telling them lies, to frighten them."

"Don't concern yourself," he assured her. "I trust you. Be our guest. You're welcome to paint here in the school at any time you wish, mornings when the little children are here, or afternoons when it's quiet, just the older students. I'll vouch for you."

Don Roberto escorted her through the courtyard, where strings of plastic pennants were fluttering in the breeze and students were sweeping with homemade brooms. He stopped to tell a boy to tuck in his shirttail. He addressed the students by name and told them how lucky they were that a real artist from the United States was coming to paint in their school. Catherine felt reassured that she was, once again, welcome in the town. Little children shook her hand and hurried off to class, chattering in Mam.

She set up her easel in the courtyard, under the porch roof in case of a shower. Soft clouds clung to the mountaintops, visible over the school building across the courtyard. The sun sparkled on the plastic pennants. Girls in vivid colors walked by between classes and looked shyly at her work, fascinated by her brushes and paints. Then they dashed to join the boys, to play basketball and ignore her. In quick strokes she added the basketball players to her sketch, the boys in their red pants dribbling the ball, the girls running and leaping, undeterred by their narrow skirts and plastic slippers. The morning hours sped by.

* * *

From his classroom in the far corner of the school, Baudilio watched the gringa at her easel across the courtyard.

He stood at the blackboard in front of his fourth grade class instructing them in mathematics. Columns of his well-formed numbers stood out, sharp and clear, in white chalk against the black of the board. He enjoyed teaching multiplication and division. The rules of calculation were predictable and unyielding, as were, to Baudilio's mind, the rules of orthography and calligraphy, and the facts of geography and history. It was his responsibility to instruct the children entrusted to him with the clarity of his ideas.

Baudilio's ideas didn't change with the wind like others' did, for they were based on a simple understanding of truth, of what was right and wrong. He never tried to be what he was not, to pretend he was a leftist when the flag of Ché went up over the town square and everyone danced in the brief delusion that soon they would be free. Because he wouldn't dance with them, the guerrillas had wanted to kill him. He had fled to Mexico rather than change his opinions. He came back as poor as he'd been when he left. Some people, even people who had backed the guerrillas, had stayed in town while the army occupied it, and had grown rich as a result. Now these double-talkers owned hotels and businesses. All Baudilio had was a diploma certifying him to teach primary school. His job at Urbana Mixta, teaching fourth grade from eight in the morning until lunch at one, was hard. The classes had grown larger every year, swelling from thirty-five to sixty-five. In the afternoons he preached. And the people who'd danced under Ché's flag came to him and said, you were right. We were betrayed. Those guerrillas were not who we thought they were. They came from Cuba with their promises of land and jobs for the poor, but they couldn't deliver. They could hide in caves in the mountains, they could beat an old man to death with stones, but they couldn't win a revolution. Those guerrillas were not good men. And Baudilio's congregation grew with people who realized, like him, that the solution to the country's problems was a clear distinction between right and wrong, and a firm hand.

Neither teaching nor preaching paid well. Many years had passed before he'd been able to buy a house on the main street, where he lived with his wife and seven children. Now, other than the house, he had only two things: his gift of oratory and his mission. He hypnotized his audiences when he spoke of his vision of the future and the dangers that lay in store if they opened the town up to influences from the outside, to lawlessness, to gangs, and to the money-grubbing family that owned the Hotel Todosantero, and its head, Benito, his chief rival. Baudilio wanted to be mayor, not for his own glory but to bring the kingdom of God to Todos Santos. It infuriated him that Benito, who had already brought such filth upon the town, was running against him. Not only that, but the corpulent and gregarious innkeeper had a large group of supporters, despite the well-known fact that his son was a drug dealer and troublemaker not even his own parents could control. Baudilio's face bore the evidence. A bandage covered the wound from his fight with Desiderio yesterday. A bandage could hide the cut, but not the humiliation. Something had to be done about that hoodlum.

And now, the gringa was here in the school again, a clear and present threat to the children in his care. She had defied him. She would not back down. He tried to control his rage. The words of the Apostles ran through his mind: "The anger of man does not achieve the righteousness of God." James. He worried that he had let his passions get out of hand yesterday, when he tried to put the fear of God into the woman. The presence of sin did that to him, drove him mad. He knew it was his weakness. He thought of Paul, possibly a greater Apostle than James: "Let all bitterness and wrath and anger and clamor and slander be put away from you. Be kind to one another, tender-hearted, forgiving each other, just as God in Christ also has forgiven you." Would Paul counsel him to forgive this foreigner spreading sin among his flock? He searched the Scriptures in his mind for guidance, and came back again to James. "Prove yourselves doers of the Word, and not merely hearers who delude themselves."

He had heard the warnings, broadcast by radio from Huehue, and he had seen the signs sent unmistakably from God, like the owls he had seen circling the mountaintops. The children were in danger. The gringa's presence at this time could not be an accident. His duty was clear. To be a doer of the Word, he must act. Since Don Roberto had been no help, he must go to the mayor as soon as school was out.

* * *

Believing that Baudilio had not seen her revisiting the school, Catherine moved her easel into an empty classroom after the primary students and teachers went home to lunch. There she attacked the perspective problem of rows of desks and benches against the squared tiles of the floor. Plotting the complexity of angles, she puzzled over another enigma: yesterday's encounter in the bar, when she'd come close to succumbing to the music and rum and to the young male body pressed against her, wanting her, urging her on. If her hunger hadn't been for Desiderio, then for what?

A cluster of middle-school girls invaded the classroom, and she was ready for a break from angles and complexities. She offered to give them an art lesson. She wanted to gather these lovely teenage girls around her and instruct them in the simple physicality of paint, of mixing and applying colors, to avoid the more troubling physicality of the human body and its longings. *"Entren, muchachas!"* she invited them.

She wiped her palette clean and put aside her painting. "Here, you try," she said putting a brush into a girl's hand. "What's your name?" she asked the girl.

"Rosa."

"We'll make the color of your name," Catherine said, squeezing out a fresh blob of white paint and a dark coil of alizarin crimson that glistened, nearly black. They watched as though she were a magician. "Mix them!" she told the girl.

Rosa touched the brush tentatively into the paint, from the dark to the white. The girls gasped when a streak a brilliant pink appeared. Catherine laughed and tore out a page from her sketchbook so Rosa could paint a flower in shades of crimson and pink. She let each girl have a turn at mixing colors: add ultramarine blue to crimson, she suggested, to make magenta or violet, the colors in your *huipil*. With cadmium lemon use cerulean or pthalo; ultramarine is too warm for the crisp coolness of green. Titanium white overpowers; flake white brings colors alive. The girls tested their colors on more pages from her sketchbook. The sparkle of the girls around the easel, dipping the brush from one lump of color to the next, far outshone anything on the palette. Their fresh beauty brought sudden tears to her eyes, which she brushed away without their noticing. They tittered and chatted. When some boys appeared at the door to watch, the girl at the easel dropped her brush and stepped back.

"What's wrong?" Catherine demanded. "Keep painting. You're doing fine." The girl, Magnolia, had drawn a fairly-rendered parrot in brilliant green, and was experimenting with the brush, making the line go thick and thin. She refused to go on as long as the boys were there.

"She's in love," one in the group explained while the others smothered laughter and whispered among themselves in Mam. "She doesn't want her boyfriend to see her picture. He'll tell her it's ugly."

"Oh no!" Catherine said. "Ignore him, Magnolia. You can't let a boy tell you that. You'll treat him like a king and he'll get you pregnant." Although she'd been in Todos Santos a short time, she knew from long conversations with Nicolasa what was in store for these demure maidens. "Then you'll have to leave school and you'll never get anywhere. Don't listen to the boys! You girls have to have some confidence in yourselves." How easily she gave advice to others that she wasn't so sure she could take herself. The girls laughed and poked Magnolia, shoving her toward the easel. She picked up the brush and dabbed at her painting as her friends urged her on.

The bell rang and they had to go to class. Catherine watched them go and sighed, alone again. She packed up her easel, sliding the canvas paper taped on its board into the slots in the lid of the box. That would keep the wet paint from coming into contact with the brushes, tubes, and bottles stowed inside, held in place by the freshly wiped palette. Each thing fit. She suddenly longed for order, for the polished silverware she'd arranged in its felt-lined box, the winter clothes she'd hung in the cedar closet before she'd left Iowa.

She walked back toward the Todosantero and stopped outside one of the stores with a phone for public use. She hadn't talked to Isaac since last Friday. That seemed like so long ago. She needed to hear his voice. She wanted to know that he was fine—that despite whatever had happened to her yesterday, or earlier on the mountain when she'd walked with Oswaldo in this high place so far from everything familiar, her ties to her old life had not been severed. She went inside the store. But her phone call to Antigua wouldn't go through. Afternoon clouds had lowered into the valley, cutting off the tenuous cellular connection Todos Santos maintained with the world.

Damn, she thought, damn these mountain walls. Damn clouds. "*Guard your children!*" a voice in the store shrieked at her. Startled, she located the source of the voice, a radio: *Keep them indoors throughout the period of danger. The satanic cult will arrive while the moon is full.* How bizarre that radio waves could penetrate the mist when her call could not.

"Is that broadcast coming from Huehue?" she asked the storekeeper.

"No. The Todos Santos station gives us all the news," he answered.

Including, Catherine thought, dire prophecies. She retreated from the store and continued up the street through the fog. She passed the town jail, a small concrete building with two cells that opened directly onto the street, like something out of the Old West. A drunk in one of the cells leaned against the bars and looked out at her, howling mournfully. She averted her gaze and made her way to the hotel.

She entered the dining room and there, sitting at a table, reading a newspaper and drinking a Coke, as though her wishes had conjured him up out of the gloom, was Oswaldo. He looked up and saw her. She felt a leap of gladness and surprise. This was only Wednesday. He wasn't due to pick her up until the weekend. He was early! How very nice.

"You're late," he said, flashing his grin and standing up. "I've been waiting for hours. Was your painting going well, or did some crazy preacher have you locked up?"

Catherine's forehead wrinkled in confusion.

"Nicolasa told me what's been going on here. This Baudilio, waging holy war on you," Oswaldo explained. He pulled out the chair next to him. His face and tone darkened. It was odd. "Sit down. I've come up here with some news from Zelda. You must be brave." Why? she thought, but she obeyed and sat down beside him. He took her hands. Later she would remember how warm his hands were, and how hers trembled, as though they knew before she did. He let the words out slowly, rationing them, as if to soften them, as if he were trying to keep the words themselves from doing her harm. "Isaac is missing. Someone has taken him." As if he were trying to keep the words themselves from cutting her apart. "You must not worry. Your son is alive. He's well. Zelda talked to him on Monday, when the kidnappers called." As if she could understand the words coming out of his mouth. "We'll just do as they tell us and nothing will go wrong. They called again yesterday, to say they're coming here, to Todos Santos. We just have to wait for them."

"Missing?" She felt her blood turn to air. She saw blackness swirling in front of her. "What do you mean, missing?"

Oswaldo held her hands. He told her that Zelda had called him to help, that Elliot had wired money. Zelda had decided she would stay in Antigua to get the kidnappers' telephone calls, while Oswaldo came to Todos Santos with the money for the kidnappers. He spoke slowly, in simple words, to soothe her fears. She looked at him with dry eyes, trying to understand this new language he was speaking, and even after she had deciphered the words, trying to put them into some order that had meaning. She couldn't do it. The words filled her with fury.

"No!" she shouted. "You're mistaken. This can't be true." She trembled and gasped for breath. She thrust his hands away from her, stood up, and strode across the dining room. "You're wrong!"

He didn't say anything. She came back and faced him, her hands on her hips.

"We have to do something. Have you called the police? Are they looking for him? Where is he? We have to find him. Let's go."

"There's no place to go. We don't know where he is. Sit down, Catarina."

She stared at him, her chest heaving, then crumpled into her chair and leaned against him. His arms went around her, and he was talking again, telling her they could not act rashly, they must be calm. They had to wait. Wait! How could she? How could this catastrophe have struck without her knowledge, not the least suspicion on the radar screen of a mother's intuition? With all the other parents in town fearing for their children's safety, she had never once worried for Isaac. Shouldn't she have known he was in danger? A rebellious boy in a lawless place. Wasn't her selfishness to blame? A good mother doesn't just go off to search her soul when her child is in crisis. A good mother doesn't let her son get kidnapped. She couldn't bear to think about what they might be doing to Isaac right now. She couldn't bear to think she might never see him again. She was too scared even to cry.

Oswaldo stroked her hair and tried to stop her shaking. What he hadn't mentioned in his detailed explanation of recent events was his determination to stay by her, to help her if he could, to get her son back to her, no matter what it took. The moment he had gotten the call from Zelda, and through the hours of the long drive west, he'd known this was his appointed task. He had aimed straight at it, like a missile to its target. Nothing would tear him from it, if he had to cross mountains and seas. This was nothing he could mention now, when he was trying to convince Catherine that things were not so bad as they seemed, that all would turn out well. Because it made no sense. The sensible thing would have been to tell Zelda that he had other commitments, and to steer clear, since no possible good could come of getting caught in this woman's orbit. Even if they found Catherine's son, and the chances of that were not nearly as rosy as he had painted them, then what? She was a person entangled, the mother of someone else's son, a woman whose language he didn't speak, whose culture, so far as he could tell from its movies and tourists, was irreconcilable with his own. She would never be patting out tortillas in his kitchen. He should never have agreed to come back to Todos Santos. It contradicted all his rules of the road: proceed with caution, look in the rearview mirror, don't trust the curves. These rules had kept him alive on the Guatemalan highway in dangerous terrain, and unscathed by any brush with an attractive tourist up until now.

"Don't worry," he said again, as impossible as he knew that was. "These things are common here. The kidnappers will get their money and go. Isaac will be back."

* * *

Baudilio, crossing the square toward the mayor's office, almost ran into the American woman. The guide was with her. Baudilio hadn't known he was back. He planted himself in front of the two of them.

"You!" he said to the guide. "Do not consort with the Hittites and Canaanites. The foreign devil will cause you to sin and bring ruin to your countrymen. Cast her away!"

The man didn't answer. He put his arm around the woman's shoulders and they shoved past Baudilio with an air of utmost urgency. The woman's white face looked deranged, as if she were already possessed by Satan.

The preacher's errand was more imperative than ever. Yet he had to wait for hours in the mayor's office for the return of Domingo Pablo Pablo, who had gone to Huehue to a meeting of regional mayors for the purpose of discussing security in light of the threatened arrival of the cult that weekend, when the moon would be full. An argument had erupted over where the greatest need for extra police lay. The mayor of Huehue wanted to pull in forces from the surrounding towns to protect the department capital. It had been impossible to convince him that the real danger lay in Todos Santos.

It was already dark and raining hard when the mayor's car pulled up next to the plaza and his driver let him out. Domingo Pablo Pablo was not pleased to see the lights still on in his office, but he could not upbraid the guard when he saw who was waiting to see him.

"*Compadre*," he greeted Baudilio. "You won't be pleased. Huehue has refused our request for extra police. Six inept womanizers for a town of six thousand citizens, that's all the protection the authorities will give us. They don't believe our intelligence, that the devil-worshippers are coming to us, not to Huehue." The two men left the guard standing in the waiting room and went into the mayor's inner office.

Don Domingo sank down into his chair. The trip back over the altiplano had taken over an hour in the heavy rain, even though his chauffeur was the fastest driver in perhaps all the highlands, famous for making it to the capital in less than four hours, a journey that usually required seven. Domingo was tired. He would like to have offered Baudilio a drink from the bottle he kept in his desk drawer, but he knew that the preacher did not partake.

"The situation has grown more serious," Baudilio said. "The North American woman, the artist, was at the Instituto all day. Why is she spending so much time with our children? There must be some connection with the Satanists. Perhaps she was sent to select which children they will take. We cannot know whom among the foreigners in town may be planted here by the malevolent ones." He paused to let the mayor's imagination work. "This leaves us only one reasonable option."

"What's that?" If there was a safe way to keep Domingo Pablo Pablo off the hook when trouble arrived, as it always did sooner or later, he was all ears.

"We must close the hotels. Expel all the foreigners from town until the danger has passed."

"What! How do we do that?" Although he got along well with Baudilio, out of necessity, since the preacher controlled a large number of his Evangelical constituents, Domingo was in no hurry to anger the hotel owners, particularly Benito, possibly the next mayor and a powerful presence in their political party. Domingo hoped to go on to bigger things since the law prevented him from running again as mayor of Todos Santos.

"It won't be difficult. You've just come from Huehue with department orders. The hotels have licenses that can be revoked if they disobey directives from the government. Let their owners explain to the tourists that this is not a safe time to remain in Todos Santos. It will only be a few days. If you don't act now, the foreigners may start grabbing and hiding children right away in preparation for the dark rites."

To avoid an unacceptable risk, the mayor agreed to this plan of action. He would go around to the hotels first thing in the morning. The evangelist rose to go.

"You must stand firm." He clasped Domingo's shoulder in a firm hand. "Gird your loins with truth; put on the breastplate of righteousness. I will pray for you. With God's help, we'll prevail over Satan."

Domingo felt a little better that, in the absence of reinforcements from Huehue, at least he had Baudilio's prayers working for him. He hoped they would prove effective against a multitude of problems.

* * *

That evening, Catherine sat like an invalid by the stove in the kitchen, but its heat couldn't warm her. Nicolasa made her tea and scrambled eggs, but she couldn't eat. Marvella tried to get her to play peek-a-boo, and Nicolasa scolded, "Not now, *mi'ija*. Cata's not in the mood for games."

Rolfe talked quietly to Oswaldo about the tension in the town. Rain beat on the tin roof, drowning out their voices. Leaving food on her plate, something she normally would not do in Guatemala, Catherine excused herself to go.

"If it stops raining, knock on my door," Oswaldo said. "We can try calling Antigua again." More than anything, Catherine wanted to talk to Zelda. Repeated attempts on Oswaldo's cell phone had failed to go through. She was desperate to hear her sister-in-law's voice. If only those cursed microwaves could get over the mountains. Maybe Zelda, strong and confident, could keep her from losing her mind.

She went upstairs to her room, past the open door to the dorm with its eight single beds crammed in at odd angles, awaiting the arrival of the young backpacker tourists. She tried to read in bed, but it was hopeless. She couldn't focus on the page. She turned out her light and shivered under her thin blankets. Images of Isaac appeared out of the dark. Isaac as a newborn, his face wise and peaceful. She and Elliot had called him the three-day-old Perfect Master. At the age of two he was plump, with cherubic curls, rocketing down the street in front of her. Every time he saw a cigarette butt, he exclaimed, "Yuck!" He stomped the nasty butt with his sneaker. *Yuck* was his favorite word at two.

He'd been a demanding toddler, prone to tantrums. Elliot had criticized her when she gave in to them. What else could she do? Isaac wouldn't sit on a step for a "time out" as other children would. He wouldn't go to his room. He wouldn't back down. He knew how to get his way. She couldn't conquer his will, even at three. She admired that.

Isaac, hungry for knowledge, had started at a young age to make pronouncements. After she had read to him dozens of times a little science book on the beginnings of life on earth, he looked up at her one day and said, "There would be no life on earth without bananas." His favorite food at the time. She loved the way his mind worked and wrote down his words in a little book she still kept.

The rain lashed at the dark windows of the hotel. The cold bit through the four blankets she'd piled on her bed. She felt so hopeless, so alone. If only she could reach Zelda. Not Elliot. He would blame her. He had wanted to march Isaac off to summer school where he'd learn the consequences of his bad attitude. Maybe Elliot had been right. Her mind raced with the thought that he was always right. It was her fault Isaac misbehaved at school. It was her fault he was gone. Guilt crept under the covers with the cold. She curled herself into a ball and tried to hold in her body heat.

Footsteps sounded on the bare wood floor of the hall. Doors opened and closed. She listened to the voices of the tourists in the dorm room. She had seen the room in the mornings when the maids cleaned it of the detritus left by the stream of guests traveling on a shoestring. Backpackers whose lives were so free and unattached, they dropped parents and boyfriends and girlfriends like the litter they left in the dorm. They were so young, they had no one whose life meant more to them than their own. She envied them. She heard Oswaldo's door open in the room next to hers. She listened to him move around his room and continued listening after the sounds stopped and the hotel was devoid of human noises.

Darkness and anxiety pressed down on her. Wind and rain rattled the windows. Her shivering grew more violent. Sleep was out of the question.

She got out of bed and went to her door. She battled indecision for a moment, then opened it and looked out into the hall. The light was on in Oswaldo's room, streaming out of the cracks around his door. She knocked softly and waited. The door swung open. Oswaldo was still up and dressed.

"I can't sleep," she said.

"Come in," he said, and closed the door behind her. She touched his chest, his down jacket.

"Cold, isn't it?" she said, and kissed him. He kissed back, the kiss she had been waiting for, not short and Spanish, but long and hungry and at the same time comforting. This kiss felt right. After a while he left her lips and kissed her face, paying attention to every part of it, the eyebrows, the forehead, the bruise on her cheek, the earlobe, the neck, at which point she said, "This is crazy."

"We can stop," he said.

"No. I don't want to."

He backed up and sat down on the edge of the double bed, the *matrimonio*, pulling her to stand between his legs.

"Take this off," he said, tugging gently at the shoulder strap of her summer nightgown, so ineffectual against the highland nights.

"Okay. But remember, I've had a child. My body's not young anymore."

When she stood before him, naked except for her underpants, he said, "You are beautiful."

"My husband doesn't think so."

"He's mistaken." Oswaldo kissed her nipples and her belly with its Cesarean scar. She shivered.

"Let me warm you up." He pulled her onto the bed and covered her body with his clothed one and she felt his heat and smelled the stuff he put in his hair to make it stand up and dug her hands under his belt into his pants and felt his penis. It was erect, urgent. It told her she was wanted.

She unbuckled the belt. "Your clothes are a problem." He got rid of the clothes and turned out the light as she slid under the blankets. And later, when his warm skin was against hers and his penis was inside her and she was rocking with his rhythm and his heat was surging into her, tears came to her eyes. And she had no idea for whom or what—Isaac, Elliot, her marriage, or the wondrous amnesia of desire fulfilled—she wept.

11.

Still thinking about giving his so-called kidnapper the slip, Isaac noticed that no matter how easy-going Carlos appeared, he was always watching. It gave Isaac that prickly feeling in his spine again. Thursday morning Carlos roused him before dawn to board a bus. All roads in Guatemala lead to the capital. So they headed for Guatemala City. Five hours later they changed buses. By mid-afternoon they had already been on the road for ten hours, listening to hawkers selling miracle cures down the aisle of the buses, to beggars' tales of misfortune, to the shrill patter of women carrying baskets over their heads as they squeezed past. "*Chuchitos! Chuchitos de pollo de carne de frijol, chuchitos, chuchitos!*"

Carlos bought four chuchitos and handed two to Isaac.

"Delicacy time, Isaac. Nothing but the finest cuisine here on the Pan-American Highway."

Isaac imitated Carlos, unwrapping the corn husk,

eating the mealy little handfuls of steamed corn dough stuffed with some kind of meat, trying to keep the juice from leaking into his lap. Then, like everyone else, he threw the wrapper out the window.

By the time they pulled into the terminal at Huehuetenango, Isaac was stiff and weary. They dodged puddles from the afternoon rain across the mud space where buses were lined up at low cinderblock sheds. Carlos seemed to know what he was doing. He chose a green-and-gold-spangled bus and herded Isaac on board. The seats were already packed with men and boys in red-and-white-striped pants, women and girls in matching outfits, as though they were all marching in the same Sousa band. The bus driver jumped up when he saw Isaac and started speaking in rapid-fire Spanish. Isaac didn't catch much except "*Cerrado, todos cerrados,*" over and over.

Carlos calmed the driver down and pushed them along the aisle, finding an empty seat near the back. "What was that all about?" Isaac asked.

"Some kind of weird shit coming down in Todos Santos. Devil-worshippers on their way. We're going up into the boonies, man. People believe all kinds of superstitions. Bus driver says all the hotels in town are closed, they don't want no tourists coming in. I told him not to worry, we not tourists, got friends in town, a place to stay, etc. etc. That's all we need, devil-worshippers."

A man crowded into the seat on the other side of Carlos, who slid over, crushing Isaac into the window. As the bus climbed up switchback after switchback, scaling the massive face of the mountain range, the temperature plummeting the higher they got, Isaac was actually glad to be pinned up against Carlos at such close quarters. He shivered in his thin T-shirt.

"Hoo boy. I forgot how cold it gets up here," Carlos said. "You got a jacket in that backpack of yours, Isaac?"

He didn't. He's been packing for the Caribbean, not the Arctic, when he and Bernie had left Antigua. Almost a week ago.

"Never mind. We'll get you something warm in Todos Santos. Got to show your mom we taking good care of you, my boy."

Sure, thought Isaac. The ransom demand would really convince her of that. He wondered how Carlos planned to get the money. How do you arrange a money drop in a place with practically no phones? And in a town that was all excited over devil-worshippers. Wouldn't that make people more alert, on the lookout for the criminal element?

Carlos must have been worried, too, even if he didn't show it. About an hour and a half into this leg of the trip, the bus left the paved road and started bouncing over muddy ruts. Chicks in a crate on the rack over Isaac's head burst into peeping, raining feathers down on him.

"Shit," said Carlos. "The road has gotten worse since the last time I was here. Feels like we in a cement mixer. I'm thinking, maybe we bail out early. How'd you like to check out one of the most scenic spots in all Guatemala? La Torre, highest peak in Central America, according to the guidebooks, if you don't count the volcanoes."

"It's too late for mountain climbing, don't you think?" Isaac said. Nearly five o'clock, in fact.

Carlos laughed. "Can't pull nothing over on you, man. Tomorrow's a better day for a hike, no doubt. But I got a friend up here in this godforsaken tundra, an old geezer I did a favor for once. Let's visit him and check things out before it gets dark."

Tundra was a good description for the scene outside the bus window. The treeless plateau spread out to distant mountains, cold and empty except for a few scattered hovels. They passed an adobe hut overshadowed by a huge gray rock formation, like some petrified giant glowering through the mist at the puny signs of human life. When they came to a cluster of houses that looked like a Siberian outpost, Carlos stood up and clambered over the guy beside him into the aisle.

"This is our stop," he said, "La Ventosa—the windy place—pearl of the altiplano."

Isaac followed Carlos off the bus. Mist shrouded the village. The bus rattled away. Isaac's spirits sank even lower.

Carlos refused to be daunted. "Hey man! Keep an eye out for a Best Western."

They walked along a dirt track among the adobe houses. Turkeys gobbled furiously, hustling out of their way. Children peered out of dark doorways.

"*Niños,*" Carlos called to them. "*Quieren dulces?*" Do you want candy? He pulled small Snickers bars out of his pockets and held them out. The ragged, dirty children gathered around.

"Don Jerónimo. *Está en casa?*" Carlos asked. Is he home? The children didn't answer so Carlos switched to another language, not at all like Spanish, strange and guttural. This time the kids responded.

"It's good to know the local lingo," Carlos said in English with a wink. Isaac wondered how a Garífuna from Lívingston knew how to talk in this place. He wondered what else Carlos knew. Every day he spent with Carlos, instead of getting to understand him better, just seemed to deepen the mystery.

The kids followed them through the village, past the last house, then on a narrow path that wound through a pasture, past big boulders and spiky magueys. "Don Jerónimo, he's a big honcho around here," Carlos explained.

"A *chimán*, like a witch doctor. He does Mayan ceremonies, sacrifices chickens, the whole shebang. Folks around here don't make a move without consulting old Jerónimo." Ahead of them the pasture steepened and disappeared into cloud. That was the mountain, La Torre, Carlos said.

They came to a clearing in the rocks. Smoke rose from the clay-tiled roof of a small adobe house. The whole roof seemed to exude smoke. There was no chimney. "*Hola!* Don Jerónimo!" Carlos called out.

A man with white hair and a wispy beard poked his head out of the door. He looked ancient, like his tattered red-striped pants and faded wool jacket. In spite of the cold, his gnarled bare toes stuck out of antique leather sandals. His face crinkled into an almost toothless grin. "Carlitos!"

There was more of the Indian language Isaac didn't understand, but he got the impression that Don Jerónimo was happy to see them. He waved them into the dark house. Its one unpainted adobe room was blackened by smoke. An open fire burned in the center of the dirt floor. Smoke rose from it, filling the room and escaping through gaps at the tops of the walls, under the roof beams. An old woman knelt on a straw mat by the fire, rolling out dough on a stone mortar. Blankets were jumbled on a bed in one corner. Two wooden chairs, several low stools, and a rough wooden table covered with assorted cooking pots, utensils, and candles completed the furnishings. They sat down on the stools close to the fire.

"This is Doña Tecla," Carlos introduced Isaac. "They only speak Mam. I stayed with them a while when I was hanging out in Todos Santos, a few years back. Good people."

Doña Tecla gave them mugs of sweet, watery coffee. Isaac cradled his in his hands, savoring its heat. Don

Jerónimo chattered away with Carlos while his wife patted out tortillas and tossed them onto the griddle balanced on three rocks over the fire. Soon she plucked them off the fire and handed them around.

"This is dinner, Isaac," Carlos informed him. "Simple but nourishing. Have all you want. The more you eat, the better our hosts feel."

The hot corn taste of the tortillas was delicious. Isaac was hungry. Doña Tecla kept the tortillas coming.

After dinner the old man took them outside into the dark night. He carried a lantern and showed them the outhouse at the edge of the compound, then took them to a wooden shed beside the house. He unlocked the door and led them inside. He lit a candle on a table against the unpainted wooden wall. Isaac saw in its flickering light a bunch of clay bowls and pots, more candles, and an unpainted cross, its arms of equal length, notched at their ends.

"That's the *chimán's* sacred table, where he does his magic thing," Carlos said. "You're in luck. He says he's got a ceremony scheduled for tomorrow night. Some kind of cleansing shindig, he tells me. You gonna experience some local color, Isaac. Probably we should rest up for the event. They can go on all night, and this is our bedroom. I stayed here before. Not too bad, if you have enough blankets."

Carlos dropped off pretty quickly. Isaac could hear his snores. Lying under four blankets on his pallet on the dirt floor, he couldn't make out anything in the dark windowless shed. Things were getting weirder and weirder. Ten thousand feet above sea level, witch-doctor next door, devil-worshippers on their way, and Carlos on another pallet beside him. There was no way he was getting away from Carlos now.

* * *

Catherine woke up alone. Sometime before dawn she had left Oswaldo's room and fallen asleep in her own bed. Sunlight streaming in through her window dispelled fragments of vivid dreams. Just as well. She had a feeling she was coming unhinged. Dreams—whether of Isaac, Elliot, or Oswaldo—could only push her over the edge.

She was on the terrace drinking coffee when Benito stormed in from the street. Faustina looked up from the basket of beans she was shelling under the peach tree and asked what was wrong.

"The mayor has closed the town to tourists," Benito said. "He threatens to take away our license if we don't put all our guests on the bus for Huehue today."

"Ay, *Dios*! How does he expect us to do that?" Faustina exclaimed.

"Lock your doors, that's what Domingo Pablo Pablo said. The tourists won't stay if they have no beds. 'Forgive me, old friend,' he had the nerve to say. 'These orders do not come from me.'"

Nicolasa yanked hard on the weaving she had tied to the porch post. "No doubt these orders come from Baudilio. They have that smell about them."

"The mayor says it's just to last through the weekend. Until the danger from the baby-snatchers has passed." Benito spat on the terrace floor.

"If Baudilio has his way, the hotels will never reopen. The tourists will forget all about Todos Santos. They'll go to San Juan Atitán or Nebaj instead." Faustina wore her perennial frown that would never let them forget that life was hard. She seemed unsurprised by this bad news, as though bad news were all she ever expected to hear.

"The bus drivers have been told to inform tourists in Huehue that Todos Santos is closed to visitors, for their own safety, by INGUAT," the national tourism agency, Benito said. "Lies, I'm sure of it. INGUAT never turned away tourists, not even during the *Violencia*. But what can we do? We can't be the ones to defy orders. Suppose when the cult arrives we were found harboring devil-worshippers? Tell the guests they have to go."

Catherine noticed that Benito assumed that the devil-worshippers were on their way, that the rumors were true. Even Benito, who was so down-to-earth, shared in the collective superstition. Sighing and shaking her head, Faustina left to go upstairs and knock on doors.

"I can't leave. Isaac is coming here," Catherine said to Nicolasa and Benito.

Marvella had been listening to the grownups with more understanding than Catherine would have believed. Now she piped up, climbing uninvited onto Catherine's lap, looking up into her face, and putting her sticky finger to Catherine's nose. "You're not leaving. *You're* staying here to paint my picture."

"Did you tell the mayor about Catarina's son?" Nicolasa asked her father. Marvella jumped out of Catherine's lap.

"If the mayor knew that the cult has Catarina's son, he would inform the police, maybe even the US Embassy. He doesn't want to be responsible for the troubles of foreigners. He would tell the Americans, 'This is your problem. Send CIA to deal with it.'" Benito pronounced the acronym in Spanish, *See-ah*, so it took Catherine a minute to understand, and when she did she felt alarm. "He would love that, to get CIA in here, finding the kidnappers, protecting Todos Santos."

"I don't want that," Catherine objected. "I don't want the authorities involved."

"No," Benito agreed. "You want your son back alive,

you don't tell them. That's what I figured. So I said nothing to the mayor about you. But you don't have to leave. No one can prevent us from offering hospitality to our friends without charge. The cult is coming here with your son. You may stay with us. We'll take care of you."

"Papá," Nicolasa said. "Perhaps it's best she and Oswaldo stay up at my house. It's out of the way. No one in town needs to know."

"Everyone in town will know whether they need to or not," Benito said. "But it will be better if they're not in the hotel. You don't need a license to have guests in your house. Good idea."

"Thank you," Catherine said, grateful to them both. "I have to talk to Zelda before I decide what to do. She may have some news from the kidnappers." Who undoubtedly are *not* a satanic cult from LA but a band of perfectly run-of-the-mill criminals from Guatemala City, she thought, but how could she tell them that, these people who were taking care of her? How could she ask them to throw off their long tradition of rumor and superstition? And how generous of Nicolasa to offer her new house to Catherine and Oswaldo. What did Nicolasa know, or suspect? Getting up from the table, Catherine said, "I'm going to the store with the phone. I'll be back soon."

* * *

When Oswaldo came down to the terrace, he found Nicolasa with a machete in her hand, attacking a large shrub that grew on the terrace under the window to his room. She hacked at the long white bell-shaped flowers that hung from the plant. He picked up one of the flowers from the ground and stared at its fluted opening, taloned with delicate barbs.

"What are you doing?" he asked.

"Getting rid of this *campanula* bush. Smell it."

Oswaldo didn't have to raise the flower to his nose. The strong perfume dominated the environs of the bush.

"That scent in small amounts brings sleep to the insomniac," Nicolasa said. "An overdose can cause insanity. There's too much madness in this town already."

"You think so? Too bad. The flowers are so pretty."

Nicolasa told him about the mayor's order.

* * *

Catherine went to the store that had its phone in a wooden booth, so that she could close the door for some privacy. Although no one in town spoke English to her knowledge, she didn't want eyes on her during this conversation. The phone in Zelda's house only rang twice.

"*Haló,*" Zelda answered in Spanish.

"It's me," Catherine said.

"Did Oswaldo get there?"

"Yes. He told me everything. Have you heard from the kidnappers?"

"Not yet. I talked Elliot out of calling the police. The cops here are all bozos. You don't know which side they're on. And the CIA is worse. You don't want them. How are you holding up? Do you want Elliot to come? I told him to wait in Iowa until I heard from you, but he could catch a flight down today."

"I'm not sure his presence would do a lot of good, Zelda." Catherine stopped, unable to explain further.

"I know what you mean," Zelda cut in, although Catherine doubted she could know the full extent of it. "He's a pain. Yelling at me for letting this happen. He's more useful in Iowa than he would be here. Isaac might try to call there. Better that Elliot should man the phone at home than bull his way around in a country where he can't even speak the language. But I'm sorry you have to wait this out alone, Cat. I wish I could be there. Sending Oswaldo was the best I could do. I know he's reliable."

"I'm okay. Sort of. I can't stand this waiting. I want to do something."

"You can't. We'll probably hear from them today to get instructions. This ought to be over soon. Just try to keep it together. You don't sound too good. Call me again this afternoon. Since Oswaldo's phone doesn't work up there, I can't call you. You'll need to give them the money as soon as they tell us how."

After Catherine hung up she stood in the store, staring at the glass showcase full of candy and pens and bottles of pills, knowing she should call Elliot. She didn't think she could take talking to him right now. She'd try later.

She wasn't sure how things would stand with Oswaldo until she saw him in the morning sun on the terrace, drinking his coffee, smiling up at her with his gold tooth sparkling. "You were up with the roosters, I see, while your lazy guide was sleeping in," he said. "Maybe you should fire me."

She managed a laugh. "I don't think I will," she said.

* * *

"Look what I got for you, sleepy head!"

Isaac opened his eyes. Cold air and morning sun came through the doorway of the shack. Carlos closed the bottom half of the double door and held up a worn red-and-yellow ski parka. "The latest style in La Ventosa. Just off the racks."

He tossed it to Isaac. "Breakfast is waiting," he said. Breakfast was coffee and tortillas again. Isaac hugged the parka around himself, even while he sat next to the fire. Carlos chatted in Mam to Don Jerónimo, who cackled at what must have been jokes. Then he told Isaac, "More good luck. The old man is offering to take you with him this morning while he gets stuff for the ceremony tonight. Wild shit—medicinal plants, feathers, berries, *chimán* stuff. He'll take you up the mountain while I go into town and check things out. You'll have a great time, see the scenery, and I'll be back for dinner. Sound good?"

Isaac figured it didn't much matter whether it sounded good to him or not, it was clearly Carlos's show. "Are you going to talk to my mother?" Today was the day she was supposed to have the money ready for the drop. How was that going to work, Isaac wondered.

"No, man. Your mom never going to lay eyes on me. I'm gonna get that all worked out today. No one going to get upset."

Upset, thought Isaac. What did that mean? *Hurt?*

The little Indian lady, Doña Tecla, pressed another hot tortilla into his hand. She patted his arm and said something in Mam.

"She wants to know if you like the jacket. She got it for you this morning, borrowed it from a neighbor."

"Tell her thanks," Isaac said.

"You tell her. *Chejonta tey.*"

Isaac repeated the phrase. Doña Tecla bobbed her head with delight.

"See? Now you talk their language. You'll be fine," Carlos said.

After the last tortilla, Carlos left to catch the bus to Todos Santos, and Isaac followed Don Jerónimo up the trail past the compound toward the peak, now visible in the clear morning. The old man had changed his sandals for high rubber boots, but his step was light and sure up the steep, rocky trail. Isaac had trouble keeping up. The air was thin, and he had to stop often to breathe. The *chimán* would wait for him, searching through the brush for small alpine blossoms, pointing out their brilliant reds and pinks to Isaac. Sometimes he would find something to slip into the crocheted bag he carried over one shoulder. He would tell Isaac the names of the things he found, speaking in Mam. If Isaac could make out the strange sounds, with clicks and stops between syllables, he would repeat it. Don Jerónimo would nod encouragement. The old guy was cool, almost Zen-like, even if Isaac couldn't talk to him. He wished Bernie were here. Bernie would definitely be into a Mayan ceremony.

Mostly they climbed in silence. The trail took them through stands of tall pines and open places where Isaac could look down at the altiplano stretched out below them. In the distance the rolling hills plunged down into clouds. Occasional peaks of volcanoes stuck up out of the billows of white. Don Jerónimo pointed these out, pronouncing their names.

After two hours of hard climbing, they reached a rocky knoll. Behind it, the forest spread out in a level grassy place that looked to Isaac like parkland. Don Jerónimo patted a big rock and put down his bag. Isaac sat down and watched the old man take the machete from his belt. He set to work, hacking away at the bark on the pines around them, gathering a pile of small sticks. The gashes he left on the tree trunks oozed sap. The pile of sticks grew larger. Finally, Don Jerónimo tied a rope around it, and picked the whole bundle up onto his back with the rope around his forehead. He gave Isaac the crocheted bag to carry, and pointed down the trail they had come up. Isaac guessed Don Jerónimo had all he needed now for whatever was going to happen tonight. Isaac wondered what Carlos was doing. He didn't like the idea of Carlos running into his mother. The thought of Carlos near his mother scared him.

12.

"*Still* no news from those assholes? I can't take this, Catherine. This sitting here by the phone, waiting for it to ring. I can't get any work done, and I have a show to ship out in ONE MONTH. Some wet-behind-the-ears punk from the State Department calls, wants to question my son about the death of a kid in a place I never heard of, asks what my son was doing there, and I DON'T FUCKING KNOW. Zelda doesn't know either, didn't even know Isaac was unsupervised in Lívingston. Who's minding the store down there, letting a defiant fourteen-year-old go tooling around on his own in a dangerous country? He should have been in summer school, learning some discipline."

Elliot's voice crackled through the phone, his anger like electric shocks striking Catherine's ear. She sorted through the barrage of words, seizing the one word that grabbed her. "Who died, Elliot?"

"Some kid named Bernie. You don't know about this? What are you DOING down there for chrissake?"

"You don't have to make me feel even worse. All I know is that Isaac was kidnapped. Who's Bernie? How did he die? When?" Horrible suspicions took over. Would Isaac be the next to die? The question paralyzed her with the phone clutched hard against her ear, straining to hear over static.

"Some troublemaker Isaac was palling around with. A winning combination. His parents thought they were with Zelda, she thought they were with the parents. Great. Not too hard to pull the wool over theoretically adult eyes where you are. Seems to be a real asleep-at-the-wheel crowd."

"Stop it, Elliot. Just tell me, how did this boy die?" She felt tears welling in her eyes and forced herself not to sob aloud.

"He drowned. The authorities don't know how."

"Do they think the kidnappers did it?"

"The cops don't know about the kidnapping," Elliot said. "Zelda insists on keeping them in the dark. I think maybe it's time to get some professionals on the case, the FBI, the CIA. You're in a fucking banana republic. It's time to knock some heads."

"The CIA doesn't have a good record here. Listen to Zelda. She knows what she's talking about; she's lived in this country thirty years."

"She let our son go AWOL."

Our son. Elliot seemed to be inviting her to blame Zelda with him. Catherine knew that his tirade was a cover. Just waiting in fear and anguish, powerless, was an untenable position for Elliot. She wished she could join his team, that they could ride through hell together. She wished she didn't feel like slamming down the phone. She was crying silently now, tears streaming down her cheeks. She dug into her jeans pocket for a Kleenex.

"This isn't helping, Elliot."

Maybe he heard the quaver in her voice. "Do you want me to come down? I could get on a plane first thing in the morning. I'm not getting anything done here anyway. Just tell me what you want."

There had been a time once when all she wanted was Elliot's voice, Elliot's touch. Through the terrifying pain of Isaac's birth, Elliot had held her hand. With each contraction she had looked into his green eyes and believed, having his love, she could bear anything. That time was long past.

"Don't come now," she said. "It's safer for you to stay there. In case Isaac calls."

She didn't want him to come. She didn't want to meet Elliot's eyes.

The guests had all left the hotel since the mayor's order that morning, packing up their suitcases and backpacks, some sullen, some obedient, dismayed at their sudden expulsion. Only Catherine and Oswaldo were left. After supper, Nicolasa gave them stacks of supplies: sheets and blankets, baskets of tortillas and fruit and eggs. They piled the stuff into Oswaldo's van along with their bags.

"You're doing us a favor, trying out the house," Nicolasa said. "We'll move in as soon as you've got everything ready."

Rolfe and Nicolasa had decided to stay in the hotel as usual that night. They said it was for Marvella's sake; they didn't want her first night in her new house to be filled with fears of devil-worshippers. Nightmares. A bad omen. In Todos Santos there was a custom for inaugurating a new house, a ceremony of neighbors bearing water from the sacred spring in Los Matías, a fiesta with ritual drink and marimba music. They would move when the time was propitious. Not now. The mood in town was too unsettled. Marvella watched them packing the van.

"Everybody's running away," she said. "Aren't you scared?"

"I'm not scared," Oswaldo told her. "We'll be safe, and so will you."

Oswaldo and Catherine drove up out of town. They passed darkened houses, small cinderblock or adobe *ranchos* butted up close to the road, with just enough space for a patch of dirt, an outdoor sink, and a narrow porch. Oswaldo pointed out the carpenter's shop, the house of the tailor Don Gregorio, who had a beautiful garden, the charred remains of Doña Olga's *típica* shop that had burned down recently, with all its hand-woven fabrics, leaving her destitute, and her husband in the States not sending her any money.

"You met a lot of people today," Catherine laughed. She suspected that his gossip was intended to keep her mind off Isaac and the mayor's orders. She liked that. They passed the ruins, pulled to the side of the road, and parked.

"I thought we were hiding," Catherine said. "People will see the van."

"You can't hide in a town like Todos Santos," Oswaldo said. "When the kidnappers get here, someone will know. That's why I'm making as many friends as I can."

With flashlights they picked their way down the dark path through tall corn to the shuttered house. Catherine thought of Marvella. This would be a spooky place for a little girl tonight.

Everything was in order in the new house. While Oswaldo built a fire in the kitchen wood stove, Catherine made up beds. She did her best with sheets that were rough and a little too small on the big double in the room next to the kitchen and Marvella's small bed on the second floor. The room was cozy. When she came downstairs, Oswaldo was opening a bottle of wine.

"Where did you get that?" she asked. Wine was unavailable in Todos Santos, where stores, bars, and cantinas only offered beer, the local *aguardiente*, and, for the especially extravagant, whisky.

"I brought it from Antigua. The corkscrew, too. I thought it might help to improve your courage just now."

"What a good idea," Catherine said.

They turned off the electric light and sat by the fire with just a candle, drinking the wine out of water glasses. The circle of light held the night at bay, as though Oswaldo's presence in the ruddy kitchen, and the strong wooden door built by Rolfe, were enough to keep her terrors out. They talked about things that were far away. When the bottle was empty, she said, "I'll sleep upstairs."

Whether sleep was possible, whether leaving Oswaldo to climb the stairs alone was advisable, remained to be seen. The alternative, to slip again into his protective arms, as though he were a lover she could count on in distress, seemed rash.

"As you wish," he said lightly. "I'm only your guide. I obey your commands, like the *genio en la lámpara*."

"Genius in the lamp?" she repeated the phrase in Spanish.

He hummed a tune from *Aladdin.*

"Oh. Genie." She laughed. "You're out of the bottle now." For some reason the thought struck her as hilarious. She couldn't stop laughing, perhaps because laughter released her from the oppression of her fear. Oswaldo sang from the Disney movie, in Spanish, adding to the absurdity. He pulled her up and they danced around the room to his singing until they both collapsed in laughter. At which point she realized it was easier to surrender to his embrace than to face the demons in the dark. It was easy to let him lead her into the bedroom, easier to yield to flesh on flesh and quiet her thoughts. And whether they would have been of Isaac or Elliot, she didn't know, because now her world stopped at the edge of the candlelight and she didn't have to wonder where her son was or whether she had somehow betrayed him. Her world was only there under the blankets. Her whole world was Oswaldo's body, his hands and mouth on her, the candle sputtering out and covering them in darkness.

She woke up nestled against him, surprised she'd slept. Sunlight and birdsong filtered into the room. It took a moment to remember where she was, for her anxiety to return. She got up carefully, not waking Oswaldo, and looked out the window at mist rising across the valley, shimmering in the early light.

In the kitchen she found a small Italian coffee pot and the coffee they'd brought up the night before. She had to guess at the proportions, packing the coffee grounds into the middle section, filling the bottom with boiled water, putting it on the range top. The coffee came out strong, the way she wanted it, not the way they drank it in Guatemala. She carried it outside to the porch, where the sun had just risen over the mountains, cutting the coldness of the morning. Oswaldo came out to join her. She poured him a cup of coffee. He tasted it and made a face.

"I know," she said, and pushed the sugar jar across the table toward him. "It's like American women, not sweet enough."

He grinned and spooned in the sugar. "True. But I can do something about that."

The taste of strong coffee in the morning freshness, sunlight sparkling on the flowers in Nicolasa's yard,

Catherine wished she could enjoy it, wished she could spend a honeymoon morning pondering the intoxicating new presence of Oswaldo, without the dark emptiness left by Isaac. Impossible.

Oswaldo handed her a roll of sweet bread from the basket. "Eat," he said.

"I'm not hungry."

He didn't insist. "Oh well, more for me."

That was good. He knew when to be serious, when to joke. They had nothing to do now except wait for word from the kidnappers. It wouldn't help for him to tell her not to worry or ask her how she was doing. Instead, after breakfast he looked around at the flowers blooming in front of the porch and said, "Looks like Nicolasa's garden needs weeding."

They set to work among the bougainvillea and gladiolas, nasturtiums and impatiens, and other flowers Catherine didn't know the names for. The smell of earth and plants reassured her. The sun warmed her back as she stooped over to yank the weeds. Oswaldo worked beside her. They didn't talk, except sometimes to consult with each other on which was a weed, which a desired specimen. They found that each had some expertise on gardens. The task of bringing order into nature that would have, under other circumstances, been an ordinary and pleasant one to share with a fellow gardener, became for Catherine that morning a rite of hope. They had made a pile of weeds and were feeding them to the rabbits when Nicolasa appeared coming up the path from town. A thought sprang into Catherine's mind. Could Nicolasa be coming with good news?

The hope was crushed by Nicolasa's ordinary greeting. "Thank you! The garden needed attention, and lately I've been spending all my time at the hotel." She put down her basket and helped them carry the weeds to the rabbits' cage. Disappointed, Catherine reminded herself that where they were, good news could not just arrive. There was no phone at the Todosantero. There was only slow and excruciating waiting, until her next call to Zelda, her only contact with the kidnappers.

"Now that we have no guests, I can relax." Nicolasa slipped off her plastic shoes and sat down on the grass. Catherine sat beside her and Oswaldo disappeared behind the house.

Nicolasa reported on the situation in town. "All the children are indoors today. Baudilio broadcast warnings on the radio this morning. Keep your children home from school. Don't let them out of sight."

"How long can this go on?"

"The cult will come this weekend. By Monday it will be over." Nicolasa sounded matter-of-fact. The cult *will come*. Did she believe it too? Did she share the town's insane paranoia, or was it possible that the devil-worshippers were real, and that they had Isaac? Catherine was beginning to be confused. Here in these mountains the lines between reality and superstition blurred. Ghosts and Satanists appeared more credible than elevators and indoor plumbing.

"What will happen to Baudilio if the cult doesn't come?" Catherine asked. "If it's all a bunch of rumors he's using to intimidate the town."

"Nothing," said Nicolasa. "The people will go on as before, looking for something to gossip about, believing every evil they hear. That's the problem with Todos Santos. That's why I want to leave this place. Close up the new house and go to Germany."

"Small town people are like that everywhere. In Iowa we have Evangelicals too. And city people aren't much better. If you think they are, you'll be disappointed in Germany. Ignorant and superstitious people are everywhere."

"The schools are better in Germany," Nicolasa countered.

Even though she thought that was probably true, Catherine, contemplating her possible losses, wanted to win this argument with the Indian woman. She wanted Nicolasa to know the value of what she had, not just the house her husband had built with love, but her family, her people, her past.

"You shouldn't go," she said, for the first time. "You'll regret it. Marvella should grow up here, in her own country. She should learn to weave and make tortillas and cook those wild greens that grow in the mountains. It's her heritage. You don't realize how precious that is, more precious than anything she'll get from school." And she waited for Nicolasa to retort, *Who are you to give advice? What do you know? Your life is a mess.*

But her friend only patted her hand. "Maybe you're right." Oswaldo came back around the house toward them. "Maybe you'll find happiness here," Nicolasa said with deliberate mischief.

Catherine wondered what Nicolasa had guessed. Was that why she had insisted that her family stay at the hotel, giving her house over to the two of them?

"Are you women going to chat all day?" Oswaldo asked, "Or will there be time for lunch?"

"Lunch is waiting for you at the hotel," Nicolasa replied, getting up.

* * *

Catherine hurried through lunch, desperate to call Zelda. Nicolasa went with her to the store with the phone, to protect her from the curiosity of people staring at the one tourist left in town. The absence of children was eerie. No urchins playing in the dirt pleaded as she went by, "*Una foto? Un quetzal?*" No kid darted by without seeing her, intent on a game, batting a tired ball up a steep street with a stick, laughing if the ball hit her in the shins. No shoeshine boys accosted her as they crossed the square, "*Lustre!*" It felt like the aftermath of some plague that had taken from her not only her son but every living child. She moved through a still world. The fountain was turned off. On top of it, a large, plump bird sat motionless. She was startled when the bird swiveled its head around to glare at her, its face like a cat. Round eyes and sharp little ears. An owl.

"Look." She pointed it out to Nicolasa.

"Bad." Nicolasa said. "You know what the people say."

"About owls?"

"An owl in daylight is a sign of misfortune to come," Nicolasa said.

Catherine remembered Baudilio's speech in the *salón*. She shivered. Now she was beginning to see portents. She was losing her mind. "Do you believe that?"

"It doesn't take witchcraft to see bad things going on in Todos Santos today."

Clouds obscured the mountaintops and began to move down into the valley. They needed to make the phone call before it was too late. Catherine stepped up her pace.

"*Ay, Dios!*" Nicolasa stopped at the top of the stairs leading down from the plaza. In the street below people were getting off the bus from Huehue. A dark man looked up at the two of them and seemed to take note, his fingers twisting his long, kinky hair. He wasn't a local.

"What's wrong?" Catherine asked.

"I know that man. He was in Los Angeles with my brother. He came here two years ago to sell drugs and caused lots of trouble. Desiderio ended up in jail in Huehue for two months. That one, his name is Carlos, got clean away. It's bad news that he's here now."

"Do you think he's tied in with the cult?" Was it possible they'd already arrived, sneaking into the town one by one?

The man moved up the street, looking back over his shoulder at them, as if waiting to see where they headed.

"Who knows?" Nicolasa said. "Come on." She took Catherine's arm and led her down the stairs.

Catherine felt the familiar anxiety constricting her throat. She had to talk to Zelda. Then she had to find out more about this Carlos.

* * *

Carlos sat down at the bar of the Sin Nombre and ordered a beer. The girl behind the bar brought him a Gallo. The place was quiet, just a couple of Todosanteros at the table in the corner, not lively with tourists the way Carlos remembered it. Of course, it was early. He asked the girl, "Is Desi in?"

She looked at him blankly, like maybe she didn't comprehend his Spanish.

"Desiderio, *muchacha*, the fucking owner, is he around?" Carlos repeated.

She got it and disappeared into the back. A minute or two later, Desiderio came out. "*Hombre!*" Carlos greeted him.

Desiderio gave him that same blank look, like maybe he'd forgotten the last time Carlos had been in town on business, about two years ago, or further back when they were together on the streets of LA. Then he shrugged. "Carlos, *vos*. What's up?"

"Have a beer on me, man. Doesn't look like you're too busy to sit down with an old friend."

Desiderio pulled a Coke out of the refrigerator, poured it into a glass, and came around to sit down next to Carlos.

"What," said Carlos. "You gone Evangelical?"

"Maybe. I'm just trying to run a bar here. I'm out of the business. You picked a bad time to come up to the cold country. No tourists in town."

"So I heard. That must be rough for you. Someone in town trying to give you a hard time?"

Desiderio nodded. "You're always a sharp one, Carlos. That's right. Someone's trying to run my family out of town. And I'm not going to help him by getting involved with you."

"Don't worry. That's not what I'm here for. I'm heading north, was hoping you'd take me across the border. You haven't gotten out of that business, have you?"

Desiderio swirled his glass and stared at the bubbles. He took a sip. "When do you want to go?" he asked, finishing his Coke. "The price has gone up."

"In a day or two. I can afford it."

Desiderio got up and went behind the bar. He stashed his empty glass in a plastic bin and wiped the spot where it had rested with a towel. Then he put a CD on and turned up the volume. Not that he was worried about the two men in the corner overhearing their conversation. Everyone in town knew who the coyotes were, and no one cared. Taking people across the border was considered a legitimate business.

"I can probably do it," he said. "The way things are, Leti can cover the bar."

"Doesn't look like there's much to do here," Carlos observed. "With the tourists all gone." He let that sentence mingle with the music, Manu Chao's hypnotic words—*Qué voy a hacer, je ne sais pas, Qué voy a hacer, je ne sais plus, Qué voy a hacer, je suis perdu*—repeating over and over in a haunting rhythm. Then he added, as if it were an afterthought, "But they're not all gone. I saw one crossing the square when I got off the bus. A gringa. Who's she?"

Desiderio shrugged again. "Just some North American. An artist."

"She staying at your mother's place? They told me all the hotels were closed."

Desiderio paused as if calculating what this interest in the North American could mean, but then divulged the information, perhaps figuring it was available anyway from any busybody in the street. "She moved up to my sister's new house outside of town."

Carlos stood up, pulled a couple of bills out of his pocket, and put them down on the bar. "Talk to you later, *amigo*. Thanks for the beer."

Walking back down the main street toward the square, Carlos noticed all the changes in the town. A lot of new houses were rising up to overshadow the old adobe, big houses made of cinderblock with arched porticoes and fancy windows and elegantly tiled floors. Money was pouring into this town, he thought. Undoubtedly dollars coming from the *norteños*, Guatemalans working in the United States. No wonder the price for crossing the border had gone up. The coyote business was good.

He stopped into a pharmacy to ask where he could make a phone call. Two years ago there hadn't been a single phone in Todos Santos. Now, the pharmacist directed him to three different stores and commented on the price of making a call and quality of connection of each. These were not matters that concerned Carlos. He visited all three of the stores before he found the one where the phone was not out on a table in the middle of the store but tucked away in a booth where the caller had a bit of privacy. There he pulled out a slip of paper from his pocket and dialed Zelda.

* * *

Zelda had just hung up from yet another conversation with Catherine in which she'd told her sister-in-law there was still no news. Midday on Friday, and still the kidnappers hadn't called. It was up to Zelda to keep everyone— Catherine, Elliot, herself—sane, if that was possible. She had told Catherine to call her again at five. Then the phone rang. She picked it up, thinking this was it.

"*Haló.*"

"Is the money in Todos Santos, like I told you?" The same voice spoke, in his faintly accented English. She knew he came from Lívingston. She wondered where he was now, and if he had met up with the gang that was supposed to be on its way to Todos Santos.

"It's there. Where is Isaac?"

"Don't worry. He very safe and comfortable right now, but he can't make it to the phone right this minute. You do just what I ask, he have no problems. You listening?"

"I'm listening."

"The money is in hundred dollar bills?"

"Yes. We've done everything you said. Fifty hundred dollar bills."

"Good. Your sister, she gonna put all those bills inside a copy of *Prensa Libre*, she can buy the paper right in town, she gonna do it nice so it just look like a newspaper, not like a lot of money, and she gonna put it inside a *moral*, one of those colorful bags the guys in Todos Santos carry around all the time. You got that?"

"I've got it," Zelda said, a little impatient with such careful instructions for something so straightforward.

"Tomorrow morning an old guy, a Todosantero, gonna call on her at home. He know where she is. She gonna give him the bag. Then he gonna leave. She stay put, no funny business, no cops show up, and her sonny boy be home in time for supper."

"I want to talk to Isaac."

"You talk to him tomorrow night." And the phone went dead.

* * *

Oswaldo wasn't around when Catherine and Nicolasa got back to the Todosantero. That was fine. Catherine had a plan. No more waiting around. She had to find Isaac. She didn't want company. She left Nicolasa on the terrace with Esperanza and the children trying to act as though it were just a normal afternoon with no owls gathering in the plaza, and went alone up the main street toward the Bar Sin Nombre. She hadn't spoken to Desiderio since the fight in the street and the kiss in the bar, and had only seen him in passing, going into the kitchen of the hotel and disappearing quickly out the door, ignoring both her and his wife. Now she had not only to speak to him but to use her gringa magic, the fascination all the locals, not just Desiderio, had for foreigners. She needed to uncover his secrets. Was he what he had seemed that afternoon in the bar, a misunderstood man striving against odds to succeed on his own terms? Or had she been deceived by the alchemy of music and chivalry? Was he what people in town thought, a drug dealer involved with gangs from the US? Could he know the kidnappers? The thought chilled Catherine. Maybe her connection to Nicolasa had snared Isaac in the cult's web.

She opened the door to the bar with trepidation, half expecting to see Carlos and possibly even a band of devil-worshippers. But the room was empty except for two Todosanteros in the corner and Desiderio behind the bar. She went up to the bar and sat down on a stool.

"I didn't expect to see you in town today," he said, looking right at her. What was in his eyes: concern or challenge? The jewel in his nose, the lion's claws around his neck, looked like gangland talismans. Desperation made her bold.

"I never thanked you for defending me against Baudilio the other day. You were very brave." She used what she thought was her most seductive voice, lower than normal.

"You told me I was foolish."

"That too. But considering everything that's happened, I should at least have thanked you."

"You picked a strange time." He continued to stare at her as if unconvinced. Gringa magic wasn't working. There was nothing to do but forge ahead. She returned his look and didn't flinch.

"Nicolasa and I saw a friend of yours arrive. A man named Carlos."

"Is that why you came here?"

"Have you seen him?" Maybe it was naïve to think he would just come out and tell her the truth. Just because he'd bathed her face in warm water and renounced Yankee dollars. Could he have betrayed her son?

"He was just here," he said.

"What did he want?"

"He wants to go to the North. That's all. Do you want a beer?"

She tried to read the truth in his eyes. They were black and opaque, like all the eyes in here, his face a mask, like all the faces. This was a fool's venture. She pressed on.

"Does he have Isaac?" she asked.

"Carlos is not a kidnapper. I knew him well in Los Angeles. He stayed away from fights, sold a little marijuana, not much. He was never violent."

"So why did he show up in town just now?"

"It's a coincidence." Desiderio opened a beer for her without being asked.

"Coincidence! Desiderio, please. Nicolasa told me the man got you jailed. Why be loyal to him?"

"I'm telling you what I think. If you want to speak to Carlos, there's a place he might have gone. But it's an hour's drive from here. You would need a vehicle. The last bus left not long ago."

"We can use Oswaldo's van. Will you take me there? Now?" Catherine's heart raced with excitement and hope.

"If you wish," Desiderio said. "It will be a slow night here, nothing that Leti can't handle."

"I'll be back."

Oswaldo hadn't returned to the Todosantero, and Nicolasa didn't know where he was. Catherine waited for him on the terrace. He had the keys to the van, the key to finding Carlos. Time passed with deadening slowness, as it had ever since she had found out Isaac was gone. It was as though time itself were her enemy, elongating itself while she waited for the kidnapper's message. She felt stretched as taut as time. Mist settled into the valley in a dense mass. Nicolasa called her into the kitchen to sit by the fire. The women were preparing supper. Marvella tried to distract her without success. Catherine had told Zelda she would call again. First, she had to find Carlos. What a time for Oswaldo to be out on one of his wanderings. Finally she decided to go look for him at Nicolasa's house.

In the fading light she walked up the hill out of town, picking her way up the rough cobblestone street. With each step her anxiety mounted. Oswaldo's disappearance disturbed her. He'd been by her side without fail for two days, always knowing just how to help her, just what to say, what to do. How could he have abandoned her right when she needed him most? Where was he? What would she do if he wasn't at the house? How had she come to need him so much?

She tried to think of alternatives. There were other cars in town. She would find someone, Nicolasa would know a driver she could hire, she would go tonight to find Carlos, who, the more she thought about it, must have Isaac. What would she do if she found him? She'd take the ransom money with her. But would he take it and let Isaac go? Suppose he was with the group, the whole cult? Suppose Desiderio was part of it? Her thoughts raced. Mist closed in thick around her. It was getting dark. She had no flashlight. She came to a bridge over a stream and an unfamiliar fork in the road. She paused to study the crossroad, climbing up beyond the stream toward the ridge. Strange she'd never seen it before; she'd been up this road a number of times. Was Nicolasa's house behind her? Had she missed the path to the house? A woman's voice spoke soft and low in her ear. "That's your road. Take it."

Catherine whirled around. She peered into the swirling mist, in the last of the twilight. She saw no one. Where could the woman be? Why would she hide? Perhaps she had only imagined the voice, so close. She was about to start back down the road, when she heard the voice again, very clear, gentle, but very insistent. "Look! There it is. Take your road!"

Catherine looked up the road toward the ridge. It was straight and broad, illuminated by a cold light, although there was no moon. Eerie. The voice was very compelling, very sure of itself, as though it knew what was best for Catherine.

She was tempted. The voice was sweet. The road was glowing, silver and attractive. Isaac could be at the end of it, she was almost sure.

Ridiculous! she thought. What's happening to me? Out loud she said, "I know my road. I know where I'm going!" and she started down the hill, walking as fast as she dared, peering through the gloom at the ghostly shapes of small houses, trying to figure out where she was. Nothing she passed looked familiar. She walked close to the left side of the road, searching for the path to Nicolasa's house. Surely even in the dark she would recognize the little stone step set in a mound of grass where the path entered the cornfield. Somehow, though, she missed it again because she came to the Mayan ruins, a place at last that she knew. She sat down on a rock, feeling faint and disoriented. She knew she was in the ruins, but when she studied the dark shapes of the buried pyramids, trying to remember them, she couldn't. Below her the lights of the village appeared, chaotic and disordered. They should have been familiar. Which was the main street? It should have been obvious. The mist rose up out of the valley. The moon came out from behind a cloud, round and full. Catherine fought against panic. Gazing steadily at the sprinkle of lights below, trying to make them make sense.

"Catarina." Oswaldo's voice called through the pines. There he was, at her side, his hand on her. "I've been looking for you."

She stood up and leaned against him, shaking with fear and relief.

"What happened?" he asked. She couldn't answer. It wasn't until over an hour later, after he'd led her back to Nicolasa's house, lit candles, and built a fire, that she could speak enough to explain. She told him about the voice in the mist.

"It was so close. But I couldn't see anyone. Where was she hiding? And where did that strange road come from? Am I insane?"

"Let me tell you a story. It will explain," Oswaldo said. He made them both tea and sat next to her by the fire. "Once there was a beautiful Indian girl, as sweet and shy as she was lovely. She was also very poor. Without money in this world, no matter what your other assets, you are nothing."

Catherine listened to Oswaldo's soothing voice, and watched the firelight flicker on his face. She waited for her fright to pass so she could go out again, this time to search for Carlos and Isaac. Oswaldo drew the story out.

"One day a handsome young man rode into the village on the back of a half-wild horse. A young Don Juan, that's who he was, the son of a rich Ladino planter, as proud and wild as the horses he liked to ride. His eyes fell on lovely Perfecta and he decided he must have her. Before long, Don Juan was visiting her little adobe hut by night to sing love songs at her window. As sure as rain follows sun, they were engaged and married. Soon they had two children, a girl and a boy. Perfecta was happy. So happy. Ah . . . too bad such happiness cannot last. Once his wife lost her girlish beauty and developed the big belly and breasts of a mother, Don Juan got tired of her. He took to spending more and more time away from home, riding his wild horses and carousing with other rich men for months at a time. He came back to Perfecta's house only to visit the children. He was a doting father, but he ignored their mother. She became wretched. She longed for the caresses he bestowed on the little ones and withheld from her."

I know how she felt, thought Catherine. She rested her head on Oswaldo's shoulder. It was getting so late. They should leave. But still she felt too weak to interrupt, too weak to stand.

"Perfecta's misery turned to anger. The next time her husband visited, she demanded that he remain with her and their children. Don Juan informed her that he was leaving her, to marry a rich woman. She should not cry because he would always give her money to live. But cry she did, wailing her heartache until she thought she was going mad.

"The very next day as Perfecta and her children were walking by the river, Don Juan came riding by in a carriage. Beside him sat an elegant lady. He stopped the carriage to greet his children with hugs and kisses. He told them that after his wedding they would come live with him in his beautiful new hacienda. He spoke no words to Perfecta. Then he raised his whip and drove away, leaving Perfecta in a cloud of dust. At that moment she really did go mad." Yes, Catherine could imagine that. She took Oswaldo's hand.

"If he wouldn't have her, then he wouldn't have the children either," Oswaldo continued, stroking Catherine's hand. "She grabbed them up—they were still quite small— one at a time, and threw them into the river to drown.

"As soon as the children sank beneath the current, the mother realized what she had done. She ran after them down the river, screaming and crying. But it was too late. She watched their little drowned forms tumble and scrape the bottom of the river and chased helplessly along the bank beside them until she dropped from exhaustion. There a traveler found the next day the dead body of a beautiful woman." Oswaldo stopped.

"That's some story," Catherine said. It was bizarre how she felt, as though the fable were meant for her. As if she were guilty of losing her son.

"It's the story of the *Llorona*, the crying woman. Ever since then, she has haunted rivers and streams, crying for her lost love and searching for her lost children. She tries to lure travelers with her beautiful voice to join her search. You heard the *Llorona*."

His lips brushed her cheek reassuringly, as if he had just told her something perfectly normal. "It's a good thing you didn't follow her. You would never have come back."

13.

"*A* y *Dios, ay santo mundo, ay santa mesa!*" The voice of Don Jerónimo droned on and on in a rhythmic whine. It was past midnight. Isaac's butt hurt from sitting on the narrow wooden bench for hours. He tried to relieve it by leaning back against the wall, but he was sandwiched between Carlos and some guy from the village and couldn't squirm too much. He couldn't go to bed, since the ceremony was taking place in the shed where he slept. A dozen local people were in there, crouched on benches made by resting planks on cinderblocks or rocks, all staring silently at Don Jerónimo. A fire burned on the dirt floor in the corner of the room. Every time the fire was about to die down, Doña Tecla threw more stuff on it. Heat and smoke, pine scent and incense filled the shed. Isaac felt lightheaded. It seemed like forever they'd been listening to the *chimán*.

Don Jerónimo sat facing the audience and chanting. Beside him screens made of bamboo poles had been set up around his sacred table. An open front in the enclosure let Isaac see that the table had been covered with a cloth and fixed up as an altar, with candles burning on it next to bottles of clear liquor and packs of cigarettes people had brought in with them and placed there. Offerings to the gods, Carlos told him. Each person would put their offering on the altar, kneel in front of it on the dirt floor covered in pine needles, and mumble a bunch of stuff in Mam. Prayers and requests for the gods, Carlos said. *Why does my ear hurt? Should I go visit Granny in Gracias a Dios?* Carlos translated everything that was going on in whispers to Isaac. Once everybody was settled, the little old white-haired shaman got started with the praying. Mostly the chanting was in the harsh and incomprehensible sounds of Mam, but sometimes Isaac recognized Spanish words mixed in, and a lot of *ayayay's*. The priest had a short length of heavy chain in his hand that he rattled as he droned. After a while, he said something to Doña Tecla, over in the corner. She brought him a bag that he held up to show to the people in the room.

"He says that's sugar, the sweetness of life that mother earth gives us in the blood of plants," Carlos, sitting next to him, whispered in Isaac's ear. "Now we getting to the good part. Watch this."

The shaman cleared away the pine needles on the floor in front of him and poured out a circle of sugar, talking to the crowd while he worked. "That symbolizes the world, *santo mundo*," Carlos translated as Don Jerónimo continued pouring two straight lines, crossing in the center of the circle. "That's the Mayan cross, arms of equal length, oriented by the compass. These old guys, they always got a compass in their heads."

The shaman put down the bag of sugar and brought out five long candles of different colors. He laid the red candle down on one arm of the sugar cross, pointing its wick toward the center of the circle. "Red points east, to the sunrise," Carlos whispered.

The black candle went opposite the red. "He say the negativity of black has big power. The Maya used to use it for good before the Spanish came along with their black magic."

The yellow candle went on the southern axis and symbolized the wind. The white candle pointed to the north, where clouds came from. Finally, Don Jerónimo put a green candle across the center of the circle and Carlos said it was the nature candle.

Next Doña Tecla brought him a long package bundled in leaves that Don Jerónimo unwrapped in his lap. He took out rough black lumps of *copal*, the Mayan incense that Carlos told Isaac came from the blood of trees. He unwrapped bundle after bundle of *copal* and piled it into the four quadrants of the circle. He sprinkled *copal* dust over the green candle in the middle of the pile. He started handing out small bundles of *copal* and small candles to all the people in the room. Isaac got five of the little candles: red, white, yellow, black, and green. Don Jerónimo had dozens of these candles, and arranged the rest of them on the pile, spoke-like, each on its own color quadrant. Then he sat back on his heels, took a cigarette out of his pocket, and lit it. He puffed on it, blowing out mouthfuls of smoke.

"The smoke going up to the Lords of the Hills, and to the ancestors. He's praying to them. He call on them like this: Caballero K'oy, give me health. Caballero Xolik, give me food. Caballero Cilbilchax, give me patience in this life. Caballero Bach, give me advice. These are the names of the mountains where the Lords live."

The chanting ceased. The *chimán* seemed to drop into a trance. The people in the shed sat silently without moving. Suddenly, the *chimán* took the cigarette out of his mouth and used it to light a candle. He leaned forward and touched the candle to the pyre. It exploded into flame. Wax and *copal* sure were more flammable than the average firewood, Isaac thought. Don Jerónimo raised both hands to the people sitting around the roaring blaze.

"He's inviting everybody to put their candles on the fire and pray."

Isaac didn't have much truck with deities, but he joined the line of folks who were circling the fire and putting their candles carefully onto the correct color piles while the priest moaned and muttered in Mam. When everyone was sitting down again, Don Jerónimo opened a bottle of liquor, *aguardiente*, Carlos said, and poured some on the fire. It flared up like a Christmas pudding. It likes its drink, Isaac thought. It seemed to be gobbling up the offerings, as if the candles and incense were food. Don Jerónimo took a few pulls off the bottle. The fire didn't seem to mind sharing. He gave the bottle to someone near him. It got passed from person to person in the room, each taking a drink. When it got to Isaac, he put it to his lips and took a slug. He nearly spit it out again; the strong, foul-tasting liquor burned his mouth and throat. Carlos, watching him, grinned and winked.

Don Jerónimo began to hum a wordless tune. It had that sad and simple sound the marimbas made wherever Isaac went in Guatemala. People started to hum along with him. The tune was easy to follow. The *chimán* closed his eyes as he hummed. Isaac studied his copper-colored face, his strong nose curving down to widely flared nostrils like features from an ancient Mayan carving. He seemed powerful and distant, a lot different from the little old guy who had led Isaac up the mountain in the morning. Suddenly he stopped humming and began to speak in

Mam again, his eyes still closed. His speech increased in force and tempo until it was a fusillade. He hardly seemed to pause for breath. He rocked slightly back and forth, his face illuminated by the fire, sweat appearing on his forehead and rolling down his cheeks. He raised his fist and rattled his chain angrily. Isaac worried that he would pass out, or have a heart attack.

The fire suddenly went out, transforming the room into dusk, lit only by the embers and candles on the sacred table. Don Jerónimo's eyes opened and glared at Isaac across the room. He said something. It sounded to Isaac like an accusation. All eyes turned to look at him.

"He say, someone in this room bearing a heavy load. Evil hanging over his head. He thinks it's you. He want to know, you got a question for the gods? This is your chance, man. Ask the unanswerable. Penetrate the mysteries of the universe. Jive him a little bit. Ask the dude a question. It'll warm his old heart. I'll translate for you." Carlos made it sound like a game, a ride in the amusement park, not some insane Mayan ritual in the wilds of nowhere.

Isaac didn't have time to think through all the possible consequences of asking the question most pressing on his mind. With a nervous look at Carlos, he said, "Ask him if I'm ever going to make it home."

Carlos slapped both thighs and rocked back with enjoyment, as though this entire night were an entertainment made for him. "That's a good one, man. That's perfect." And he repeated the question for the shaman and the assembled worshippers.

Don Jerónimo barked a command at Doña Tecla. She rose and left the shed. Don Jerónimo stood up and went inside the enclosure around the altar. He loosened a blanket that fell over the open entrance, cutting him off from view. The chanting started up again. Doña Tecla came back in carrying a large white rooster clamped under one arm so it couldn't flap its wings. She and two men went into the enclosure, which had to be pretty crowded at that point, Isaac figured. He couldn't see what happened in there, but he heard the rooster squawk and the chanting rise in volume.

"They sacrifice Mr. Cock-a-doodle-doo, slit his throat, drain the blood out and mix it with the *copal*. Then it all goes up in smoke to feed the old Lord of the *Cerro*, who's in there now with the *chimán*," Carlos whispered. A few minutes later, Doña Tecla came back out with the body of the rooster, limp and bloody. Don Jerónimo stayed inside and the praying continued. The smell of incense mingled with another, sharper odor that Isaac guessed must be the rooster's blood. Finally the praying stopped. A man came out of the enclosure and went outside. Isaac heard a skyrocket go off.

"That's it," Carlos said. "That signifies the Spirit's gone. The Lord's gone home to his mountaintop. Now we gonna find out what he said." Don Jerónimo opened the curtain and signaled. "Come on," Carlos said. Isaac followed him inside the enclosure. The three of them knelt in front of the altar on the pine-covered floor. Isaac, crowded next to the *chimán*, noticed that he was dripping with sweat. He stole a look at the altar. A clay pot held a gooey mix of *copal* embers and dark blood. Don Jerónimo gave him the bottle of *aguardiente*. He took a small sip and handed it to Carlos. Next, they passed a cigarette.

"We offering thanks to the Spirit for coming to Don Jerónimo," Carlos explained. "When we smoke and drink, the Lord of the *Cerro* get some too." Carlos and Don Jerónimo talked in Mam while they passed the cigarette.

"He say your problem is you got a death you got to atone for. Soon as you're done, you can go home. Not a bad performance, huh?" Carlos grinned.

* * *

"Oswaldo, do you believe in ghosts?" The late hour had forced Catherine to abandon the idea of going to find Carlos that night, much as she itched to do so. Oswaldo had agreed to go first thing in the morning. There was a teasing tone in her voice that Oswaldo was relieved to hear. She was recovering from her fright. Oswaldo knew how dangerous a *susto* like that could be, the terror that came from close contact with the dead. So he'd drawn out the history of the *Llorona* and told it like a tale from another time and place. He'd watched her easing down while he spoke. That was his job now: to take care of her, to protect her from Satan-worshippers, preachers, and spirit voices. He had taken on this job, against his better judgment, when he had come back to Todos Santos.

"I grew up in a house full of ghosts," he said. "My mother kept them around for protection. My dead grandmother, *santa Abuelita*, was always dropping things in the next room. *Pom!* The racket she made. All us kids would jump. Mamá would cross herself and say, *santa Abuelita* is annoyed with you. No more quarreling. Sometimes my grandma came in the night and stripped the roses off the bush in the garden, left them scattered around the patio. Then my mother would cry and pray out loud to *santa Abuelita*. 'Don't blame him, Mamá, he can't help it. He's a man.' And we'd know that my grandma was angry at my father."

"Why would you know that?" Catherine asked.

To the rational mind, this made no sense. Oswaldo knew that. How to explain a whole different order of logic?

"The nights we were visited by spirits would be nights my father didn't come home. My father's a *mujeriego*; he loves women. He always had girlfriends. My mother put up with it, the late nights and early mornings he came home drunk and smelling of perfume, the rumors brought to her by her women friends of where he'd been seen, with whom. She didn't complain for herself. But she would put her chin up high and her lips in a thin line and give a big sigh and say to him, 'You killed my mother and now you won't let her lie in peace.'"

"How did he kill your grandmother?" Her tone of skepticism had changed to fascination.

"She claimed he caused *Abuelita's* rages, that she died from rage and haunted us from rage. And my grandmother wasn't the only ghost in the house. My mother had a whole battalion of dead female ancestors creating havoc. Tipping over vases, hiding keys, spoiling the soup with too much salt. To this day, my parents are still at it. My father doesn't stay out all night any more, but he still chases girls, younger and younger ones. My mother hears, and her ghosts come. If you don't believe, you should come to my house and see for yourself."

Catherine looked at him with those laser eyes of hers that stared right at things and saw only what was there. That's what Oswaldo had noticed about foreign women from the first, their attention to matter, molecular detail, Newtonian forces.

"Is that why you never married?" she asked. "Because of your parents' battles?"

"Perhaps." He got up to put more wood in the stove and poke the glowing embers until they flared up again, sending out the rich smell of that cedar that only grew up here so high, so far from the house in the capital he'd gone home to after the *Violencia*. She was right. He couldn't bear the spirit war of his parents, or the pathos of his mother. Some people said that these days the tortilla had turned over, that women were growing bolder, more direct in demanding their rights, less dependent on feminine wiles and ghosts. But he didn't see that in his mother or her friends or the girls in the capital he was told to court. Only the foreign journalist he had met in boarding school and the tourists from Europe and North America would tell a man what they were really thinking. That was what drew him to these women, that and the certainty that they threatened no permanent entanglement.

"Where were you this afternoon?" Catherine broke into his thoughts. "I looked for you." She held out her palms to the fire, as though still feeling the chill of her scare, hours earlier, from the *Llorona's* voice.

"I walked around town talking to people. I was looking for anyone who had seen Isaac, or knew something. A man up by Calvario said he'd seen a blond boy. Then it was his cousin who'd seen him. I had to find the cousin. I kept chasing rumors, going from one to the next, like a dog chasing his tail. In the end, nothing turned up."

"I needed you." He felt the bluntness of her accusation.

"I'm sorry." It bothered him, because he knew it was true, had known in the afternoon, when he'd strayed farther and farther from the terrace at the Todosantero, that she needed him. Even at the time, he'd thought maybe he wasn't so much searching for Isaac as getting away from her need for a while. But when he'd got back to the hotel and gone to look for her, finally finding her in the ruins, alone and frightened, he had realized it was too late for him now. His course was set.

"First thing in the morning we'll find Desiderio and go to Carlos," he reminded her, as if she could forget. And now here she was looking beautiful, her face flushed from the fire, her cropped hair curly from the mist. To distract himself from the ache she aroused in him, he picked up the newspaper he'd bought earlier in the day, the *Prensa Libre.*

"Look here," he said, perusing a third-page article. "A hotel in Huehue had to seal off one of its rooms. A guest found a strange blue light coming from under the bed. You still don't believe in ghosts?"

"Really, Oswaldo!" She laughed weakly. "How do you know it wasn't an extraterrestrial?"

* * *

While people hung around drinking coffee and smoking cigarettes, Isaac crawled over to the blankets piled in the corner and dozed. He'd hardly slept when there was Carlos again, putting a cup of coffee in his hands.

"Mornin', Isaac! Bus comes in twenty minutes. You done enough atoning. Time to go find Mommy."

It didn't look like morning when they went outside. Pitch black and icy cold, with a million stars overhead and a low round moon. To Isaac's surprise, Don Jerónimo walked with them down the path to the road. He thought the old man should be exhausted after the long night, but he seemed just as energetic as he had been the morning before, climbing the mountain. Living so high must make people tough. The houses of La Ventosa were dark and silent in the empty altiplano. The three of them stood by the road, waiting, Isaac stamping his feet to keep his toes from going numb. He hugged the borrowed jacket close. "What's the plan?" he asked Carlos.

He knew Carlos would have one. Sure enough.

"It couldn't be easier," he said, his voice still buoyant with the high spirits of the night. "I talked to your aunt yesterday. She a nice lady, very sensible, no bullshit. We communicate just fine, not gonna have any problems, Isaac, don't you worry." Carlos was talking in English, so that Don Jerónimo could have no inkling of what he was saying, although Isaac had begun to think the shaman knew a lot of what was going on. Maybe he had second sight; maybe he was in on the scam. It was hard to tell. He nodded and smiled while Carlos proceeded to talk about him. "Our friend here gonna pick up the cash. You just have to stay out of sight on account of all the craziness going on in Todos Santos now. I got the perfect spot. You can get some well-deserved shut-eye while we take care of business. Quick as a wink, you having lunch with your mom, and Carlos is just a pleasant memory you can tell someday to your grandkids. Okay?"

Isaac had to hope it was okay. It wasn't like he had a choice. Out of nowhere he heard a horn. Headlights approached out of the darkness. The bus appeared, rounded a curve in the dirt road, and stopped in front of them. They got on. The seats were packed with dozing passengers. Bundles were crammed into the overhead racks.

"Market day in Todos Santos," Carlos explained. "Everybody in the whole damn countryside on their way to market."

They had to stand in the aisle, grasping the backs of seats, as the bus started the twisting descent. The sky lightened and turned pink. Isaac saw the walls of the valley rise around them. He watched giant clouds edged with pink pass at eye level, hanging in the ravines. Cornfields plunged from the side of the road. The bus kept stopping to take on more passengers, men and women bearing bundles, babies, and children, pushing him further back, crushing him into the crowds of red pants and dark skirts. Finally the road leveled off and they crossed a bridge. He saw a sign for Todos Santos.

Isaac tried to make out where they were, in case it could be of some use to him. He felt himself on the last leg, at the critical end of their odyssey. The outcome was close at hand, whatever it was. He felt danger. He still didn't know if he could trust Carlos. He wanted to. He needed someone he could count on, someone who could talk English and get him out of here. After all these days of being kind, joking with him, taking care of him, Carlos couldn't turn on him. Could he?

Buildings came into view, crowded together and painted garish colors, flowers spilling out of yards and containers on porches. Suddenly Carlos whistled loudly.

"*Bajamos!*" he shouted and fought to the back of the aisle, Isaac and Don Jerónimo in his wake. He thrust open the rear door of the bus as it halted. "This is where we get off."

He jumped down onto the cobbled street, turned, grabbed Isaac's hand, and then the old man's to help them down. The bus rumbled on and left them standing in the main street of town, in front of a building with purple-curtained windows and a sign over them reading "Bar Sin Nombre." Its metal door was shut tight, with no sign of life at seven in the morning. They passed it and went to the next door, a heavy wooden one painted in designs of blue and pink and yellow. Carlos took out a key and opened it. He flipped on a light.

Inside were shelves stacked with cartons of Coke and cases of beer. A storeroom. In the corner stood a large, ornately carved double bed. Decorations hung on the walls: a Mexican hat, a calendar showing a Swiss chalet, a diploma.

"Here you go, Isaac," Carlos said. "A perfect hidey-hole. Kick back, take off your shoes. Help yourself to the Cokes, I'm running a tab. A few hours, I be back."

Isaac sat on the edge of the bed.

"Carlos," he said. He didn't know what to say next. Carlos waited, patient. "Be careful."

"You know it! Nobody gets hurt. Relax." Then he and Don Jerónimo were out the door. Isaac heard the lock click. His stomach turned over. He waited a few minutes, then tried the door. It was locked. There were no windows in the storeroom. Just thick adobe walls and the solid door.

* * *

Saturday morning sparkled. Mornings, Catherine had learned, were the best time in Todos Santos. The strong tropical sun burned off the evening mists. You could so easily imagine a Michelangelesque God sitting on a cloud at the head of the valley, dispensing justice and mercy. It was possible to have hope in the morning. Hope seemed to live up on the rim of the valley, perhaps in the place the locals called Puerto del Cielo, door of heaven.

This morning there was no time to linger. She must speak to Zelda, as soon as possible, to find out if the kidnappers had called yesterday. Then she would resume the aborted search for Carlos. The sun had barely crested the valley's rim when she and Oswaldo walked down to the Todosantero. They left the van behind, knowing the street became impassable on market day. Already vendors were setting up stalls in front of the hotel. Catherine and Oswaldo ducked into the kitchen of the hotel, away from the prying eyes of neighbors who might wonder why a foreigner was still in town on this dangerous day, two days after the mayor's order, might even pass the word to the mayor himself or, worse yet, to Baudilio. The family was at breakfast. While Faustina gave Oswaldo a plate of eggs and tortillas, Nicolasa would go with Catherine, who couldn't possibly pause to eat, to the store with the phone. Not even Baudilio would dare physical challenge in the presence of the formidable daughter of the Todosantero.

Marvella wanted to go. Nicolasa said no. Another day she would have to spend indoors.

Catherine left Oswaldo in the kitchen with Desiderio, who would take them to look for Carlos on her return.

"Don't disappear," she told Oswaldo.

"Don't worry," he said.

* * *

It was way too early for Don Jerónimo to pay a call on the American woman in the house of Desiderio's sister. The fact that Isaac's mother was staying there worried Carlos a little. When he had found out about it the day before, he'd wondered what Desi knew about the kidnapping, and whether he would put together the pieces and tie Carlos into it. Small towns were places where everybody knew everyone else's business. But he and Desi went way back, and there didn't seem to be any problem between them. Desiderio trying to stay out of trouble now was cool; that business two years ago had turned out pretty well for Desi, except for the inconvenience of jail, and now he had his nice bar and was making it like a man in his home town, not bearing any grudge for the screw-ups that he knew weren't any fault of Carlos. Carlos had helped Desiderio out as a young wetback on the streets of LA, and now all his old mentor needed was a little trip *al norte*, easy to provide, and paid for.

Carlos steered the old man toward the market so they could do some shopping and wait for the appointment time. They poked into the market building together, stopping in all the stalls, and the *chimán*, who knew just about everybody in town, shucked and gabbed and had a good time. Don Jerónimo always came into Todos Santos on market day, so Carlos didn't worry that this would seem anything out of the ordinary.

Out on the street again, getting closer to appointment time, they watched a large black tour bus make its way up the street toward the parking area in front of the church. Bigger than a chicken bus, as big as the long-distance Pullmans to the capital, but shiny and clean and new, unusual in Guatemala. People stopped to stare at it passing.

"You seen anything like that before, uncle?" Carlos asked Don Jerónimo. It was the kind of bus Carlos might expect to see in Antigua or Tikal, the tourist meccas of the country, but not up here in the backwoods.

"No. I never saw a bus like that in Todos Santos," the old man answered.

The tinted windows of the black bus didn't let you look inside. Carlos could see the expressions on people's faces watching the strange bus go by. They thought it came from someplace foreign, unknowable, possibly evil, like a spaceship from a hostile planet. He and Don Jerónimo walked up the street after it and saw it stop, open its doors, and let people off. The people coming out of the strange bus were strange too, shrouded in black and gray, in fashionably cut black overcoats or black and gray sweaters and stylish jackets, tasteful black and gray pants. Their faces were covered by the large brims of hats; some wore white veils over their noses and mouths. They looked Asian, trim and neat. Carlos guessed they were Japanese. They certainly looked out of place in Todos Santos, as though they had taken a wrong turn out of Paris.

While the tourists fanned out into the market, Carlos explained to Don Jerónimo the little errand that he needed, just to pick up a bag from his friend the American woman. He would do it himself, but you know how these things are, he'd had a misunderstanding with the woman's husband and agreed to stay out of the picture. This was no big deal. She was just returning a little item he'd left behind. Carlos would wait for Don Jerónimo in the plaza, then they'd finish at the market and be off.

The shaman agreed without question to the task and trotted away up the street toward the house Desiderio had told him about, where the kid's mother should be waiting with the money stashed in the folded up newspaper so the old guy would never know that the item he was carrying was really fresh green US currency. Not that it would matter if he did. He was an honorable old dude, in tune with the gods, and wouldn't know what to do with all that money. As long as he had his beans and tortillas, he was a happy man. Carlos liked the way he blended in with all the other red pants going up the street. You really couldn't tell one guy from the next in this town. That was to his advantage.

The Japanese tourists making their way past Carlos to ogle the wares spread out on mats on the street—now *they* stood out, their black clothes contrasting with all the bright colors around them like some dark patrol from the underworld. It didn't surprise Carlos, the looks they were getting from the locals, averted eyes, hands over mouths. Apparently they hadn't heard that no foreigners were allowed here this weekend. Carlos was used to Japanese tourists. He knew the hats and veils were intended to keep out the tropical sun and dust. But to the local bumpkins they sure could pass for members of a satanic cult.

Carlos bought a cup of coffee at the newsstand and eyed the headlines on the *Prensa Libre*. Then he put down his cup and climbed the stairs to the plaza to wait for Don Jerónimo. He picked a bench facing the fountain where he could keep an eye out for the old man's return. That's how he spotted the American woman, coming out of the hotel across the street and down into the plaza.

The minute he saw her, his mind went into high gear. Of all the possible fuck-ups, which one was the most likely? The father, or the aunt, or somebody, had called the cops. The whole devil-worshipper thing was a fabrication. The army had sealed off the town. All to capture one low-key kidnapper. But Carlos knew the limits of American power and zeal. More likely that the kid's mother hadn't gotten the message. She didn't realize that right now while she was strolling past the fountain with Desiderio's sister, the old man was knocking on her door, expecting to pick up a bag. Whatever had happened, the plan that had seemed so simple and foolproof was blown out of the water. He had a bad premonition. He didn't want to be around when all hell broke loose.

While these mental calculations were going on, the woman caught sight of him. The flickering expressions on her face mirrored everything that had just happened in his own mind: surprise, recognition, fear, a rallying, a gathering together of facts and suspicions, observations and guesses. He watched her pause, grip the arm of Desiderio's sister, and now they were both looking at him, both staring, like hunters at their quarry, or maybe more like the deer, frozen at the moment it first sees the dog, its teeth bared.

Carlos watched all this going on like it was a movie in slow-mo, stretched out over time, as two female Japanese tourists appeared out of the corner of his vision, snapped pictures of the fountain, then passed between him and the two women, interrupting the electrical current that connected him to them. The Japanese kept on; now the women were visible again, and Carlos saw that the American woman had reached a conclusion and was coming at him, her face set with determination.

He stood up to meet her advance.

14.

As soon as Isaac heard the lock snap into place, he realized what he was dealing with. Trapped in the storeroom—thick adobe walls, solid wooden door. No getting out. Carlos was a kidnapper. For real. That whole friendly thing Carlos had going was just a front. He'd had the whole operation planned from the first night in Lívingston, when he'd moved in on Isaac like a barracuda to its meat. The drinks, the drugs, the cute way he'd raised the topic of kidnapping, like it was an idea that had suddenly occurred to him, just an option, like Isaac could say no if he wanted to, had all been a setup to lure him into going along with the plan. Like there was something Isaac could do to stop it. So instead of causing trouble, instead of going to the police in Lívingston, he'd signed on. He'd helped Carlos rip off his parents for five thousand dollars. Maybe that wouldn't be the end of it. Maybe Carlos would up the ante, keep asking for more. Maybe he'd take everything his parents had. While he, the accomplice, the worm who'd caused Bernie's death, was locked in a cell. Death row?

Fighting his exhaustion, he kicked the door with all his might. It didn't yield. No way he could stop things now. He was a partner in crime. He groaned and sat down on the bed. The room spooked him. No windows, earth walls. He could see the dirt poking through the plaster in places. He felt like he was buried underground. Shadows of the Mexican hat on the wall stretched out and contorted like an apparition, taunting him. Strange things were happening in Isaac's mind and body. He kept hearing the sound of dripping water, just at the edge of his consciousness. He wasn't sure if it was from being up all night or from something else. Who could say what was in the smoke up there in La Ventosa, or in the shaman's coffee? The sound of water might be a hallucination. No matter where he went, there was always water. An omen. A reminder. He lay down on the bed and a wave washed over him.

* * *

Isaac's eyes popped open. He didn't know how long he'd dozed. In the harsh electric light in the storeroom it could be noon or midnight. No daylight seeping through the cracks around the heavy door. He sat up and swung his feet off the bed. The nap had cleared his thinking. He had to get out of there before Carlos came back. He got up and tried the door again. Definitely locked. The kind of lock that required a key to open, inside or out. He pounded on the door until his knuckles hurt, hoping someone would hear. Nothing happened. What did he expect? Even if someone did hear, did wonder who was inside trying to get out, did decide to lend a helping hand, what could they do? Carlos had the key. Isaac stopped banging and started looking around for tools to force the door open. Just cases of drinks on the shelves, a few rough, wooden chairs, a small table with stuff piled on it in the corner. He looked through the stuff: plastic bowls, broken cup, enamel pot. He opened a drawer in the table and found a metal spoon. It was an ordinary stainless teaspoon, a little cheesy, with a handle decorated by some curlicues. A straighter, thinner handle would be better, but he'd give it a try.

No matter what he did, he couldn't force the handle of the spoon into the crack of the door. After tearing up the wood a little and bending the handle, he gave up and threw it on the floor. He kicked the door again, bruising his foot.

Near the bed was a large wooden box painted emerald green with big yellow stars and trim on it and little yellow legs. In other circumstances he would have admired its funky handmade look. He opened it, hoping for treasure: not doubloons, but a screwdriver and hammer. All he found was a ragged pair of blue jeans and a Grateful Dead T-shirt. That was it for the contents of the room—storeroom, bedroom, whatever it was, there was nothing in it to pry him to freedom.

The only thing left was his backpack, still with him after all this. He rifled through it and pulled out his passport. He fingered the stiffness of its cover with the lamination coating his photo, his name and information, and the bold lettering, *United States of America*. Not as good as a credit card, but he didn't have one. It was worth a try.

He slid the passport cover into the crack of the door and felt for the lock. The flimsy cardboard butted up against the bolt and crumpled. Again and again Isaac jammed the passport against the lock and jiggled the door, but the bolt wouldn't give. Again and again. He refused to give up. He didn't have anything else. He looked with desperation at the damaged passport, the cover starting to shred under his assault. He begged it to work. Minutes were ticking by. Carlos would be back soon. He doubled the cover of the passport back on itself, the thing his mother had told him countless times never to do to a book, and slid the double thickness back inside the crack in the door. Up against the bolt again; this time he felt a little give. Another jostle of the lock handle, and the door sprang open.

He grabbed his backpack, stuffed the ruined passport in it, and stepped outside into morning sun. He glanced around for signs of Carlos. The dun-colored street was lined with shops, doors and windows standing open, people milling around, all locals. Up the street to his right, the people thickened into crowds. That would be the market. He started in that direction, with no clear idea of what he was looking for, only that in the center of town maybe there would be a policeman or some sort of authority he could go to, and that if he saw Carlos he would duck into a store. The closer he got to the market, the more people there were. They looked at him out of the corners of their eyes. They made remarks in Mam he couldn't understand. He remembered that something weird was going on in Todos Santos, they were expecting a devil invasion or something. They probably thought he was a devil. He hoped the cops weren't superstitious.

The sidewalks ahead were full of vegetable and fruit stands. He had to move out into the street. Here he felt more exposed to the stares of the people and the possibility of running into Carlos. He kept looking for someone in uniform. Never had the police seemed so appealing. He thought of asking someone where the police station was, but was afraid to draw more attention to himself than his blond hair and white skin already attracted. At a corner where a side street skirted a large concrete building and he could scarcely pass through the crowds around French fry and taco stands, he saw a welcome sight. Tourists, bending over a display of fruit spread out on blankets on the cobblestone street. So the town wasn't closed to outsiders after all. Two guys, Asian by the look of them, probably Japanese, since that's what Asian tourists generally were in this country, loaded down with cameras. The younger guy lifted his camera to snap the woman selling the fruit, but the woman startled at the sight of the camera as if it were a gun, and her baby stopped nursing and began to cry. The older tourist, a white-haired guy wearing a surgical mask over his mouth, reached out to touch the crying baby. The mother clutched it to her breast and started screaming.

Screaming like she was being murdered. Isaac couldn't understand the words, but the people around him sure could. They surged toward the two tourists, pulling Isaac with them, all shouting at once. A few words in Spanish separated out of the din. "Baby-stealers! The baby-snatchers are here!" People grabbed the old man and started hitting him with their fists. He bent double and threw his arms over his head, possibly having a heart attack. More people rushed toward him, carrying big sticks. Isaac was just a few feet away now. He saw the savage faces of the attackers, crazy with frenzy. His heart slamming against his chest, Isaac pushed forward and grabbed the old man's arm. He yanked him away from the sticks, and the old man practically fell against Isaac. He was small, frail, trembling violently. The other Japanese swung his camera at the attackers in an effort to fend them off. Immediately the crowd turned on him. Isaac saw the sticks flailing, heard the shouts and screams blend into a deafening uproar, and pulled the old man through the press of bodies, toward a side street. They broke free of the crowd, the old guy grabbed Isaac's shoulder, and Isaac put his arm around him to hold him up. He half dragged him up an incredibly steep street, over paving stones that were round and slippery. He stumbled with the weight of the man clinging to him, almost collapsing. People rushing down the street toward the roaring crowd below went around them. Isaac straightened, and kept on heaving the old guy up the hill, his lungs bursting with the effort. They made it to the top, to an intersection of narrow streets, more like cobbled paths. Isaac pulled the old guy around the corner, into the niche formed by a doorway, and stopped, leaning up against the closed door, gasping for breath.

15.

A few minutes earlier, Catherine and Nicolasa had pushed their way through the vendors kneeling in front of the hotel. Already the street was packed with people who had come in from the surrounding countryside for their weekly shopping. People leaned over displays of foodstuffs, hardware and trinkets, cassettes and CDs, baskets of live chicks and ducklings. The two women crossed the stream of crowds with difficulty and climbed the stairs into the square. There they saw something unexpected. Two tourists, stylishly outfitted, one in tailored gray pants and a black sweater, the other in a long trench coat, a white veil hanging from her broad-brimmed black hat, were taking a picture of the fountain. So, Catherine was not the only foreigner in town. But where had these two come from, and when?

"Probably Japanese," Catherine whispered to Nicolasa. "They wouldn't look so odd on the streets of Tokyo."

"Why the veil?" Nicolasa whispered back.

"To keep out the sun?" Catherine looked past the fountain. There, sitting on a bench facing her at the other side of the square, was Carlos.

She grabbed Nicolasa's arm. "Look!"

Now Nicolasa saw him too. They both hesitated for just an instant, staring at their quarry, delivered by sudden providence. The two tourists walked past. Catherine felt a rush, as of vestigial hackles rising. She would not let him out of her sights again. "Hurry. Let's talk to him," she said.

He stood up as they approached. His face lit up in a winning smile. He greeted Nicolasa like an old friend. "*Hola, mamacita.* Where's your baby girl? She must be big by now. I saw your brother yesterday, looking good, very good. Nice place he has."

"Carlos," Catherine said, zeroing past formalities, not waiting for an introduction that rarely came in Guatemala, getting right to the point, "Nicolasa tells me you're from Lívingston. My son was just there last week. Maybe you met him, a blond boy named Isaac, fourteen years old." She spoke Spanish, but pronounced Isaac's name in English, the way Isaac himself would have said it to the kidnapper. What did the kidnapper know about Isaac? His age? His mother's name? He must know plenty. He knew Zelda's phone number in Antigua.

Carlos answered smoothly, his face telling her nothing. "Sorry. I didn't have that pleasure. You should be careful though. This is a dangerous country for kids. Keep an eye on him."

"Someone called, telling me Isaac and a friend were coming to Todos Santos. Someone from Lívingston. Even if you don't know Isaac, I bet you know this person. I would give you money for the information. I wouldn't ask how you got it, if you would help me find my son."

"I wish I could help you."

She was sure he was holding back. She had to break through that suave façade. "Five thousand dollars in cash. American dollars. I have it with me right now. If you could take me to Isaac, it would be your reward. No questions." She checked the impulse to pull out her wallet and dangle the money before his eyes, right there on the spot, there in the square, where she was protected by crowds of onlookers and Nicolasa at her side. That would be her next move. Before she could make it, before she could even gauge his reaction to the cash offer, a roar erupted from the street below the square. Everyone in the plaza froze. Heads turned toward the sound coming up from below, a chorus of yelling and screaming, a sound signifying something terrible.

Suddenly there was movement all around Catherine, people surging toward the edge of the plaza, a flow of people coming between her and Carlos. Nicolasa held onto her. They were caught up in the crowd, moving with it to keep from being trampled. Catherine kept her eyes fixed on Carlos. She reached out to grab him. But people came between them. She tried to push her way through them to the kidnapper, dodging around shoulders and hats and bundled babies on backs. But she couldn't fight the force of crowds pressing toward the edge of the plaza. Abruptly, Carlos disappeared into the mob. She felt her frustration and anxiety rising with the screams. She clutched Nicolasa's arm and found herself shoved against the railing. Below her was a mass of people running up the street toward them. People in black and gray followed by a tidal wave of red pants, red and purple *huipiles*, as if a war of colors had broken out, a blotting out of darkness by the colors of Todos Santos. She heard shouts of "Baby-stealers! Devil-worshippers! The Satanists have come!"

"*Dios*," muttered Nicolasa.

"Carlos is gone! We have to find him." Catherine searched the tidal wave of people for a sign of the fleeing kidnapper. She didn't care what happened to her. All that mattered was the man who could take her to her son. People around her raced toward the stairs to join the red flow. Carlos must be down there. She moved to follow.

"Wait!" Nicolasa stopped her. "Don't go down into that. It's not safe."

They clung to the railing and watched men, women, and children emerging out of houses to join the throng, people pouring toward the space in front of the church, where the buses and trucks that had brought people and goods to the market were parked, toward a large black bus that by its grim hue stood out from the others. A man came out of the black bus and was almost knocked down by the people in black and gray running toward the bus and scrambling on board. The man was surrounded by the red wave, which closed around him like whirlpool. Catherine saw long sticks and clubs rising and falling over the place he had disappeared. She saw people hurling stones into the vortex. She heard screams rising even over the cacophony of the crowd.

"We have to find the police," Nicolasa said, turning away from the railing. Together they ran across the plaza. In front of the colonnade of the municipal building, the mayor stood in a knot of people. Nicolasa's father Benito was beside him.

"Papá, Don Domingo, what's going on?"

Before either man could answer, a voice thundered over the square. "Evil has arrived. The baby-snatchers are here. The vengeance of the Lord is upon us."

The group around them started moving toward the parking lot, except for Benito and the mayor, who stepped out from under the portico and looked up for the source of the voice. There on the second floor of the colonnade stood Baudilio with a bullhorn.

"*Ay, Dios!*" Nicolasa exclaimed. "Do something, Don Domingo!"

"They're no devil-worshippers," Benito said. "I saw them in the street. They're tourists. The people are out of control. Somebody could be killed."

The bullhorn blared on over their heads. "The Satanists have entered the bus. After them, all you who are righteous! Defend our town! After them, Todosanteros!"

The mayor just stood there. Catherine snapped. "Somebody has to stop that idiot!"

She raced toward the portico stairs. She ran up the wide metal stairway that gave access to the second-floor offices of the *palacio municipal* and dashed along the spacious balcony. Baudilio was turned away from her, facing the church, so intent on his message of doom that he didn't hear her coming. She ripped the bullhorn from his hands. She exploded with fury, against him, the kidnapper, and the chaos that had swallowed Carlos. "You lunatic! Look what you've done."

With a snarl, Baudilio tried to snatch the bullhorn back. Catherine held it with both hands and used it to bang him across the side of the head. He reeled back with a yelp.

"Stay away," she hissed. "Next time I'll hit harder."

He gripped the balustrade and glared at her like a caged jaguar, measuring the seriousness of her intent. She looked past him toward scene in front of the church.

People were attacking the bus with sticks and stones. She couldn't see through the black-tinted windows to the people inside. What could be happening in there? Where was Carlos? Was he in the mob? She couldn't let him escape. How would she find him in this melee? Someone in red pants yanked open the door of the bus as she watched, and the red wave rose up and entered.

A hand grabbed the bullhorn from her. Benito and Domingo had come up behind her. Domingo shouted into the bullhorn "Todosanteros! This is your mayor. Calm yourselves. There are no devil-worshippers here. They are innocent tourists on the bus. Stop now. You have nothing to fear. Look around you. Is there anyone whose child is missing? There are no baby-stealers. Put down your weapons. Put down your sticks and stones. Come out of the bus. Stop now." The voice of Domingo Pablo Pablo went on, repeating the same message over and over.

Even while flames leapt up around the rear of the bus.

* * *

Isaac didn't know where to go next. The old guy hadn't loosened his hold, but at least he'd stopped sucking in air like a dying goldfish. Tears streamed silently down his cheeks. The street they were on now was deserted, a block above the maelstrom. They could still hear the screaming, coming from below.

"Come on," Isaac said.

This time they walked, Isaac looking around nervously. They came to a jail cell, open onto the street. A man in red pants stood behind the bars, drool hanging from the corner of his mouth. A stench of beer and urine came from the dirt-floored cell. The man was peering out at the sound of the riot.

"Hey," said Isaac. "Which way to the police?" This was one guy who should know, he thought.

The prisoner squinted at him fuzzily, then waved a trembling arm. Isaac followed the direction of his gesture.

In front of them was the town square. Cautiously, Isaac nudged his leech-like companion toward the open cross street. The old man let go of Isaac at last, shaking his head vehemently and saying something in Japanese. He was afraid to leave the shelter of the jail. They could hear the screaming of the crowd coming from just out of sight.

"Come on," Isaac said in English. "We have to get to the police. Police," he repeated, hoping the old guy could at least understand that one word. He grabbed his hand and pulled him forward, darting past overturned baskets and knocked down tables. No one saw them. The people were all down below. Isaac saw the pounding hordes streaming past the bottom of the street, past the raised square. He pulled his frightened companion up some stairs to the empty plaza. Concrete benches and railings painted toothpaste green surrounded a tacky fountain. On the far side of the fountain, the only people in the plaza were gathered in front of a long building with a two-story arcade, the kind of building they seemed to have in the center of all these Guatemalan towns he'd passed through on the bus, little dirtball towns with visions of grandeur. In front of the arcade was this little cluster of a few guys in red pants, a woman in Indian dress, and—Isaac had to blink a few times to make sure of what he was seeing, that it wasn't just a mirage like those pools of water on the flat stretches of Interstate 80. Standing out in that clump of short, black-haired people, like a beacon, was one person who didn't belong there. His mother.

The first thing Isaac noticed when he realized he was really looking at his mother, was a transformation. In all the muscles and nerves, tendons and stuff in his body, things released that had been pulled taut as catgut for he couldn't remember how long. But other things pinged in and tightened up. He couldn't just whoop with joy and rush over to her. The square was open. Carlos could be anywhere, looking out for his ransom money. He had to think things through. His mother was here, just like Carlos had said. She was alive and okay, in the middle of this craziness. If that much was true, what else about his so-called kidnapper could he trust? Maybe she'd paid the ransom, and Carlos was gone, and it was over.

Just like that? Carlos—vanished? Without saying goodbye, sorry about kidnapping you, kid, good luck with your life. Even if he was a kidnapper, hadn't he rescued Isaac, never judged him for his crime, fed, clothed, and in his own way nurtured him through hell? Isaac had never thought it would end that way, so suddenly. His loss felt like a big hole somewhere in his chest.

A voice on a loudspeaker boomed out over the sound of yelling, and the little group in front of the arcade broke up. He watched his mother disappear into the arcade. That did it. Tugging on the Japanese guy's hand, Isaac crossed the square at a trot.

* * *

The voice of the mayor combined with the smoke of the burning bus to create confusion in the crowd that had swept up the hill in a wave of fear and rage. Now that the wave had come crashing down on the dark bus that had landed like an alien spacecraft in the area in front of the church, it swirled and eddied in disorder. The presumed devil-worshippers, driven by heat and smoke and panic, poured out of the bus, clutching their dark robes and white veils, even as the words in Spanish and Mam echoed over the heads of the townspeople: *They're tourists. You have nothing to fear.*

The townspeople dropped back. Mothers checked the babies bundled in shawls on their backs. Fathers counted the little ones who had managed to cling close to them even in the stampede. Older siblings appeared out of the throngs, toting toddlers. As a column of terrorized Japanese fled the flames, a census was taking place, and a realization. By the time Benito appeared to herd the disaster victims to safety, an understanding was dawning. No child was missing.

* * *

"*Hijo de puta!*" Benito had sworn at the sight of the flames. Moving with speed that surprised Catherine, he dashed toward the stairs. Almost knocking down someone coming up, he disappeared from her sight. To be replaced by a vision. Three people rising from the stairwell and gliding along the balcony toward her, as though on ethereal wings. First came Nicolasa. Then a small, white-haired, stooped-over man in a dark suit and a surgical mask. And then Isaac. Catherine gripped the balustrade behind her to keep from keeling over. She watched, speechless. Domingo was still roaring beside her into the bullhorn, not paying attention to the angels advancing along the balcony toward them. Nicolasa's mouth was moving, so for all Catherine knew, she might have been talking. But she couldn't hear, couldn't speak, couldn't breathe, until Isaac was right in front of her.

"Hi, Mom," he said.

She dove for him, clutched him to her, buried her face in his hair. He hugged her back. Breathing in his golden sweetness, Catherine felt herself in the calm spot in the eye of the hurricane. She'd never experienced such joy, didn't know it was possible, that rapture like this was within human grasp.

Never again would she let her son go. In a flash she vowed that whatever it took, whatever she had to pay, whatever crime she had to commit, whoever she had to sacrifice, she'd make their lives whole again. Nothing else mattered.

Nicolasa, at her side, was trying to get her attention, taking her arm. "Catarina, *vamos*. Let's get you and your son out of here."

Movement had started up again, people swarming up the stairs into the square below the balcony, as though the force that had sucked them all to the space in front of the church had reversed and was spitting them out again. Now the movement was chaotic, people heading in every direction, not knowing which way to turn. Nicolasa shepherded Catherine, Isaac, and the old Japanese man down the stairs, through the confusion, past the stalls in the street where vendors were picking up spilled baskets, piling fruit in shawls to wrap up and sling over their backs, protecting their meager livelihoods from the wave that had broken on their shore.

* * *

An hour later, some thirty tourists were sitting on the terrace and in the dining room of the Todosantero. Some were crying; others were speaking rapid Japanese in angry voices. Their clothes were torn and dirty. Cuts and bruises showed on their faces, arms, and knees. Faustina, Nicolasa, and Esperanza brought them hot tea and cold *licuados*, and basins of water to wash their wounds. Catherine joined them, trying to help. She spoke to them in English because they didn't speak Spanish, translating their requests, trying to comfort them.

"We're so sorry," she translated Faustina word for word. "This was a terrible misunderstanding. The mayor is looking for vehicles to take you back to Huehue. Meanwhile, please rest. Please accept whatever comfort we can offer you. We're so sorry. Our people are not really like this. We apologize for Todos Santos."

An old woman carrying a basket came out onto the terrace. Faustina said to Catherine, "Explain to the Japanese that Doña Juana wants to help them with her *ruda* plants. She wants to cure them of their fright."

Some of the Japanese permitted the *pulsera* to try her cure. She chewed the leaves of mint called *ruda* that she took out of her basket, took a mouthful of clear liquid that smelled strongly of medicine from a bottle, and spat a fine spray at a tear-stained face. Her subject started back. She moved to the next and spat again.

"It works best if the person isn't expecting it," Nicolasa murmured to Catherine. "Doña Juana does it to newborn babies, who people believe are very susceptible to fright in their first month. She does it to fresh-hatched chicks and turkeys, any fragile new creature. For adults who know the cure, she'll sneak up behind them to surprise them."

"I don't think that would be a good idea in this case," Catherine said.

"No," Nicolasa said. "These people will never recover from their fear. It will possess them in nightmares for the rest of their lives. They will leave Guatemala as soon as possible and never come back."

* * *

After the Japanese had left, Catherine went upstairs to check on Isaac. She opened the door quietly and he stirred in one of the two twin beds. She came in and sat down on the empty bed, waiting for him to rouse from his nap. He stretched out from his fetal curl under the blankets, opened his eyes, and looked at her.

"Hi," she said. "Feeling refreshed?"

"How long did I sleep?"

"About three hours. I've been helping take care of the Japanese injured in the riot. The mayor found a bus to take them to Huehue."

"Is my little dude okay?"

"Physically, he's fine. He's very grateful to you, Isaac. He believes you saved his life." When the old man had found out, through translators, that Catherine was the mother of his savior, he'd held her hands between his and wept.

"You are blessed," he'd said. "You have a good son."

"I'm so proud of you," she told Isaac now. "Dad is, too. I talked to him on the phone. And Aunt Zelda. We're going to Antigua tomorrow. Dad's meeting us there." Catherine was determined: she was putting this family back together.

"How did all those Japanese get here?" Isaac asked.

"They came on a tour. Their bus driver hadn't heard that the town was closed. One of the tourists was killed."

"I saw it," said Isaac. He'd straightened out and was staring up at the ceiling, his arms folded on top of the blankets. "That's how we got away. They turned on this other guy."

"The Japanese ran for their bus. Their Guatemalan bus driver was inside. When he saw the mob coming, he got scared and tried to escape. They killed him too."

"Jeez," Isaac said. He hiked himself up in the bed and leaned against the wooden wall.

"It's very bad in Todos Santos right now. Terribly sad. The townspeople are in shock. They're bringing flowers to the places where the two men died, and lighting candles. Lots of people are crying. The police are rounding people up, trying to find the ones who did it." Catherine paused. There were things she had to know before they could celebrate their personal joy. "In the confusion, Carlos got away." She watched Isaac's reaction to the name.

"Did you give him the money?" he asked.

So she'd been right. Carlos was the kidnapper. "No," she said. "I was ready to. Then the lynching happened."

"Lynching?"

"That's what they call it here. *Linchamiento.* The word they use for all vigilante killings, not just hangings. Did Carlos . . ." She looked for the right word, the one that would gently unlock the door on his experience. "Did he hurt you?"

"Carlos?" Isaac said. He flopped back down in bed, buried his face in the small pillow, and sobbed. Catherine, her imagination wild with fears, moved onto the edge of his bed and stroked his head as she had when he was a small child. His shoulders shook. She tried to rub his lanky adolescent back through the blankets.

"Sweetheart," she murmured. "I'm sorry."

His crying began to quiet. He turned his head away from her and spoke toward the wall in a low voice. "No. You don't understand. Carlos didn't hurt me. The kidnapping thing was sort of to help me out." His voice trembled. He sniffed hard, rallied himself, and went on. "I'm sorry, Mom. Something really bad happened in Lívingston."

"I know your friend Bernie drowned. Was Carlos involved?"

"No!" His answer was a cry of pain. "It was an accident. I took him out in a boat. It was my fault. I was afraid Aunt Zelda would be mad at me. I lied to her about Bernie's parents taking us to Lívingston and I got Bernie drowned." He sobbed again and said through his tears, "When Carlos came along with the kidnapping idea, I didn't know what else to do, so I agreed to it. I helped him." He wrapped his arm over his head, his face still to the wall. He had confessed.

Catherine stared at her son, wrapped in a cocoon of blankets. She was stunned. She'd never imagined this. "What do you mean, you got Bernie drowned?"

Bit by bit, she coaxed the story out of him, between sobs. Not what they were doing on their own in Lívingston, that could wait. But the day of the storm, Isaac's enthusiasm to take the canoe out, Bernie's reluctance, Isaac's failed attempts to swim out to him, the wave. He uncurled from the wall and lay straight, staring up at the ceiling, glancing at her every so often as if to see her judgment of him. At the end he had stopped crying. She looked through her bag and found a Kleenex. She gave it to him, and he wiped his face, blew his nose, and turned toward her. She was still sitting on the edge of his bed. His eyes were red and swollen.

"Did you know that Bernie wasn't a good swimmer?" She was afraid to ask but had to know.

He had to think about it, as if the question had never occurred to him. "Not really," he said at last. "We went swimming the day before. He seemed fine. But the water was shallow. No waves."

"Maybe you've been too hard on yourself, Isaac."

He sat up and brightened slightly, as if sensing the first hope of reprieve. They would have time, she thought, to work it out, to come to terms with their separate ordeals, time that Bernie's parents wouldn't have. She put her arm around his shoulders and he sagged in toward her.

"Mom?" he said.

"Yes?"

"I'm hungry."

* * *

The rain held off that afternoon. The clouds hovered at the ridges, allowing shafts of light to break through, as if in recognition that there are times when mortal strength falters and heaven needs to deliver a modicum of peace. Marvella danced out onto the terrace while Catherine and Isaac were finishing lunch. The little girl stared at Isaac with relentless interest. She had little experience with golden-haired boys in Todos Santos. "Are you from Germany?" she asked.

Catherine introduced them. "Let's play," Marvella said.

"Sure," Isaac said, and sprang up from his seat. "What do you want to play?"

She dashed away, disappearing into the kitchen. Minutes later she reappeared with Celestino and a rubber ball that she handed to Isaac. "Come on!"

He tossed her the ball. She missed it. Celestino scrambled after it and gave it back to Isaac. He showed Marvella how to cup her hands to receive the ball, and bounced it to her gently. She missed again. Catherine watched Isaac's patience as he bounced the ball over and over to Marvella and sometimes rolled it to Celestino, keeping the two little kids laughing. She thought of the endless hours she'd spent throwing a ball to him when he was little. How easily frustrated he had been then. How trapped she had felt, in the backyard, her green prison, with nothing but the ball, her son, and his tantrums. Later it had been Little League, those games that went on forever, she on the sidelines with the other moms. Now he was the one throwing the ball, the tantrums and trophies behind him. It was for this she'd endured those hours on the bleachers. And the agony of the past few days.

Oswaldo came out onto the terrace.

"I took your bag up to your room," he said. He'd gone back to Nicolasa's house to retrieve their suitcases and the van.

"Thank you." She looked him in the eye. It was obvious to her that some things were over. She was going back to Elliot. He must have known that would happen. There would be no recriminations. They would be friends. "For everything."

He raised an eyebrow, nodded, and sat beside her, not too close. They watched the children playing ball. A beam of sun hit the terrace. Esperanza tied her weaving to the porch post and knelt down to work. *Esperanza.* Her name meant hope. Catherine loved that. Names with meanings. Desiderio, Benito, Celestino, Marvella: *desired one, blessed one, celestial, marvelous!* Names signifying hope.

The servant, Cecilia, having cleared the lunch dishes, came out with a load of laundry to wash in the sink on the terrace.

"He's a good boy, your son. Good with the little ones. You must be very happy," Oswaldo said quietly.

"Happy?" Tomorrow she would leave Todos Santos. Her few days with Oswaldo would fade like the mists in the mountaintops, like a vision induced by shamans or altitude. Other marriages had survived worse crises. Her future was mapped out plain to the Iowa horizon.

"As happy as a person in your state can expect," he elaborated.

"What state is that?" she asked, watching the little smile creep to his lips.

"Married."

16.

The bus terminal of Huehuetenango appears before you reach the town. Perhaps it is this place—an open space of dust or mud, depending on the season, between two long rows of dirty concrete sheds, crowded with colorful, rusting buses, their windows so often cracked and shattered, their hoods open while drivers struggle to eke another year of service out of exhausted engines—that gives Huehue its reputation with tourists as a spot devoid of charm. Charm was never the intent of the forces that created the terminal. Convenience and utility are its strengths. The new market building stretches out behind the bus offices and *comedores*. Stores line the terminal, selling plumbing supplies, paint, stoves, mattresses, and other cumbersome items that can be bought and loaded directly onto the tops of nearby buses for transport to outlying villages. People come from miles around to shop in the market and the terminal for goods either unobtainable or unbearably expensive in their villages. They never have to enter the old town of Huehue at all. Tourists on their way to Mexico never have to see Huehue's central plaza with its gazebo of bougainvillea, beneath which a dozen men offer to shine your shoes for two quetzales. Nor its lovely arcade and band shell of delicate salmon pink, its neoclassical church, its strolling groups of fresh-scrubbed teenagers in neat school uniforms, arm in arm.

Church bells were ringing on Sunday morning when Elliot Barnes followed his driver out of Bugambilia Café, across the park from the church. If he noticed the sun sparkling on the lemon tree overhead or the loud chatter of tropical birds, he was not impressed. Exotic locations did not appeal to him, particularly after having been up all night in a taxi on the lonely highway between the airport and this highland outpost.

By the time his flight from Dallas had landed in the Guatemalan capital, Elliot's patience had long since worn out. He'd lost it somewhere between Cedar Rapids and Chicago, or Chicago and Dallas, or possibly years earlier. He'd called Zelda from the airport and told her he was going straight to Todos Santos. He'd lost confidence in his wife and sister to manage the situation down here, and he wanted to see his son right away. Fine, Zelda said. Take a taxi.

The trip by cab had been unbearably slow. The car, a Toyota sedan from the early eighties, was well past the age of reasonable retirement. When they had finally crawled into Huehue, Jesus, the driver, had insisted on stopping for breakfast. Quick, the guy had said it would be, as near as Elliot could tell from his broken English. Not quick enough. Now, forty minutes later, they returned to the parked cab. Elliot brushed off the seat with distaste before he got back in. The upholstery was crumbling, the springs that were poking through it covered by a dirty cloth. Handles, knobs, belts, everything in the interior was broken. A large spider crack in the windshield splintered the view from the driver's seat. Jesus appeared undeterred. The engine coughed to life, and they pulled out of the parking space. A few blocks from the center of town, they stopped at a gas station. Jesus buried his head under the hood, came back and told Elliot, "Need to fix. Okai?"

Did it really matter if it was okay by Elliot? The car so evidently needed to be fixed. They left the gas station, drove to the end of a street, and pulled into what looked to be an abandoned field. Several cars in all stages of decay were parked outside of a long, open roof of corrugated tin held up by posts. A mangy bitch slept under one of the broken cars, while her puppies played in the dirt and grass of the field. Elliot got out of the car and paced around the field for a while, avoiding the puppies that nipped at his ankles. He was sure that they were crawling with fleas. He watched as a mechanic emerged from the shed with glacial slowness, jacked up the car, and removed a front wheel. Jesus and a boy who appeared out of nowhere helped the mechanic replace a brake pad and reassemble the wheel. Then he moved to the other front wheel.

Fifty minutes later, they were on the road again. The car stalled repeatedly on the way out of town. By the time it was running reliably, they were climbing the face of the mountain range. The car slowed to fifteen miles an hour. At one point, the key fell out of the ignition. The car kept going. Jesus picked the key up off the floor and stuck it back in.

Later in the journey, when they had left the paved road, the car filled with the smell of gasoline. They jolted over ruts and rocks. Elliot thought about sparks. He envisioned the interior of the car engulfed in flames. They began a long, steep descent. He was glad they had replaced the brake pads. It was beyond his comprehension what could entice anyone to this place.

* * *

At the far end of town, overlooking the River Limón and the valley down to San Martín, a dense cluster of concrete structures painted in glowing turquoise house the dead of Todos Santos. The dead are allowed to rest for only seven years in their above-ground tombs, after which their bones are exhumed and burned to make room for more. For these seven years at least, the dead remain part of the lives of those they have left behind, who bring them flowers and plastic streamers and burn candles and fires on their graves. Once a year, on November second, the whole town turns out to party with their departed loved ones. They drag marimbas into the cemetery and set up concession stands selling snacks. They set off fireworks among the tombs, the marimbas play, and people drink beer and dance with the dead. The fireworks explode over their heads and rain down on them, and many people carry umbrellas to ward off falling chunks.

Today November second was still several months off, and the valley was gray with clouds. Perhaps the sun was ashamed to show his face. The cemetery was somber. Church bells tolled in the distance. Two small boxes sat on the ground between Domingo Pablo Pablo and the priest. All around stood the townspeople, crowded into the narrow aisles between the tombs. Catherine, shivering beside Nicolasa, listened to the mayor speak.

"We come here today in a solemn procession to bury the blood of two innocent men. The blood of a Japanese tourist, a young man, thirty-one years of age, a visitor to our country, and the blood of a countryman, a bus driver, a father of Guatemalan children. Blood has stained the soil in these two boxes, soil of Todos Santos. The priest has blessed this blood-stained soil, and shortly it will lie with our ancestors." The mayor raised both hands as if in a gesture of blessing, then turned his palms toward his audience.

"But the stain of blood will remain on all our hands." His voice boomed and he let his arms drop. "On the hands of all Todosanteros, those who live in town, and those from the countryside. There has never been a lynching in Todos Santos before. In other parts of Guatemala, yes! We hear of people who take the law into their own hands, people who are frustrated and impatient with our justice system, people who believe that wealthy criminals go free while the prisons fill up with the poor. Lynchings are common in Guatemala. Ignorant people express themselves with violence. But not here, never in Todos Santos." The mayor looked around at the faces in the crowd. Heads dropped in shame. His voice softened.

"Here we welcome outsiders. They live in our homes. They study in our Spanish schools. They come to our fiestas. They buy our products, our weavings, our *morales*, our *traje*. They stay in our hotels. They eat in our *comedores*. But now? Will they come now?"

There was anger in his voice again. He shook a finger at the crowd. They shuffled under his glare. "We always thought we were good people. Now there's blood on our hands. All of us are guilty of this crime. All are in need of grace. We have allowed our fears to close our hotels and our houses and our hearts to the visitors who have helped sustain our local businesses. Our visitors are gone. They take with them a fear that can't be cured. This fear will follow them back to their country and they'll pass it on to others, and others will be afraid to come to Todos Santos. The Peace Corps has withdrawn its volunteers. Foreign governments are warning their citizens to stay away." Catherine wondered if this was what angered Domingo Pablo Pablo, as well as the horror of the murders. And yet, she could hardly blame him for being as concerned for his town's livelihood as for its crime.

"Shame on you! Shame on all of us! The young mother who started the violence is in jail." The words shocked her. The young mother in jail? Surely not in the foul cell open to the street where, like the drunks, she would be on public display. "More will follow her. The guilty must be punished. Japan and INGUAT already are demanding arrests. The army is here." Catherine had seen them arrive, men in camouflage ostentatiously bearing arms, pouring out of military trucks in the center of town.

"I ask that you cooperate, that you come to me if you have information on those who participated in this violence. For the good of our town, we must know who raised a staff or stone against the tourists and the bus driver, who lit the fire that burned the bus. Anyone who withholds this information, who refuses to turn in his neighbor or his brother, shares the blame in these brutal murders. Anyone who hides these criminals in his home or *rancho* shares the blame. Anyone who passes rumors, who talks of devil-worshippers, who speaks evil of tourists, shares the blame." Catherine thought of Baudilio, whom the mayor had taken into custody yesterday. The poor terrified mother seemed as much his victim as the dead men. Maybe they were all victims of their brutal history, of their polarized society, of their corrupt institutions.

"Light candles," the mayor said. "Bring flowers." He slid the two small boxes into the open crypt at his feet while the priest made the sign of the cross in the air. One by one townspeople moved forward to stuff handfuls of flowers into the crypt and pile them around the tomb. And then, all at once, as if at an unheard signal, they turned away and headed toward the exit of the cemetery.

They know it's over, Catherine thought, without being told. As if they all think with one mind. She saw copper-colored cheeks wet with tears. As if they feel with one heart, she thought. They had accepted the blame and mourned. None of this was new to them. Here on the ground where year after year they buried their own, they were familiar with tragedy. It was not something that happened apart from them, on a highway, in a hospital, in the sanitized American setting Catherine was used to. Death had touched each one of them personally many times, and now they mourned the deaths of two strangers, together, in a collective, as they had attacked the day before.

"This should be the end of Baudilio's tourist-bashing career," she said to Nicolasa when they passed through the gate out of the cemetery.

"Let's hope," Nicolasa sighed. "He's already free. He has too many supporters to be locked up for long."

"I can't believe it!" Catherine let her outrage show. "You're right to get out of this place. Guatemala will never solve its problems. Take Marvella to Germany." Their children were back at the Todosantero. Nicolasa hadn't wanted Marvella to see all the tears. Isaac was still sleeping, as though he could sleep forever.

Nicolasa shook her head. "I changed my mind. Last night. I talked to Rolfe. We're not going. Too many people are leaving Guatemala. Someone has to stay, to work for change."

Those had been Catherine's words. She wished she could take them back. She gave her friend a worried look.

Nicolasa shrugged. Catherine bit back any reply. They walked together through the town, past the space in front of the church where candles burned at the foot of a small white cross, newly erected. They passed the open door of the church. Catherine thought about how many deaths had been mourned here, how many times priests had been sent up from Huehue to perform holy rites in this building that was already old when the *Mayflower* landed at Plymouth Rock.

They went on up the hill toward the hotel. Isaac should be up by now. They had a long trip ahead of them. She wanted to start for Antigua before noon. That's what she had told Oswaldo, when they had met early that morning over instant coffee on the misty terrace. He hadn't wanted to go to the cemetery. He didn't like funerals, he said; too many women crying. She remembered what he had told her about growing up in a house full of ghosts. How much she'd come to know about him in two weeks. Now he seemed distant. Already she missed his gold-toothed smile.

"Consider this," she had said. "You've acquired a new skill. Kidnap victim recovery. Highly marketable in this country."

He looked at her with both eyebrows raised. "You've made a joke?" he asked.

"What do you think?"

"It's as bad as mine." He had given her the grin she'd wanted.

So she and Nicolasa had been the only ones to go to the cemetery, and now they were back, passing through the dining room of the hotel. Across the terrace she saw Oswaldo and Desiderio wrestling a propane tank into position outside the shower. The Todosantero boasted the only gas-heated hot water in Todos Santos, hotter and more reliable than the ubiquitous electric heaters attached to shower heads that terrified Catherine with their dangling bare wires. The tables on the terrace were empty due to the gloominess of the day. She glanced to her left, under the balcony overhang, and looked right into the eyes of her husband.

He was sitting across the table from Isaac. She stared in surprise. His eyes were shadowed; his face, a little gray; his sandy hair rumpled. He looked cold in a thin khaki sports shirt and khaki pants, dressed for the tropics, so uncomfortable on the terrace of the Guatemalan hotel. So odd, unexpected, unwanted. She had planned to go to him, meet him in Antigua, and there, on neutral ground, she would take up the harness again, or shackles, or whatever her marriage was. Not now. She hardly knew what to say.

"Elliot! How did you get here?"

He answered her question, perhaps not noticing the omission of a more tender greeting. "In a taxi. Let me tell you, it was not a pleasant experience. It's a miracle I survived. I've been up all night. Forgive me if I'm not at my best."

He stood up to kiss her. She tensed. She felt so exposed, Isaac looking up at them, with Nicolasa by her side, not understanding what they were saying but knowing more than Elliot did, Nicolasa walking past them, past her brother and Oswaldo and the propane tank and into the kitchen. She knew that Oswaldo, too, would be aware of the family drama, would have known before she did what lay in wait for her at the end of the funeral, the end of the morning.

"Isaac's been filling me in on what went on here," Elliot gestured vaguely at the terrace with its spectacular mountain vista. Did he see it? "The bloodbath. Nice place. Next thing you know they'll be opening a Club Med. Just make sure your life insurance is paid up before you come."

She lowered herself into the chair next to Isaac. The remains of breakfast lay on a plate in front of him. "It's not that bad, Dad, once you get to know the people. You didn't need to come down. Don't you have stuff to get done that's more important? You're getting ready for a show."

"Isaac. What do you think is more important to me than my own son?"

Catherine heard the strain of the ordeal in Elliot's voice, and saw the glow in Isaac's face. So that was why he was sopping up the last of the egg on his plate with a tortilla, a contented smile on his face. His father had left his studio and crossed international boundaries for him, the prodigal son, forgiven by his father. And beginning to forgive himself.

"I figured something out, Mom," Isaac said. "Why don't you stay and finish your work? I want to go back to Iowa with Dad and do summer school. If it isn't too late. If Aunt Z will let me out of my job."

Catherine knew that it wouldn't be too late for Isaac. If he was willing to work, he could finish eighth grade in weeks.

"I'm getting you both out of here," Elliot said, sounding masterful, despite the thinness of his clothing, his inadequacy for the job. "This country's not safe."

He didn't realize where the danger lay, not in angry mobs or violent crime but in the clarity of light, the thinness of air at eight thousand feet, a different sky. Catherine saw it, even through the mist.

Elliot had not sat down again. It seemed he couldn't wait to leave. Even after all the hours of travel, he appeared tense, ready to spring.

"Let's go for a walk," Catherine said. She got up. "Be back soon," she said lightly to Isaac, and led Elliot out of the hotel.

* * *

Oswaldo watched them go. If he had steeled himself for this moment, inevitable from the start, it didn't help him now. The sight of the husband had done it to him, the sight of them together as a family, had caused him the kind of pain he'd always thought reserved for others. The pain that could cause a man to swallow poison rather than live without his love. Or to challenge his rival to a duel. He wanted to run after the couple who had just walked out of the Todosantero and out of his dreams, to challenge the husband, to tell him he'd wasted his chance, his turn was over.

"Are you going to let her go away with him?" Nicolasa had come back out of the kitchen. She startled him.

"What are you saying? Why not?"

"It's simple," Nicolasa said softly, so that only he could hear and not the boy sitting across the terrace from them. "A woman must follow her heart."

"Not so simple. She has a son, and a home in the North." Oswaldo tried to make his face a mask. He wanted no tinge of sorrow to show.

"You give up too easily. Fight for her."

"Please." He shook his head and smiled bitterly. "I'm not a violent man."

"I don't mean with violence. Give her what he doesn't."

"What can I give her? I have no wealth."

"I think you know what I mean," Nicolasa persisted.

As if there were no limits to the power of love. Oswaldo thought he knew better. How many times had he seen them come, these women from northern lands, and leave again, taking their hearts with them? "She's a foreigner," he insisted. "She'll go back where she belongs."

Nicolasa would not let him have the last word. "I know about foreigners. Ask her to stay."

* * *

Up the hill from the hotel Catherine turned into a path between houses, between banks of impatiens and glads and stands of calla lilies. Did Elliot see the flowers, or did he only notice the broken glass and plastic wrappers and dog turds in the mud?

"Where are we going?" he asked.

"There's a Mayan ruin just up the hill. It's a quiet place. We can talk."

Elliot was gasping for breath. They reached the ridge below the ruins and turned up the dirt road between low adobe houses hugging the ridgetop. Cornfields dropped steeply on either side, down into the town. From here they could see the entire valley ringed by mountains, bearing the weight of clouds. They passed women at their *pilas* and children playing in the dirt. "*Buenos díías. Adióóós,*" they sang, like a lament.

The dirt road cut right between two grass-covered pyramids. A few years ago, Catherine had heard, when the road was built, two skeletons had been unearthed, buried standing up, gold teeth still shining. The two ancient Maya were tall, unlike the Maya of today, dwarfed by poverty and hardship. The mayor at the time, perhaps ashamed to be desecrating the holy ground of his own ancestors, had ordered the skeletons reburied in the cemetery and allowed the project to go on destroying the past. That's progress, Catherine thought. The sound of marimbas came up from below. After five centuries of suffering, people will shrug and laugh and play their marimbas.

She and Elliot climbed up above the road cut and stood looking out over the misty valley. She remembered when they had liked to walk together, when their silences were companionable communication. No longer. Now she had to speak.

She had practiced the speech silently, climbing up to the ruins. *We have to start over. We'll see a counselor, and behave better toward each other, and revive our marriage. For Isaac's sake.* But they were not the words that came out.

"I'm not coming back, Elliot."

Not coming back. He got it, she could see, like an annunciation of the apocalypse. She felt her tears welling and struggled to suppress them.

"What are you saying?" She heard the choke in his voice. "If this is about those couple of . . . superficial relationships I had with people I don't give a shit about, all I can say is, it won't happen again."

"It's not about that. The good times are all too long ago. The feeling has gone out of our marriage. It's over."

Elliot ran his fingers through his hair, as if he wanted to tear it out. "What about Isaac? Are you abandoning our son?"

She could see that after this, at every passage in Isaac's life, graduation, marriage, the birth of children, sacraments that a couple should celebrate together, she and Elliot would meet as strangers, on the opposite sides of the room, a wall of bitterness and silence between them. She looked up at the hills, scanning for salvation.

"Isaac will be okay. He's grown up a lot in the last two weeks. Take him back to Iowa. Enjoy solo parenting for a few weeks. I'll be back in a month. We'll talk to him then."

"This is crazy, Catherine." Elliot's voice rose and roared out over the valley like Jehovah's blast. Righteous rage echoed from the hillsides. "Don't do this! You've lost your mind here."

He fixed her with glittering green eyes. Could he still see into her soul? Would he refuse to accept her leaving him, would he sweep her into his arms and insist on taking her home to Iowa? She stared back at him through her tears, saw tears in his eyes too. He blinked, turned away, paced to the edge of the grass.

"I'm getting out of this place. Come back when you've regained your sanity." He slid down the muddy path to the road cut, almost falling, cursing, and stalked off the way they had come. She watched him go past chickens scratching in the dirt road, past the women at their *pilas*, until he disappeared.

Finally the sun emerged. She felt it strike, burning off the mist and part of her sadness. She felt a lightening, relief. She looked down the valley toward San Martín, where the clouds were breaking up, and further off, where the mountains rolled in endless succession, uplands and valleys hiding dozens of villages, each with its *traje*, its stories, its secrets waiting to be explored. She'd go to Iowa in a month, but for how long she wouldn't say. There might be other books to be written here. She was free now to look for them.

Whatever happened now, she had set her sights on the unknown. Although she might fall off the edge of the earth, she would not die by degrees in Iowa. In the future, when set upon by doubts—about a book, or Isaac, or hardships she couldn't yet foresee—she would remember the clarity of this day. The intensity. Every sensation was magnified, the sharp air on her cheek, the brilliant sun in her eyes, the fluty call of the *guardabarrancos*. She felt immersed in light.

ACKNOWLEDGMENTS

I owe so much to the people of Todos Santos, whose warm welcome came at a critical time in my life. In particular, I want to thank Benito Ramírez Mendoza, teacher and community leader, in whose houschold I lived, and Edvin Figueroa Montt, school principal and friend, who has opened many doors for me. Faustino Pablo Bautista, a friend and Guatemalan artist of national stature born in Todos Santos, provided the painting for the cover.

The Two Crosses of Todos Santos by Maud Oakes, an American anthropologist who lived in Todos Santos in the 1940s and paved the way for many curious outsiders to follow, provided much useful background material, as did *Unfinished Conquest: The Guatemalan Tragedy* by Victor Perera. Two prize-winning documentaries by Olivia Carrescia—*Todos Santos Cuchumatán: Report from a Guatemalan Village*, 1982, and *Todos Santos: The Survivors*, 1989—tell the before and after of the brutal civil war in the words of the Todosanteros themselves.

I thank Nora England, Mayan linguist, who introduced me to Guatemala and the Mayan culture.

So many friends helped in this long project, reading the manuscript and generously offering their expertise and advice. I owe all a debt of gratitude, particularly Susan O'Keefe, Rebecca Williams, Charles Austin, Victoria Scott, and especially Michele Herman of the Writers Studio, as well as many others. My heartfelt thanks go to Diane Goettel of Black Lawrence Press for her enthusiasm and guidance. Much appreciation goes to Aaron Zimmerman of NY Writers Coalition, who has been an inspiration and support from beginning to end. My deepest thanks go to my children, Sam and Tess, who make it all worthwhile.

TODOS SANTOS AUTHOR Q & A

What about Guatemala fascinated you so much that you decided on it as a setting for your first novel?

Since my first trip to Guatemala in 1978, I've loved the country for its spectacular landscape, its friendly people, and its strong connection to its pre-colonial past. Our country seems very young compared to Guatemala. I was drawn to the contrast between a small, homogeneous, mostly indigenous, mostly rural culture with our own huge, heterogeneous, technologically advanced, powerful nation. Every time I came back to New York or suburban New Jersey after several months in Guatemala, I felt like I was looking at familiar scenes with an almost unnerving clarity, as if I'd taken some sort of strange truth serum.

By putting Catherine into this setting, where she's a foreigner in a strange culture, I hoped to give her a similar jolt. She also discovers, as I have, the commonalities in human experience across cultural borders.

How much time did you spend in Guatemala while working on the novel?

I came back from my first visit to Todos Santos, where I spent one night in 1998, and told a friend about it, at length. I must have sounded pretty excited, because she said, "That's it. That's your novel." (At the time, I didn't know I was writing a novel). I went back in 2000 and spent a month, in the hotel that inspired the Todosantero. (It's no longer there). I still wasn't working on the novel, but rather a short story set in Washington State. By the time I returned, in 2001, to stay for a year, and write the first draft of the novel, I'd already spent more time in Todos Santos than Catherine did.

In *Todos Santos*, there is a very troubling scene in which a group of tourists is attacked and one of them is lynched. Can you talk about the actual story that this is based on and how the event in your novel differs?

The lynching happened in April of 2000, just after I'd bought my ticket to spend the month of July in Todos Santos. The US State Department immediately issued a warning. I went anyway. I interviewed many people and got many versions of the story. There was no way I could keep it out of the novel. It happened very much as it is described in the novel, except that there was no Baudilio, no crazy xenophobic preacher. The town was never closed off to tourists. In fact, I encountered very little xenophobia in Todos Santos. In some rural villages there is suspicion and fear of outsiders, but not in Todos Santos.

Of course, there was no Isaac or Catherine either. The mayor did get on the bullhorn and call on everyone to count their children, to see if any were missing. The fear of baby-snatchers and devil worshippers was real; some things you can't make up. The remorse afterward was also real. However, I wasn't there, so I had to make up the details.

As a visual artist yourself, how do you feel that your relationship to elements such as color, texture, and scale informed your writing? Also, how do you think this informed Catherine's character and perspectives?

I'm always intensely affected by my visual surroundings, and when I write, I have to see the scene, as if I'm watching a movie. However, you don't have to be an artist to experience the overwhelming importance of color in Guatemala. The colors and textures of the hand woven fabrics that all the indigenous women wear go back deep into their cultural traditions. Color has symbolic meaning for them.

A small, mountainous country, Guatemala feels much bigger than it is. Maybe it's the bad roads, and how long it takes to get from one place to another, especially if you're using public transportation, which I always do there. Maybe it's the mountainsides, rising thousands of feet, making you feel small, or that fact that wherever you wander into rugged wilderness, there's always a footpath, a boy herding sheep, a piece of red thread, caught on a bush, reminding you with intimate touches that people are everywhere around you. I don't know if being an artist made me more aware of the great contrasts of scale I encountered in Guatemala, at every level, but if it did, then Catherine must have picked up on it. Like me, she's an observer.

Motherhood is a major theme in *Todos Santos*, especially the differences in Catherine's American views on motherhood and traditional Guatemalan mothering practices. How important do you think parenting practices are in cultural identity?

Babies in Guatemala spend the first year of life bound tightly to their mothers, slung either across the breast or the back. They are almost never out of physical contact. There are no play dates, no bouncy swings, no outward facing baby-packs encouraging them to explore the world. Babies and children are part of everyday life, universally adored by men as well as women. Children are criticized for being individualistic, and encouraged to conform in the communal life of the culture. In these ways, child-rearing there is different than in our culture, where children are encouraged young to pursue their uniqueness. How many times are American children told to be leaders, not followers?

In the end, however, all parents want the same for their children: happiness and success. And their worries are pretty similar, as Catherine found out.

TODOS SANTOS READER'S GUIDE DISCUSSION QUESTIONS

1. The novel's title means "All Saints." Catherine wonders on page 8 if the town's inhabitants pray to Christian saints or to "older, darker gods." Do they? What roles do religion, shamanism, and superstition play in the lives of the Guatemalans in the book? What are Catherine's and Isaac's attitudes toward the beliefs they encounter, and how do those attitudes change?

2. The novel begins with Catherine and Isaac arriving in Guatemala, a place where they are outsiders. What is the role of setting in the novel? Do you think Catherine and Isaac would have made different choices if they had stayed home in Iowa that summer? Nicolasa tells Catherine she wants to leave Guatemala; Catherine urges her to stay. Why? What do you think people who are born into poor and violent countries should do to improve their lives?

3. The story is told largely through two points of view—Catherine's and Isaac's. How does this structure serve the novel? How does Isaac see the world differently than his mother? When Catherine finds out that Isaac has been kidnapped, she accuses herself of being a bad mother. Is she? Is Zelda a poor choice of guardian?

4. Isaac blames himself for Bernie's accident. Was it his fault? How does he redeem himself? Should Catherine have been angry at him when she finds out he helped engineer his own kidnapping?

5. Discuss how the theme of good vs. evil repeats throughout the book. Baudilio stirs up the populace and attacks

Catherine. Is he evil? What about the people who attack the Japanese tourists? And the society that jails the young mother because she inadvertently started the riot? Is Carlos really a kidnapper? Or just an opportunist who was sincere in his desire to help Isaac?

6. How is nature used as a metaphor? What effects do the high altitude of Todos Santos and the sea level heat of Lívingston have on the characters? Guatemala calls itself "the land of eternal springtime." Would you agree?

7. What effect does Catherine's affair with Oswaldo have on her marriage? Compare Catherine's relationship with Oswaldo to what you know of her relationship with Elliot. Did she make the right decision in the end of the novel? What do you think the future holds for these characters? Will Catherine end up with Oswaldo?

8. On page 46, Rolfe tells Catherine that everyone there believes in the power of the *pulsera*, and that if she stays long enough, she will, too. Do all the characters believe in superstitions? Does Nicolasa? Does Oswaldo? Why does Isaac ask the shaman if he'll ever get home? How could Don Jerónimo have known about Bernie's accident? Did Catherine really meet the *Llorona*?

9. Catherine is an artist, which means she is an observer. How does this shape her character? Is she a passive observer? How does her character change through her experiences in Todos Santos?

10. Even though Zelda is Elliot's sister, she seems to be encouraging Catherine to break free of him. Why would she do that? Is she being disloyal to her brother?

11. What are the effects of history and racism on contemporary Guatemalans? What has the relationship been between the

Spanish conquerors and the Mayans? Does it seem to be changing? What were the aftereffects of the civil war that reached its height of violence in the 1980s? At the funeral for the victims of the lynching, Catherine sees the villagers mourning "together, in a collective, as they had attacked the day before." In what ways is the culture she finds in Todos Santos different from American culture? In what ways the same? What relevance does Guatemala have for Americans?